GEN. ISKAQ

The General listened absently to the white man's voice and watched the sweat pouring off him as he talked. In his mind's eye, however, all he could see was his old friend Sutan lying in a pool of bloody water, moaning and choking with blood running from his mouth and nostrils and his stomach heaving. He had told the proudly smiling men who had done it to stop for the present and let the prisoner rest; but he could not leave matters there.

Soon, he would have to tell them to go on again. Unless, of course, one of the whites should talk first.

Passage
of
Arms

Eric Ambler

BALLANTINE BOOKS • NEW YORK

ISBN 0-345-25914-9

This edition published by arrangement with Alfred A. Knopf, Inc.

Manufactured in the United States of America

First Ballantine Books Edition: November 1977

passage . . .

    9. A mutual act or transaction; something that goes on between two persons mutually; a negotiation; an interchange or exchange of vows, endearments, or the like; an interchange or exchange of blows; encounter; altercation; a fencing, as in argument; as, a *passage* at or of arms.

Webster's New International Dictionary

CHAPTER I

ALL THAT Mr. Wright, the rubber-estate manager, ever knew of the business was that an army patrol had ambushed a band of terrorists within a mile of his bungalow, that five months later his Indian clerk, Girija Krishnan, had reported the theft of three tarpaulins from the curing sheds, and that three years after that someone had removed the wheels from an old scooter belonging to one of his children. As it never occurred to him to look for a possible connection between the three incidents, he remained unaware even of that knowledge. In Malaya, at that time, there were more important facts to ponder and attempt to correlate. Stolen tarpaulins and missing scooter wheels were trivial mysteries; and, although the ambush itself was not forgotten, it was remembered more for its proximity than its novelty.

Mr. and Mrs. Wright had been at breakfast when they heard the sound of firing. It began with a flurry of submachine-gun bursts and continued intermittently for about two minutes.

The truck which took the tappers out to the work areas had not yet left the compound; and, although there was a lot of shouting and excitement, there was no panic and little confusion. Almost before the firing had ceased, the barbed-wire barricades were in position and the inner defense posts manned. During the long silence that followed, Mrs. Wright, a woman of character, calmed the servants and ordered fresh toast and tea so that she and her husband could finish breakfast.

1

At eight-thirty the patrol appeared: fifteen Malay infantry-men under a British subaltern, and two R.A.F. radio operators. They had been in the jungle for several weeks and their success that morning would probably earn them a rest period. They were smiling and talking as they toiled up the steep track to the compound.

Shortly after they arrived, Girija was summoned to the bungalow. As he went up the veranda steps he could see the officer, a downy, blue-eyed Englishman with paratroop wings on his jungle-green bush shirt. Mrs. Wright was pouring him a cup of tea.

"All Chinese, and on their way to mine the main road, by the look of things," he was saying. "We got the lot."

"Nice work," said Mr. Wright.

"Could have been better, sir." The young officer grinned. "They were all killed outright. You can't ask them questions about their chums when they're dead."

Mr. Wright chuckled and then, seeing his clerk waiting outside, beckoned him in.

"Girija, this is Lieutenant Haynes. He's just wiped out a gang of terrorists. I said we'd let him have some men to help bury them. Will you see to it?"

"Certainly, sir." Girija turned with a slight bow to the officer.

Lieutenant Haynes nodded genially. "I left two men there on guard," he said. "They'll give your chaps a hand if you send extra spades. The ground's quite soft, I think. Shouldn't take long. If you'll speak to my sergeant, he'll detail a guide for you."

"Thank you, sir. I will make all necessary arrangements."

The officer's grin faded slightly. "Seen many dead terrorists around these parts?" he asked.

"No, sir. Have not had that pleasure."

"Well, mind you spread the good news."

"I understand, sir. Two men from each kampong?"

"That's the idea. And tell them they'll be seeing plenty more before we're done."

Girija smiled politely and withdrew to organize the burial party.

He was well aware of the reason for it. The Malay villages in the area had long been suspected by the authorities of aiding the Communist guerrillas with food and shelter. It was not that the villagers approved of the invaders, but simply that the savage reprisals that could follow any refusal of aid were more intimidating to contemplate than the possibility of having fines or other collective punishments imposed by the British. They were not warlike people; their villages were often isolated; the British forces were scattered. In the past, glib official assurances that the police and army were at last gaining the upper hand and able to protect the outlying areas from the terrorists had been given too often, and too often proved baseless. Now, the villagers believed only what they saw themselves, or what had been seen by their own people. Dead terrorists had to be shown to be dead. The burial party was in the nature of a morale-building or public-relations device.

Girija found the head tapper and explained what was wanted: two men from each of the four neighboring villages, and picks and shovels. Then he went to the Malay sergeant and secured a guide. Within twenty minutes the party was ready to move. The head tapper was obviously hoping to go with it, but Girija sent him off with the truck and the remaining men to the work areas. He had decided to take charge of the burial party himself.

The action had taken place in a deep gully carved out of the red laterite hillside by the monsoon rains, and flanked on both sides by bamboo thickets, tree ferns, and dense tangles of croton undergrowth. It was a natural route for men to use on that otherwise trackless hillside, and a perfect site for an ambush.

There were ten bodies there: four within a few feet of one another, and the rest scattered along the gully for a distance of some twenty-five yards. It was easy to see what had happened. Concealed in the undergrowth along both lips of the gully, the patrol had been able to open fire at point-blank range without fear of hitting each other or the smallest chance of missing the enemy below them. One or two of the dead men were lying in attitudes which suggested desperate split-second attempts to claw their way to cover behind the roots of a fallen tree. One had been hit in the back as he turned to run. One, the farthest away, had tried to return the patrol's fire; there were empty shells scattered on the ground

by him; but he was as dead as the rest. Nobody in the patrol had been hit.

The two Malay soldiers left on guard were squatting on
their heels by a Sterno fuel stove, heating cans of tea and
smoking. They took no notice of the burial party. Beside
them, on a ground sheet, were stacked the arms and equipment collected from the dead: machine pistols, boxes of
ammunition and road mines, and canvas belts with pouches
containing hand grenades.

The soldier who had guided the party from the compound
joined his friends at the stove. Girija knew that they would
not help with the digging unless he told them what Lieutenant
Haynes had said; but he made no attempt to do so. During his brief inspection of the gully he had made two small
discoveries. They had aroused his curiosity and made him
wish to know more about the dead terrorists. He put the
burial party to work and sat down on the ground nearby.

The first thing he had noted was the fact that, although
the bodies had been searched and stripped of all arms and
equipment, there had been no cooking utensils of any kind
found on them. This meant almost certainly that they were
within a day's marching distance of their camp; which
meant, in turn, that they had probably been living off one or
more of the four villages near the estate. They would be
known, if only by sight, to at least two members of the burial
party.

His second discovery had to do with the arms and equipment. He was sure that the machine pistols were new; not
new in type necessarily, but newly acquired. His father had
been a subahdar in the British army, and Girija had spent his
childhood in barracks and cantonments. He knew the look of
a new gun and how soon it acquired the patina of use from
normal cleaning and handling. At least three of the machine pistols on the ground sheet had been so recently un-
packed, and so little used and cleaned, that traces of brown
preservative grease were still visible on them. The ammunition boxes, the mines, and the grenades were also new.
The grenades were of an old type with cast-iron fragmenta-
tion cases; but the gray paint on them was fresh and the
pins were clean and bright.

The gully was only partly shaded by the overhanging trees,

and by eleven o'clock the sun was shining directly into it. The tappers were craftsmen, used to the careful work of milking rubber trees without damaging them. Digging graves on a hillside, and in ground which, despite Lieutenant Haynes' assurance, had proved to be rock hard, was not a job which they could be expected to tackle with enthusiasm. The excitement of the occasion and the sight of ten bloody corpses were novelties that had soon paled. By the time the third grave had been dug, most of the men had lost their customary good humor. Criticism began to be voiced of the soldiers squatting in the shade and drinking tea while others cleaned up the mess they had made. There was even an exchange of remarks, meant to be overheard, to the effect that the tuan's clerk might, without serious loss of face, enhance his already considerable popularity by taking a shovel and doing a bit of digging himself.

Girija was able to ignore this unworthy suggestion with equanimity. The tappers' complaints interested him for reasons other than their substance. He was almost certain now that he knew the area in which the band had made their headquarters. Only two of the burial party had remained cheerful. Malays were not good at concealing their emotions, and although these two were trying hard to conform to the mood of the others, their satisfaction with the turn of events and the task in which they were engaged kept showing through their scowls. Girija watched them dump one of the bodies into its grave with unmistakable gusto, and then glance round guiltily when they caught themselves grinning at one another.

The two men came from a village named Awang on a river three miles away to the west. Once there had been tin mining in the district, but falling yields and rising operating costs had made the mines uneconomic. The small labor force of Awang had been gradually absorbed by the rubber estates.

Girija had been to the village once or twice to pay sick benefits to the families of men in hospital, but he did not know it well. It was at the end of a secondary road which had degenerated in recent years to no more than a cycle track. Beyond the old tin workings the jungle-covered hills stretched all the way to the borders of Thailand. In that lush wilderness, small groups of disciplined men with minds and bodies adapted to the environment could remain healthy and mobile almost indefinitely. At that period it was impossible either to police the area effectively or to halt the stream of Chinese militants filtering down the peninsular from the north. Villages like Awang became staging points for the terrorist bands cautiously working their way southward toward the politically more sensitive areas of Selangor, Negri Sembilan, Malacca, and Johore. The men now being buried had probably made their camp within a mile or so of it, going in at night to receive food, gather information, browbeat the headman, and talk earnestly to potential recruits.

Girija walked over to the two tappers and stood watching them as they filled in the grave. They had fallen silent as he approached. After a moment or two he moved in closer.

"A good day's work," he remarked.

They looked at him warily.

He smiled. "The past buries itself."

That raised a sheepish grin.

"And honest men are free again," he added.

They went on working. The body was covered now.

"The tuan was pleased," Girija said thoughtfully; "pleased that these pigs were all foreigners. To him that proved the loyalty and courage of our men here."

They looked at him again. One of them mumbled: "The tuan is a father to us."

"It is unfortunate," Girija went on, "that the lieutenant tuan does not agree with him."

They stared at him in dismay.

Girija shrugged. "He said that this gang was new to the district. He said that a week was no test of loyalty."

He had them now. Dismay gave way to indignation.

The man who had spoken before spoke again. "The tuan was right," he said firmly. "The lieutenant tuan does not speak the truth."

Girija shrugged again. "It is not important."

"The lieutenant tuan is wrong," the man insisted. "It was many weeks."

Girija made sympathetic sounds.

"Many weeks," repeated the other man emphatically.

Girija spread out his hands. "It is not my business. Perhaps you should tell this to the lieutenant tuan." He saw the sudden panic in their eyes and went on smoothly: "Myself, I do not think it necessary, or wise. The pigs are dead. They are best forgotten."

"Yes, yes. It is best. We will forget."

Girija smiled benignly and moved away. He knew that they were watching him and wondering fearfully if he would betray them to the lieutenant. He had no intention of doing so; but there was no point in telling them that. They would not quite believe him; and in any case they had served their purpose. He had found out what he wanted to know.

ii

Girija was born of Bengali parents at Cawnpore in the United Provinces of India. He had five sisters but no brothers. When he was six his father, the subahdar, went to London with a detachment of his regiment to march in the Coronation procession of King George the Sixth. During his stay the subahdar was taken on a conducted tour of the city, which included visits to the Tower of London, Westminster Abbey, the Houses of Parliament, the British Museum, the Law Courts, Battersea power station, and, for some obscure reason, a factory in Acton where bus bodies were made. He returned to India laden with souvenirs and fired with ambition for his only son. The Law Courts had particularly impressed him. Girija would become a lawyer or, failing that, a policeman.

Girija became neither. The subahdar was killed at the battle of Alamein, and Girija spent the next three years in a military orphanage at Benares. When the war ended, however, his mother wrote to a brother, who had a cotton-goods business in Singapore, explaining that she had only her widow's pension and asking if she might join him with the children. The prospect of securing this windfall of cheap labor appealed to the brother, and he replied sending passage money. In December 1946 the family sailed as deck passengers from Calcutta. With them went the subahdar's medals and the precious souvenirs of his visit to London: the Coronation mug, the picture postcards, the newspaper cuttings, the photographs, the ash tray from the warrant officers' mess at

Chelsea Barracks, and the bus-body manufacturer's catalogue.

In his last year at the orphanage Girija had been taught bookkeeping, office organization, and the jargon of commercial letter writing. The uncle in Singapore found him useful—so useful, indeed, that after three months he got rid of the bookkeeper to whom he had been paying forty dollars (Straits) a week and replaced him with Girija, to whom he paid twenty. Girija was sixteen then. He stayed two years in Singapore. During them he learned Malay and a smattering of Cantonese and made friends with a Parsee who worked in the offices of a Chinese financial syndicate.

At that time, shortage of capital, ill health brought about by internment, and sheer hopelessness engendered by the early successes of the terrorists were persuading many British rubber planters in Malaya to sell out. The Chinese syndicate was buying. It was through his Parsee friend that Girija heard that the new manager of a recently acquired estate in the north was asking the Singapore office for a clerk.

His uncle was angered by Girija's decision to leave him, and talked darkly of getting a court order requiring Girija to repay the cost of his passage from Calcutta. To his astonishment, the bluff failed. Girija, whom he had come to regard as a pliant and somewhat timid young man, not only laughed loudly and made a disrespectful noise with his lips, but also threatened to take his mother and sisters north with him unless their wages were immediately doubled. There was a shrill Bengali family quarrel during which Girija uttered a further and more compelling threat. He had made a secret analysis of his uncle's accounts which he was prepared to send to the Inspector of Taxes. The uncle wept and spoke of ingratitude, but capitulated. Girija's mother embraced her son proudly and said that he was his father's true heir.

When the time came for Girija to leave, however, he asked her for only one thing that had belonged to his father: the bus-body manufacturer's catalogue. His sisters were relieved. They had been afraid that, as a man, he would feel himself entitled to the subahdar's medals.

The catalogue was a quarto-size book with a brown cover on which the name of the manufacturer was embossed in green. Inside there were forty-eight pages of thick, shiny paper displaying the specifications of twenty different types of buses together with color illustrations of the exterior and interior of each. There were double-deckers and single-deckers, buses designed to enable the driver to collect the fares, and buses designed to carry conductors. There were twelve-seaters, twenty-four-seaters, and sixty-seaters. There were buses for long distances and buses for local service in cities, for cold climates and for hot. The cover was dog-eared from much handling, and some of the pages were loose. There was an inkstain on the title page. It was Girija's most treasured possession.

As a small boy he had sat for hours turning the pages, studying the illustrations and rereading the text. He had, in the end, come to know it by heart. At the orphanage, when he had been separated both from his mother and from the catalogue, he had found comfort in reciting it to himself, beginning with the Foreword by the Chairman (*"In presenting to our customers all over the world this, the Eighteenth Edition, of our Catalogue and Price List, we are proudly conscious that . . ."*) and finishing with the specifications of a forty-seat medium-range staging coach (available on A.E.C. or Commer chassis) *"as supplied to the Argentine Government.* Price £8,586, f.o.b. London."

One day in the streets of Benares he had seen a new bus that he thought he recognized as a modification of one of those listed in the catalogue. It had been just starting away and he had run for almost half a mile before he had caught up with it at a stopping place. Breathlessly he had searched for the body manufacturer's name plate. The bus had been moving off again before he had found it; but it had been the right plate. A wave of excitement had swept over him. From that moment he had known exactly what he wanted to do in the world. He would operate a bus service.

His first letter to the body manufacturer had been written from Singapore on his uncle's business stationery. He had been aware for some time that the original catalogue from London, precious though it was and always would be, was now very much out of date. Nevertheless, the decision to send for the latest edition had not been easily taken. For some reason that he had been unable to account for, it had seemed almost like an act of treachery.

However, the arrival of the new catalogue had given him

other things to worry about. The catalogue itself had been magnificent. Unfortunately, it had been accompanied by a courteous letter from the sales manager, informing him that the company's Far Eastern representative, Mr. W. W. Belden, would shortly be visiting Singapore and would take that opportunity of meeting Mr. Krishnan and discussing his fleet requirements with him personally. For weeks Girija had gone in fear of W. W. Belden's arrival at his uncle's office and the humiliating scenes that would ensue when the truth was known. But Mr. Belden had never come, and eventually Girija had drawn the correct conclusion. Mr. Belden had investigated the financial status of this new prospective customer and decided not to waste his time.

His prudence had been understandable. The cheapest twenty-four-seater now cost over three thousand pounds—almost double the price of the cheapest bus in the 1937 catalogue. But one thing in the new edition had caught Girija's eye: a quotation from a trade journal devoted to the interests and activities of road-transport operators. Girija had found that this journal could be obtained in Singapore and had bought a subscription. From the articles it published he began to learn about the economics of public transportation. By the time he went to work for Mr. Wright, he had acquired a reasonably realistic view of his chances of achieving his life's ambition. Unless he could find a working capital of at least twenty thousand dollars (Straits), his chances of starting even the most modest country bus service were nonexistent.

iii

Girija had a one-room atap house in the estate compound, and an arrangement with one of the servants at the Wrights' bungalow to keep it clean. There were Indian families of his own caste living in a village six miles away, and on Sundays he would cycle over there for tiffin. One of the families had an attractive daughter named Sumitra, whom he thought he would one day marry. However, during the week the curfew kept him at home, and there he always cooked his own food. Sometimes he would go back to the office after he had eaten his evening meal and do some more work before going

to bed; at others he would listen to Radio Malaya and read
and dream.

On the evening of the day of the ambush he stayed late in
the office, trying to make up for the time he had lost by
going with the burial party. The following morning he would
have to drive in with Mr. Wright to the bank at Bukit Amphu
to cash the weekly wages check, and he had not yet completed the time sheets.

The work required care and concentration, and he was
glad of it, for it postponed the moment when he would have
to entertain once more the dangerous thoughts which had
come to him in the morning.

The things he had observed at the scene of the ambush,
and learned from the two tappers, had made it possible for
him to reconstruct the recent history of the dead men with
reasonable certainty.

They had only recently arrived from the north and were
relatively inexperienced. Of that he was sure. Their use of
the easy route offered by the gully showed that. True, they
had had a lot to carry, but that did not excuse carelessness.
In an area where British patrols were being supplied by the
R.A.F., a fact which they could scarcely help knowing, they
had not even troubled to send scouts on ahead to feel the
way, but had blundered straight into the ambush in a body.

The Lieutenant's opinion was that they had been on their
way to mine the main road. Girija did not agree with that.
The quantity of ammunition they had been carrying was out
of all proportion to the needs of such an operation. And
how was the absence of cooking utensils and food supplies
to be explained if they were going so far from their base?
To Girija there seemed only one possible explanation. What
the Lieutenant's patrol had ambushed was a supply column
on its way to deliver mines and ammunition to another gang
operating farther south.

It had been at this point in his argument with himself
that Girija's heart had begun to beat faster, and that an unpleasant sensation had come to his stomach. If his reasoning
were correct, it could mean only one thing. The base camp
near Awang was a guerrilla arms dump.

He finished his work, locked up the office, and walked
slowly back across the courtyard to his house. It was a warm,

humid night. He took off his shirt and khaki drill shorts, washed himself carefully all over and then put on a dhoti. There was some lentil soup in an iron saucepan. He lit the oil burner under it and sat down to wait.

What had disconcerted him had been not so much the nature of his thoughts as the way in which they had presented themselves. He did not regard himself as being fundamentally honest or dishonest, idealistic or corrupt, law-abiding or delinquent. He did not think of himself as definable in such terms. His dilemmas had always been capable of resolution into simple questions of choice. Choice A would be wise (advantageous). Choice B would be stupid (disadvantageous). The discovery that his mind could explore enthusiastically the possibility of his committing a major crime, with only a belated and distasteful glance at the path of rectitude, had been disturbing.

And a major crime it undoubtedly would be.

He had heard about these dumps and caches. It was known that the arms were brought in by professional smugglers operating from beyond the Thai border and employing different routes from those used by the guerrillas. A number of consignments had been intercepted, but it was generally believed that a far greater number always got through. Terrorists captured far to the south in the Kuala Lumpur area had been found to be in possession of substantial quantities of weapons, ammunition and explosives of the same pattern as those intercepted in the north. It was said that there were not enough troops in the whole of Malaya to patrol the border with Thailand effectively.

Just before the burial party had finished its work that morning the Malay sergeant and four more soldiers had arrived with packing crates strung on bamboo poles. When the ammunition and grenades had been loaded into the crates, they were taken off to the compound. While the machine pistols were being gathered up, Girija had asked the Sergeant a question.

The Sergeant had looked down at the machine pistol in his hands and shrugged. "How should I know what they cost?"

"But don't you know how much your own cost, Sergeant? Supposing a man lost one."

"He would be court-martialed."

"But surely he would have stoppages of pay, too?"

"Oh, yes. Two hundred dollars perhaps."

"So much?"

"They do not grow on trees."

The Sergeant had gone. Girija had turned and looked at the row of graves. Each man had had a machine pistol, and ammunition was costly stuff. It was more than likely that what the ten men had been carrying between them was worth anything up to three thousand dollars. It would be interesting to know how much more there was where that had come from.

The soup began to bubble. He poured it into a bowl and, when it had cooled a little, began to eat.

The penalty for being found in the illegal possession of arms was death. Whether or not knowledge of the whereabouts of smuggled arms would constitute possession, and whether concealment of such knowledge carried the same penalty he did not know. One thing was clear: the illegal *selling* of smuggled arms would certainly be a hanging matter —at least while the emergency regulations remained in force. The best thing he could do was to go to Mr. Wright immediately and make a clean breast of the matter.

But a clean breast of *what* matter? He did not really *know* anything about an arms dump. He only believed one to be there. And where was "there"? Assuming that his deductions were correct, the dump was concealed in an area of jungle covering at least three square miles. It might prove quite impossible to find. Mr. Wright would not thank him for starting a wild-goose chase, and neither would the police. When the time came for him to apply for a local bus-service franchise, they might remember the trouble he had caused and hold it against him. No. The best thing he could do was nothing.

He finished his soup and felt better. He was an innocent man again, quietly digesting his evening meal. What did he want with smuggled arms? Could he ever have sold them? Of course not. Who would buy? And supposing others knew of the dump, if dump there were. Ten men had been killed; but supposing that other members of the guerrilla band had stayed behind. It might be highly dangerous to start searching in the area for their camp. Besides, there was always a

chance that one or two of the men living at Awang already
knew where it was. Not a very big chance, perhaps; the guerrillas would not have trusted their unwilling hosts to that
extent; but someone might have found out by chance.
Naturally, no man or woman from the village would dare to
go to the police with the information—or not immediately,
anyway. A decent interval would have to elapse before the
dump could be discovered "accidentally." More likely it
would just be forgotten. And that perhaps was what he
should do: forget about it. After all, he could always remember again later, if he wanted to.

There was a metal trunk in one corner of the room. In
it he kept his catalogues and trade papers and the schedule
of a projected daily bus service linking ten of the principal
rubber estates in the district with Bukit Amphu sixteen
miles away. He took the schedule out, read it through very
carefully, and then began to make one or two long-contem-
plated modifications.

iv

A month went by before Girija made any move to locate
the arms dump.

There had been no reports of any special patrol activity
in the district, and guerrilla attacks in the province had been
concentrated on areas nearer the coast. He had watched the
men from Awang carefully without detecting anything
unusual in their demeanor. But such reassurances came
mingled with doubt. If no dump had been discovered, it
could well be for the simple reason that none existed.

It was, in fact, the growing conviction that he must have
been mistaken that gave him the courage he needed to go
on. If there were nothing to find, he argued, there could be
nothing incriminating in the search.

The first part of his plan called for a satisfactory cover
for repeated visits to the Awang area. He might avoid going
through the village itself, but he would have to use a mile
or more of the road leading to it. Encounters with men who
knew him, and who might gossip or ask questions, would be
inevitable. The difficulty had seemed insurmountable at first;
but finally he had had an idea.

The latex produced by the estate went thirty miles by road down to the port of Kuala Pangkalan and from there was shipped to Singapore. Since the emergency, the trucks from the coast had had to be provided with armored-car escorts and, consequently, did not make the journey so often. Mr. Wright had been talking for some time, and writing to Singapore, about the need for additional storage sheds. The Singapore office had been reluctant to authorize the expenditure. Girija's idea was to make the new sheds an excuse for his trips to Awang.

Near the abandoned mine workings there were a number of derelict corrugated-iron buildings which had been used as offices, stores, and repair shops. Girija wrote to the head office of the mining company in Kota Bharu and asked permission to inspect the property with a possible view to making an offer for the material of the buildings.

He did not tell Mr. Wright. If Mr. Wright found out, no great harm would be done. Indeed, Mr. Wright would probably give him a pat on the back for his zeal and initiative in attempting to solve the problem of the new storage sheds. But Mr. Wright would also tell him something he already knew: that the mining company's rust-eaten buildings were not worth the cost of dismantling them, and that it would be a waste of time for him to go and inspect them.

The mining company replied with understandable enthusiasm that Mr. Krishnan had their full permission to inspect the buildings any time he liked. That was all he needed. No one person he might encounter there would know exactly how many visits of inspection he had made, or how many might be necessary. It would be assumed that he was acting on Mr. Wright's instructions. If he were ever challenged, he could produce the letter.

The following Sunday he cycled out to Awang. Just short of the village he turned off the road onto the overgrown track which led to the mining company's property. He met nobody on the way.

Ground sluicing had cleared some twenty acres of land in the bend of the river. No topsoil had been left for the jungle to reclaim, and the brown scars of the workings were still visible beneath a thin film of scrub and weed. Girija walked along the riverbank until he came to the shell of a building

that had housed a big rotary pump, and went through the
motions of inspecting it and taking notes. This was for the
benefit of anyone who might have seen him and be watching
from across the river. After a few minutes he moved away,
circling out of sight of the riverbank until he reached the
cover of some trees.

He had thought long and carefully about the problems of
searching the area. The only large-scale map which covered
it, and to which he might ordinarily have had access, was
an ordnance survey sheet marked with the estate boundary
lines. Unfortunately, a strict security regulation governed
the distribution and custody of such maps at that time, and
it had to be kept by Mr. Wright in his personal safe. Girija
was forced to rely on his none too vivid recollection of it.

The picture in his mind was one of three parallel ridges,
rather like steps, with contour lines very close together.
That meant, he knew, that the sides of the ridges were steep
and that there were deep ravines between them. It was not
much to go on; but it was something. He did not believe that
even inexperienced men would choose the floor of a ravine
for a base camp, any more than they would choose to perch
on the summit of a ridge. To that extent the likely areas of
search were limited. And there was another factor to be
considered. Even if they had had only small quantities of
arms and ammunition to store, they would have tried to
find a place for them which gave some protection from the
weather. He thought it unlikely that there were caves there;
but on the steeper hillsides there would be sizable hollows
made during the monsoons, when the heavier trees fell and
tore their roots out of the ground. Such hollows could easily
be made into shelters. All in all, it seemed sensible to start
the search by working along the upper slopes.

He attempted to do so; and that first Sunday expedition
was very nearly the last. It took him an hour to climb three
hundred yards up the side of the first ridge, and almost as
long to get down again. He tore his clothes, scratched his
arms and legs, and ended by becoming completely exhausted.
He also became frightened. If some patrolling policeman
were to ask him to account for the tears and scratches, he
would be hard put to it to invent a convincing explanation.

He succeeded in getting back to his house unobserved,

but the experience had thoroughly unnerved him and he decided to abandon the whole project. For several days he did succeed in putting it out of his mind. Then, as the scratches on his arms and legs began to heal, he began to think again. None of the ambushed men had had scratches on arms or legs. That meant that they must have found an easy route to and from their hiding place. The beauty of this deduction restored his confidence.

The next time he made no attempt to penetrate the jungle. Instead he worked his way around the fringes of it, looking for easy ways in. He found several and noted them for future reference.

The following Sunday he began a systematic probe. He had learned well from his initial mistake. When the going became too hard, he made no attempt to force a path through, but went back and tried a different or more circuitous way. He knew by now that he could never hope to cover anything like the whole area, but he had become philosophical about the search; it was a kind of game now, and although he did not expect to win, he had not yet reached the point of conceding his defeat.

Eight weeks after he began, he received his first piece of encouragement. He had been following a dry stream bed up a fold in a hillside. On both sides there were cane thickets of a kind he had learned to avoid. It was useless to try to push your way through. You had to go around them, and they often covered wide areas. Then, as the stream bed bore away sharply to the left, he paused. There were a few pieces of dead cane lying on the ground. At first he thought that they had been broken away by some animal grubbing for food among the roots. Then he saw that they had been cut.

He stood still for a moment, staring. There was no mistaking the marks on the cane. They had been made by a metal cutting edge. He examined the border of the thicket carefully. For a distance of about two feet the cane was thinner and greener, and near the ground he could see short stumps of older cane in among the new growth. At some time in the not too distant past someone had cleared a path there.

It was getting late, and he was a mile and a half or more from the tin workings and the shed where he had left his bicycle. He decided to leave further investigation until the

following Sunday. During the week, on the pretext of checking an inventory, he went to the tool store, borrowed one of
the long chopping knives, called parangs, that the estate
workers used for clearing underbrush, and hid it in his
room. On Sunday morning he wrapped the parang in newspaper, tied it to the crossbar of his bicycle, and set off early
for Awang.

He found his way back to the cane thicket without difficulty
and started hacking a path through it with the parang.
The new growth had not yet had time to harden, and the
going was fairly easy. He had no fear of running into
surviving members of the band. If this were indeed the way
to their camp, it had not been used for several months.

The path was uphill. After he had gone fifteen yards, the
cane thinned out and he found himself on a shallow ledge
from which he could see down into the stream bed. On the
ground there were some dead tree branches arranged to form
a sort of chair. It looked as if the ledge had been used as a
vantage point from which a sentry could cover the approach
along the stream bed. A well-worn track led off to the right.
He followed it, his heart pounding.

The camp was in a clearing shielded both from the sun
and from air observation by the branches of a large flame-
of-the-forest. The jungle apes had been there before him.
Pieces of clothing had been torn apart and scattered over
the clearing amid cooking pots, an earthenware chatty, and
empty rice bags. The only thing that seemed to have escaped
the apes' attentions was a metal box. It was full of leaflets,
printed in Malay and Chinese, calling upon the people of
Malaya to rise against the imperialist exploiters and estab-
lish a people's democracy.

There was another path leading down from the clearing,
and Girija followed it. It ended at the hole which had been
dug for use as a latrine. He walked back slowly to the clearing. In the long search for the camp site his doubts had
been forgotten. Now he remembered them and faced the
bitterness of defeat. Lieutenant Haynes had been right. He,
Girija, had been wrong. Sunday after Sunday he had exchanged the pleasures of tiffin with his future mother-in-
law, and the soft glances of Sumitra, for senseless walks in

the jungle and the pursuit of an illusion. There was no arms dump; there never had been.

He had started to retrace his footsteps when his foot struck something that tinkled. He looked down. Lying on the ground was a brass cartridge case. As he bent down to pick it up, he saw another one. A minute later he had found three more. He stared at them, puzzled. They were of .303 caliber. He went over the ground again and found what he was looking for: the clip which had held the five rounds.

There was no doubt about it. A .303 rifle had been fired there. But no rifle of any kind had been found at the scene of the ambush. And none of the weapons had been of .303 caliber. Where, then, was the rifle?

He searched the camp site thoroughly first. He found a small fixed-frequency radio in a teak box, but no rifle. He began to search the hillside above the camp, taking any route that looked as if it might conveivably have been used before. After about an hour he came upon a clump of bamboo from which a number of thick stalks had been cut. Then, about twelve yards away, he saw what he had been looking for.

Braced between the steep hillside and the trunk of a tree was a triangular roof of bamboo. Cane screens had been plaited to enclose the sides of the structure and form a shelter.

Girija scrambled toward it, slipping and sliding about on the spongy carpet of dead leaves and slashing wildly with the parang at the undergrowth in his path. When he reached the shelter, he stood for an instant, breathless and trying to prepare himself for the crushing disappointment of finding it empty. Then he pulled one of the screens aside.

There was a sudden, swift rustle and his heart leaped as some small brown animal rushed out past him. He pulled the screen back farther and looked inside.

The hillside beneath the roof had been dug out to make the space roughly rectangular. It was about six feet high and ten feet long and filled from floor to roof with wood and metal packing cases.

He sat down on the ground to get his breath back and stared at the cases. A number of them, he could see, were long and narrow and had rope handles. One of these was near the screen and looked as if it had been opened. He crawled over to it and prized the lid off with the parang.

Inside, carefully packed on slotted wood bearers, were six .303 rifles. Five of them were heavily greased and wrapped in thick oiled paper with the name of a Belgian manufacturer printed on it. One had been unwrapped. Girija took it out and opened the breach. It had been fired, presumably down at the camp site, and put back without being cleaned. The barrel was corroded.

Girija clucked disapprovingly. That was no way to treat valuable property. He returned the rifle to its case and began to examine the rest of his find. He soon discovered that there was more there than he had at first supposed. There were ten cases of rifles and at least thirty other boxes and cases of various sizes, in addition to ammunition containers.

He began to move some of these so as to get a look at the stenciled markings on the bigger cases, and then stopped. He would have to start back soon and there was no hope of taking an inventory that day. Besides, he had no need of an inventory.

He knew that all he had really found was hope. Of course, it would have been agreeable to dream of what was there in terms of wealth; but wealth that could only be realized, if at all, in some unmeasurable fullness of time was meaningless. It would be the hope that mattered in the days to come; and if he could draw from it the strength to go on quietly reading his transport trade journals, and turning the pages of his catalogues, and revising notional timetables, and faithfully continuing to serve Mr. Wright—if, in short, he could be patient and discreet—he might perhaps one day fulfill himself.

v

He waited, patiently and discreetly, for three years.

In the beginning it had been comparatively easy. There had been practical matters to attend to.

First, he thoroughly cleaned and greased the rifle that had been fired; then he gave some thought to the long-term problems of storage and preservation. The monsoon rains would arrive shortly, and the bamboo roof was not waterproof.

He decided to reconstruct the shelter. One Sunday he moved all the boxes out of it and laid a framework of bamboo on the ground to ensure a proper circulation of air. Over this he put a heavy tarpaulin taken from the estate compound, and then rearranged the boxes on top of it. Another tarpaulin went over the boxes and was lashed down firmly with wire rope. A third tarpaulin he incorporated in the roof. He also repaired the screens.

Thereafter, he only went to the place once a month to make sure that all was in order. He would have gone more often if he could have trusted himself, but, rather to his surprise, he had found patience easier to cultivate than discretion.

In spite of his initial resolution, it had proved hard not to take an inventory of what was in the shelter and keep it in his tin trunk. He knew that such a document was premature and pointless. He knew that if, through some mischance, Mr. Wright happened to see it and ask questions, his lies would be unconvincing. Yet the temptation had persisted. There had also been an insane desire to confide in Sumitra, to bask in her admiration and flattery, and bind her future more securely to his. He knew that she would certainly tell her mother, who would tell the father, who worked in the bank at Bukit Amphu and was a notorious chatterbox; but that temptation, too, had continued to haunt him.

During the second year he had other troubles. His mother died; and two of the cases resting on the lower tarpaulin were attacked by termites. Fortunately, he noticed the fact in good time and was able to minimize the damage. The ammunition boxes were metal, and, having given them a thick coat of bitumen paint, he moved them to the bottom of the stack. The damaged boxes he repaired with strips of teak, and sprayed all the wood containers with a powerful solution of benzine hexachloride.

The second year went by; and the third. General Templer's policy of winning the co-operation and goodwill of the people of Malaya and enlisting them in the fight against the terrorists began to succeed; and, as success snowballed into victory, curfews were lifted and road blocks removed. Areas free of terrorists were declared "white," and restrictions on unescorted civil transport movements canceled.

The day that the province in which he worked was declared

"white," Girija wrote to England for a new bus-body catalogue. The following Sunday he went to the shelter and
spent two of the happiest hours of his life, taking an inventory.

CHAPTER II

WHEN THE rubber estates in the Pangkalan district had latex for shipment, they generally notified the Anglo-Malay Transport Company at the port of Kuala Pangkalan. The company would then send their trucks to collect the latex, store it temporarily in their godowns, and finally, when instructions came through from Singapore, ship it out in one of their big motor junks.

The founder, manager, and sole proprietor of this useful enterprise was a Chinese, Mr. Tan Siow Mong.

Mr. Tan had been educated at a mission school in Macao, and spoke Hokkien and Portuguese as well as Cantonese, Malay, and English. His father had owned a fishing junk, and had divided his working year between snapper fishing and carrying cargoes of rattan up the coast to Hong Kong. When he died, in the early thirties, Mr. Tan and his two brothers had taken over the junk and turned to the more lucrative business of opium smuggling. They had been caught, in the end, by a British gunboat, and their junk had been impounded. By that time they had had a substantial sum of money saved and could accept the forfeiture of the junk with equanimity. However, a family council had considered it advisable for the Tans to leave the China Coast for a while and seek their fortunes elsewhere. One brother had gone to Singapore, another to Manila. Tan Siow Mong, the eldest, had

taken his mother to Kuala Pangkalan. There, with his share
of the family capital, he had started to deal in copra and
lend money to Malays at forty per cent. During the Japanese
occupation he had accepted a disused godown in discharge
of a debt. After the war he had tried to sell it. Unable to
find a buyer, he had eventually decided to make it pay for
itself. The Anglo-Malay Transport Company had grown from
that decision.

Mr. Tan was in the late forties now, with graying hair and
rimless glasses. He wore well-cut tussore suits, and was never
seen without a dark tie even in the hottest weather. He had
an air of well-bred dignity that was much admired in the
Chinese business community of Kuala Pangkalan.

His office was so placed that he could, without moving
from his desk, see the trucks in the unloading bay of number-
one godown and the wooden quay at which the junks discharged and took on cargo. By turning his head he could
also see, through a glass panel let into the wall beside the
door, his four Chinese assistants. Mr. Tan did not believe in
elaborate organization. Working sixty-five hours a week, the
four assistants were well able to take care of most of the
routine paper work of the business. The accounts he preferred
to look after himself.

Two of the trucks were unloading bales of latex which had
come down that afternoon from one of the Chiang Thye Phu
Syndicate estates, and he could see the Indian clerk from the
estate office checking off the weights with the godown foreman.

Mr. Tan did not like that. Mr. Wright, the estate manager,
had always, and rightly, trusted the company before. Why
had he suddenly felt it necessary to send his clerk to check
the weighing?

The clerk and the godown foreman had evidently agreed
the figures now, for, as Mr. Tan watched, the clerk smiled
and turned away. Mr. Tan had made a note to ask the foreman what reason, if any, had been given for this uncom-
plimentary change of procedure, when he saw that the clerk
was walking across the yard towards his office.

Mr. Tan looked down at the papers on his desk. It would
be undignified to be seen peering out. A moment or two later,

one of his assistants came in to say that Mr. Krishnan desired
the pleasure of a few moments' conversation with him.

Mr. Tan disapproved of Indians. He had often found them
to be disagreeably acute in business matters. He also disapproved of estate clerks, who, if they were not given occasional
presents, could delay the payment of accounts and cause
other inconveniences.

This one he remembered only from having seen him with
Mr. Wright, the estate manager. He was lean and very dark,
with bright, intelligent eyes and a predatory mouth that
smiled too much. It would be interesting to discover how
accurately he would estimate his nuisance value.

He greeted Girija with grave courtesy and asked him to sit
down.

"It is not often," he went on in English, "that we have the
pleasure of seeing you, Mr. Krishnan."

Girija smiled. "Thank you. Mr. Wright sends all compliments and best favors."

Mr. Tan congratulated himself on choosing English for the
conversation. His own, he knew, was excellent. The clerk's
was little better than the illiterate commercial patois that the
British called "Babu." It placed him at a disadvantage, small
but possibly useful.

"And are Mr. and Mrs. Wright well?"

"Both very well. We hope ditto for Mrs. Tan, self, and
family."

"Thank you, yes."

Tea was brought in from the outer office and served in minute cups. Tentative moves might now be made toward a discussion of the real object of the visit.

"This must be a busy time for you at the estate," observed
Mr. Tan.

What this banality was in effect asking was why Mr.
Wright had thought it necessary to waste his clerk's time by
sending him in to Kuala Pangkalan to supervise a normal
warehousing operation.

Girija smiled and answered in Malay. "With the rubber
market so firm, we are always busy now."

Mr. Tan nodded. He was wondering if by some faint flicker
of expression he had revealed his amusement at the clerk's

English. The Malay was fluent. Courteously, he answered in the same language.

"Let us hope the bad times are ended for good."

"Good business for one is good business for all," said Girija.

"Very true." Now, Mr. Tan decided, they were coming to the point. Reference to mutual advantage was the accepted preliminary to a squeeze.

"This tea is excellent, sir," said Girija.

Mr. Tan instantly sent for more. This again postponed pointed discussion, and further inanities were exchanged. Grudgingly, Mr. Tan had to admit to himself that the young man was handling the interview well. He found himself becoming interested.

When they were alone again, he said: "Mr. Wright is a very good manager. It must be a pleasure to work for such a man."

Girija nodded. "Indeed it is. He is, as you say, a fine manager. But he is also a man of good heart."

"I can well believe that."

"In fact," Girija went on, "when I asked him if he would allow me to come down to Kuala Pangkalan on personal business, he did not even question me before giving his permission."

"One has always known that he values your services highly." Mr. Tan was making the pace again now. The use of the phrase "values your services" would, he was sure, bring the matter to a head.

"And yet," said Girija, "I was glad he did not ask me questions." He paused.

Mr. Tan was silent. He was certain that the moment had arrived.

Girija flashed a smile. "For if he had, I would have been forced to hurt his feelings or to lie. I would not wish to do either of those things."

"Both are offenses against good taste," agreed Mr. Tan sententiously.

"Mr. Wright has been my father," said Girija. "How could I tell him that, being in need of the wisest advice on a matter of great importance, I was turning not to him but to Mr. Tan Siow Mong?"

Mr. Tan said nothing. He had nothing relevant to say. He was hurriedly revising his estimate of the situation. If the clerk were choosing this way of leading up to a request for money, he must have some absurdly large sum in mind.

Girija leaned forward earnestly. "Nowhere in Kuala Pangkalan is there a wiser head in important matters of business," he said. "It is well known."

Mr. Tan noted the qualifying phrase, "in important matters of business." He said: "You pay me an undeserved compliment."

"My friend," continued Girija, "could think of no one else whose advice on this matter would be so valuable."

"Your friend?" Mr. Tan was becoming confused again and in consequence also a little annoyed; but his tone remained polite.

"You do not know him, sir," said Girija, "and he knows you only from your high reputation. When I said that I would ask your advice on this important matter that is troubling him, he begged me not to mention him by name. The matter is highly confidential."

"Most business matters are." Mr. Tan spoke dryly. He guessed that "confidential" in this context probably meant "criminal."

Girija's smile became tentative. For the first time Mr. Tan saw him ill at ease, and decided to offer a word of reassurance. It would be irritating if the man took fright and left without revealing the object of his visit.

"If your friend respects my wisdom," he remarked, "he must also acknowledge my discretion."

Girija's smile went back into place and his eyes met Mr. Tan's. "Of course. But he is a nervous man. You will see why when I explain." He paused to choose his words before going on. "It appears that some years ago, during the emergency, when the terrorists were bringing in arms from the north, my friend found some of these arms—rifles, machine guns, ammunition." He looked up to see how Mr. Tan was taking this.

Mr. Tan smiled, but very faintly. "And so he turned them over to the police?"

"That, of course, is what he should have done." Girija shrugged. "But, as I said, my friend is a nervous man. He did not wish to call attention to himself. At the time, it seemed best to do nothing. Now he is in a difficulty."

"Yes?"

"My friend is in need of money. He thought of these arms. If he told the police about them now, there would be questions and trouble. But if a buyer for the arms could be found, perhaps his debts could be paid, and no one would be the worse. The emergency is over. No harm could come of it, only good for my friend."

Mr. Tan sat very still. "You wish me to advise your friend?"

Girija nodded. "That is what he hopes you may do, sir. Yes."

"He should still take the matter to the police. It would be very wrong to try to sell them. He need not say that he found them long ago, but he should certainly go to the police."

Girija spread out his hands. "But, sir, my friend has debts."

"It is better to go to a money lender than to risk going to prison."

Girija smiled triumphantly. "That was exactly my own advice to him, sir. To risk going to prison for a few hundred dollars is the act of a fool. I told him so."

Mr. Tan hesitated. The agreement baffled him. He knew instinctively that somewhere, somehow, he had mismanaged the conversation. He knew that he was left with only one question to ask, and that when he had asked it he would have lost a battle of wits. But he also knew that his curiosity would have to be satisfied. Mentally he shrugged off the humiliation.

"And what was his reply?" he asked.

Girija's hand went to the row of ball-point pens in his shirt pocket and drew from behind it a folded sheet of paper. He opened it out and handed it across the desk.

"This paper, sir," he said. "My friend gave me this paper."

Mr. Tan took the paper, spread it out on the desk in front of him, and looked down. It was a typed list with the word INVENTORY at the head of it. He read on:

Description	Type	Quantity	Today's Free Market Value ($ Straits)
Rifles	.303 Military S.A. Belge	54	16,000
.303 Ammo	For above	5,000 rds	6,000
Machine pistols	Schmeisser	25	18,000
.300 Ammo	With magazines for above	8,000 rds	7,000
Bazookas	U.S. Govt. pattern	4	6,000
Ammo for same	" " "	35 rds	1,000
Grenades	Mills unfused	} 100	2,000
Fuses	For same		
Land mines	Teller	40	4,000
		Total	60,000
		Equals £ (Sterling)	7,500
		Equals $(U.S.)	21,000

Note   All items in brand new mint condition in original mnfrs. packings, containers, etc.

Prices   All prices f.o.b. vicinity Kuala Pangkalan

Terms and Conditions   Items sold separate subject 20% increase.

Mr. Tan looked up.

"You see, sir," said Girija softly, "I was wrong. It is not just a matter of a few hundred dollars, but of many thousands."

Mr. Tan pretended to read the list through a second time in order to give himself time to think. He had little doubt that the "friend" for whom the clerk claimed to be acting was nonexistent. The Indian must have been desperate for money to take the risk of approaching a comparative stranger in this way, or very sure of himself as a judge of character. Mr. Tan had an uneasy feeling that the latter explanation might be the more likely. The fellow looked confident enough, and not at all desperate. Of course, he could be lying, and the whole story could be a mere trick to get money; but Mr. Tan did not really think so. In any case, it would be simple to find out. He looked up again and met the clerk's yes.

"My friend," said Girija, "would be willing to pay a commission of fifty per cent to anyone who found a buyer, and who would take delivery of the goods."

Mr. Tan shook his head. "But this would be a serious criminal matter. Does your friend not understand that?"

"That was my first thought, too," said Girija approvingly, "but he did not agree. This is not stolen property, he says. It has no owner. If it should leave the country, the police would have no interest in it. The emergency is over."

"But the laws remain."

"That is true." Girija nodded thoughtfully. "You think, then, sir, that I should tell my friend that you advise him to go to the police?"

"I think you should tell him to put the whole matter out of his mind." Mr. Tan paused and then added: "Perhaps later the law will not be so strict."

"Yes, that is so."

"Such merchandise as this is always saleable." Mr. Tan looked down again at the list. "Have you seen any of these items?"

"My friend is naturally careful."

"But do you believe him? You say he wishes to find a buyer. A list is not proof that there is something to sell. Could he produce samples?"

"He would be more than ready to do that, sir."

Mr. Tan refolded the inventory. "I know little about these matters," he said, "but I have heard that buyers in this market are not easy to reach. Contacts must be found. Time must be spent. There can be no urgency."

"My friend is very patient."

"Then, do as I suggest. Tell him to forget for a while." He looked up at Girija. "You agree?"

"Of course, sir."

Mr. Tan held up the list. "And I may keep this paper?"

It was a test question.

Girija smiled. "My friend will be happy for it to remain in such wise hands, sir."

He rose. The interview was over. When the usual courtesies had been exchanged, he left.

Mr. Tan watched him walk away across the yard, then sent for the Chiang Thye Phu Syndicate estate's files.

The first thing was to find out whether the clerk's discretion and sense of self-preservation were as lively as they had appeared to be. If he had been foolhardy enough to type out his list on Mr. Wright's estate-office typewriter, and then leave it with someone who could, if it seemed advantageous, go to the authorities and gain credit by reporting the incident, Mr. Tan wanted no more to do with him and would burn the paper at once. If, as he suspected, the young man had been careful to leave himself in a position to deny effectively all knowledge of the conversation they had just had, and of the list, then something might be made of the situation.

He looked through Mr. Wright's office consignment notes and compared the typing on them with that of the list. It was obvious that the list had not been typed on the same machine. So far so good. He read through the list once more and then locked it in his private office safe.

Later that day, when he had had further time to think, he wrote to his brother in Singapore.

ii

Tan Yam Heng was the disreputable member of the family. Such, at least, was the view of his brothers in Kuala Pangkalan and Manila.

He was one of the founders of the Singapore Democratic Action Party and organizer of a waterfront trade union which, though small in membership, had sufficient nuisance value to levy tribute on two of the bigger stevedoring companies. As the fruits of these negotiations were always handed over to him personally, privately, and in cash, he did not consider it necessary to report their receipt either to the union auditors or to the income-tax authorities. He had no time to waste on the pettifogging rituals of accountancy and other hindrances to social progress. He saw himself as a man of power, a manipulator of puppets, choosing to work

behind the scenes until the strategic moment came for him
to step forward and lead his party on to victory.

If that had been all there was to say of him, his brothers
would have been content. His political pretensions they could
ignore, and, devious men themselves, they did not seriously
object to his methods of augmenting his income. What they
did object to, strongly, was what he did with it.

Most Chinese like to gamble, and with some this liking
becomes an addiction as compulsive as those of drugs or
alcohol. Yam Heng was a gambler of this kind. Moreover, he
was a stupid gambler. Games of chance are at least subject
to the law of averages, race horses do sometimes run true to
form, and skill can often qualify bad luck at poker; but
Yam Heng's conceit and fantasies of omnipotence had in
the end demanded more esoteric gratifications. He had taken
to gambling on the "pickle" market.

This unofficial market in raw rubber is conducted by free-
booters operating outside the respectable Singapore brokerage
houses, and they are speculating on small price fluctuations
over short periods. On the pickle market a consignment
of rubber in transit may theoretically change hands several
times in the course of a day. Large sums of money are made
and lost on feverish, bull-and-bear transactions. The suc-
cessful speculators are Chinese with great experience, cool
heads, and reliable intelligence organizations. Much use is
made of the time difference between the London and Singapore markets, and a few minutes' lead on a piece of cabled
information can make thousands of dollars for its possessor.
It is the efficient who generally win; the gamblers who
generally lose.

The pickle market was no place for Yam Heng. The acquaintance who had introduced him to it was one of a
syndicate of small men, and they had been perfectly willing
to let an outsider buy in; the stronger the syndicate, the
better; but his arrogant impatience with their wariness and
caution had soon antagonized them. Eventually he had
taken his money out of the syndicate and started to operate
on his own.

If he had immediately and heavily lost, the blow to his
self-esteem might have caused him to think twice about

continuing. Unfortunately, he had won. After that, it had been too late for second thoughts.

His early appeals for loans had been received by his brothers with fraternal tolerance, and responded to in the belief that the money lent would be repaid. They had known, of course, that he was overfond of gambling, but had believed his profligacy in that respect to be confined to horse racing or fan-tan. The discovery of the true nature of the "investments" they were so innocently subsidizing had been a disagreeable shock; so had the realization that Yam Heng had been deceitfully making his applications simultaneously, and in identical terms, to both of them.

There had been worse to come. In the face of their joint refusals to lend him another cent, Yam Heng had blandly informed them that the various union funds in his charge were some thousands of dollars short, and that unless the shortages were made good before the annual audit, the consequences for the Tan name might be serious. There had been hasty consultation between Kuala Pangkalan and Manila. The brothers had paid up in the end, but only after both of them had been to Singapore and personally checked the union books. The days when Yam Heng could be trusted had gone. Thereafter, he had the status somewhat of a poor relation—a responsibility to be discharged as inexpensively as possible.

It was with this responsibility in mind that Mr. Tan had written his letter. Some weeks earlier he had received one of Yam Heng's periodic requests for money and noted a veiled belligerence in the wording. It had reminded him that the annual audit of the union books was due shortly, and that Yam Heng would soon be making his annual attempt to extort money by hinting at another raid on the union funds. Mr. Tan's nerves were strong, and for the previous three years he had successfully refused to be intimidated; but he knew gamblers, and there was always the chance that one day Yam Heng might become desperate.

At that moment, in fact, Yam Heng was merely depressed. He had had two small wins in the past two weeks and a bigger loss which had canceled out the winnings. His brother's letter annoyed him.

It contained a polite inquiry after his health, a detailed

account of their mother's most recent illness, and a proposal
that he visit Kuala Pangkalan at a convenient moment in the
near future. It mentioned that the junk *Happy Dawn*
would be unloading in Singapore the following week, and
that the master would be instructed to offer him a free
passage. It gave no hint of a possible reason for the visit.

Yam Heng knew his brother too well to suppose that the
visit had been proposed for any social or family reason.
Their mother was senile. Her current state of health could
only have been mentioned to make the invitation seem logical
to some stranger reading the letter. Yam Heng disliked having
his curiosity aroused unless he had the means on hand to
satisfy it. The offer of the junk passage irritated him also.
It was his brother's way of saying that if he wanted to travel
in comfort by train or plane, he could pay his own fare. He
considered sending a dignified reply regretting that pressure
of work compelled him to decline the invitation; but, finally,
curiosity and the faint hope of another loan decided him to
accept. He had just enough money for the train fare.

His brother met him at the station, greeted him warmly,
and drove him to the ornate brick-and-stucco house in Wil-
loughby Road. The first evening was spent in celebrating
the family reunion. Old Mrs. Tan emerged from her room,
an elaborate dinner was consumed, the young children made
their Uncle Yam tell them about Singapore, and the eldest
son showed his Voigtlander camera and some of the color-
slide photographs of birds which he had made with it. Yam
Heng found it all very agreeable. His brother remained
friendly and courteous. There were no references, oblique
or otherwise, to their long estrangement, or to the reasons
for it. He permitted himself a few restrained smiles, some
delicate compliments to his sister-in-law, and a joke or two
with the younger children.

It was not until the following day that his brother revealed
the reason for the invitation. In the morning they toured the
godowns, visited the truck-maintenance shed, and watched
one of the junks unloading fifty-gallon drums of fuel oil.
Then they went to the office and tea was served.

"And how," Siow Mong inquired at last, "is the pickle
market?"

Yam Heng gave him an impassive stare.

"I ask," Siow Mong continued after a pause, "not in a spirit of criticism, but because I want information."

For one wild moment Yam Heng wondered if his brother were contemplating a foray of his own. Then he shrugged. "Some make money, some lose."

His brother nodded sagely as if he had had a suspicion confirmed. "I did hear," he went on, "that there is another thriving market now in Singapore."

"There are markets there in most things."

"Yes. But I heard—I cannot remember from what source —that the market in arms is particularly active at present."

"Oh, yes." Yam Heng spoke indifferently. "The Indonesian rebels are trying to buy. They have several purchasing agents there."

"Several?"

"There is one from Sumatra, one from Java, another from Celebes. They are united only in their opposition to the central government."

"They compete?"

Yam Heng shrugged. "They must. There is not so much to buy. It is not easy."

"How do they pay? Rupiahs?"

"Nobody would take rupiahs. Pounds or dollars, I suppose."

"Dollars U.S.?"

"Straits or Hong Kong dollars, I would think. Why?"

"Cash?"

"I suppose so."

His brother nodded approvingly. "I would think this a very satisfactory business."

"No doubt it is."

"These agents you speak of—you know them?"

"I know who they are, yes."

"Have you not thought of taking an interest in the business yourself?"

Yam Heng smiled sourly. "The peddler cannot do business with an empty tray."

"And if the tray were to be filled?"

Yam Heng hesitated. His brother was not in the habit of making idle remarks. "That would require capital," he said cautiously.

"Not necessarily."

Siow Mong went over to his private safe, got out the piece of paper Girija had left with him, and handed it to Yam Heng.

"That was brought to me by a man who wants a buyer for those goods," he said.

Yam Heng read the list through carefully. His expression did not change. When he had finished, he glanced up at his brother. "It says that delivery must be taken in the *vicinity* of Kuala Pangkalan. What does that mean?"

Siow Mong told him about Girija's visit and summarized the conversation they had had.

Yam Heng listened without interrupting, and then read through the list again. He spoke as he read.

"Is this Indian to be trusted?"

"I think so. If he gets what he wants."

"I know very little about this market. Are these prices realistic?"

"I was able to make only one inquiry. There is a dealer in machinery here who used to import sporting rifles. Naturally, I had to be careful how I asked, but from what I was able to learn I would think these prices are three times what they should be. But in a sellers' market, who knows?"

"I could find out in Singapore." Yam Heng paused. "What is your proposal?"

Siow Mong sat down behind his desk and leaned forward across it. "You are a gambler, brother," he said pleasantly, "and you know what I think of that. Especially as, in the game you play, you cannot win. I am inviting you to try a different one."

"Selling arms is no game."

"It can be very profitable." Siow Mong's smile faded. "Let us have no misunderstandings. I have a good business here. I do not like risks. I do not have to take them. If you can find a way to handle this transaction without personal risk to me, I will help you, for a small handling charge of ten per cent. But I must know exactly what you intend to do, first. If I agree with your plan, I will put you in touch with the Indian. Is that understood?"

Yam Heng had been listening absently and did not reply to his brother's question. "There are two problems here," he said slowly. "The first is to get the goods out of the country. That is a matter of careful organization. The second problem is more difficult. They must be made respectable."

Siow Mong waited. Yam Heng might be a fool in many respects, but he could sometimes be shrewd.

"You see," Yam Heng continued after a moment or two, "if *I* were to sell these goods in Singapore, I might never receive payment. They would deal, yes; but these are not normal business dealings. There is no trust. 'Payment on delivery,' they would say. But when I had delivered, they could give me a five-thousand-dollar tip and tell me to go to the police for the rest. What could I answer in such a case? You say that these are not stolen goods, and no doubt you are right. But I would be as helpless as if they were, if I had to deal illegally."

"What is the alternative? How do you make such property respectable?"

"There must be an intermediary, someone who will sign papers, admit ownership if necessary, and take perhaps five per cent for his trouble."

"A Frenchman or an American, perhaps?"

"What sort of person? An Englishman?"

"It would be better if he were not a subject of the Federation or of Singapore. I am thinking of the emergency regulations."

"There are Americans doing such business."

"Could you approach one of them?"

Yam Heng pursed his lips. "This would be too small for those men, I think. Besides, they would want too much for themselves. We do not need an experienced man."

Siow Mong thought for a moment. Then he asked: "Have you met Khoo Ah Au?"

"Who is he?"

"I was forgetting that you have been out of touch with family affairs. He married our niece in Manila last year. They live in Hong Kong now. Perhaps he would know of a suitable American. I shall be going there next month. I might discuss the requirements with him. Possibly . . ." He broke off. "But this is all talk. You say that to ship the goods is only a matter of organization. How would you do it?"

Yam Heng told him.

His brother listened and was impressed. "It might be done," he admitted grudgingly at last.

They discussed some details, and later that day Siow Mong telephoned Girija. He referred to their recent conversation and then said that although he, Mr. Tan, could do nothing in the matter, he had heard of a Mr. Lee who might be able to give useful advice. A meeting was arranged.

iii

Girija never guessed that "Mr. Lee" was Mr. Tan's brother. Mr. Tan was refined. Mr. Lee had coarse, heavy features, a sullen expression, and a hectoring, impatient way of speaking that bordered on rudeness. Girija did not like him.

They met at a rest house not far from the estate. Mr. Lee had taken a room there for the night, and they identified one another without difficulty.

The first meeting was brief. Mr. Lee produced Girija's list and asked him if he were prepared to prove the existence of the items listed by producing a sample of any one of them that Mr. Lee himself selected.

Girija nodded. "I have already said that my friend could give a sample if required. I ask only that the item chosen should be small and light."

"How small? How light?"

"Small and light enough to be carried in the pocket. You would not ask me to cycle along the road with a rifle on my back."

"Is a machine-pistol loading clip small enough?"

"Yes. And I will bring a few rounds of ammunition with it."

"When?"

"Monday."

"Today is Thursday. Why not tomorrow?"

"It cannot be arranged before Monday."

"Very well. But I have no time to waste."

On Sunday Girija went out to Awang and made his way up to the dump. It was several months since he had last repaired the shelter, and the screens were in a bad state. The termites were back again, too. He hoped that Mr. Lee was in as much of a hurry as he professed to be.

On Monday he met Mr. Lee again and showed him some ammunition and a clip.

Mr. Lee wiped the grease off the clip and examined the German markings carefully. Finally he put the clip in his pocket.

"That would seem to be in order," he said. "Naturally, I will have to check these marks. In the meantime I must have some information. Where would delivery take place?"

"In this area."

"What do you consider would be needed to transport the goods?"

"One thirty-hundredweight truck."

"Are the goods near a road?"

"Not at present. They can be brought to a loading point fifty yards from a road, but that operation will require three days' advance notice."

"That may be difficult."

"It must be allowed for." Girija spoke with assurance. He had had three years to solve this problem in logistics, and knew that there was only one answer to it.

"You say fifty yards from a road. Would you and your friend be there to help with the loading? It would have to be done at night."

"I or my friend would be there. Two men could do the loading in less than an hour. The heaviest boxes are those with the rifles. There are nine of them, and they weigh about forty pounds each. But they have rope handles."

Mr. Lee looked at him with interest. "You speak as if you have had experience before."

"I am a businessman, Mr. Lee." Girija paused. "Perhaps, now that you have examined the samples, we should discuss financial arrangements and terms."

Mr. Lee took the list from his pocket. "These prices you mention are foolish. You knew that, of course."

Girija smiled. "I knew that you would say they were foolish, Mr. Lee. And, of course, I understand. These are always difficult goods to sell. The right buyer may not be found immediately. The demand fluctuates. Handling and storage charges are high. You must work on a very small margin of profit. That is why I am prepared to pay fifty per cent of these estimated prices to the selling agent."

"*You* are prepared, Mr. Krishnan? What about your friend?"

Girija was not disconcerted. "I am authorized to speak for him at present," he said. "I say 'at present' because my friend is considering the possibility of going to Singapore and investigating the market personally."

"Could your friend move the goods?"

"He is a patient man. He could wait."

Mr. Lee did not reply immediately. He was tired of Girija's toothy smile and the knowing lilt in his voice. "Your prices are foolish," he repeated coldly.

Girija smiled again. "Then I will reduce them, Mr. Lee. I will accept thirty thousand dollars Malay net."

"That is an insignificant reduction."

"It is the only one I can make."

"I will pay twenty thousand."

They compromised in the end on twenty-five thousand, to be paid one month after the goods were handed over. A protocol for the transaction was also agreed. Under this, each of the high contracting parties was protected against murder or trickery on the part of the other. The meeting ended in an atmosphere of goodwill and mutual respect.

The following day Tan Yam Heng took the train back to Singapore.

The following week Tan Siow Mong flew up to Hong Kong. He was there for only two days; but he was able to spend an entertaining and constructive evening with his niece and her husband, Khoo Ah Au.

CHAPTER III

TWELVE HOURS out of Kobe, the *Silver Isle* ran into bad weather and more than half her ninety passengers took to their cabins.

She was owned by the Isle Line, which operated a freight run between San Francisco and Calcutta, calling at Yokohama, Kobe, Hong Kong, Manila, Saigon, Singapore, and, occasionally, Rangoon. With the growing popularity of round-the-world trips, the company's passenger traffic had increased rapidly, and they had refitted two of their newer ships so as to enlarge and improve the cabin accommodation. The *Silver Isle* was one of these. Unfortunately, the improvements, which included an extra deck, had also added considerably to her top hamper, and in any but the calmest sea she rolled heavily.

For Greg Nilsen, however, the bad weather came as a blessing. Both he and Dorothy, his wife, were good sailors and could go down to the dining room with their appetites unimpaired. True, Dorothy did complain that the incessant rolling made her tired; but he could only view that as a minor inconvenience. As far as he was concerned, any weather conditions that kept Arlene Drecker confined to her cabin were fine.

Greg was an engineer and the owner of a precision die-casting business in Wilmington, Delaware. He and Dorothy had been planning their round-the-world trip for over two years—ever since their younger boy had gone to college.

41

They could have done it earlier if they had been prepared to fly most of the way, but Dorothy had said no. She had wanted to do it properly—by sea, and in small, slow boats.

"After all," she had said, "we're only going to be able to do it once in our lives. All the tourists go to Tokyo and Hong Kong and Paris and Rome, places like that. I think we ought to see some of the little out-of-the-way places as well; the ones most people just read about, or see pictures of in photographic books; wonderful places like Tahiti, where the cruise ships don't go."

Greg had agreed with her. However, a few evenings spent with maps, sailing lists, and an eighteen-inch globe had modified their views. They had found, for example, that if they wanted to go to Japan and Hong Kong, a one-day visit to Tahiti would add two weeks to their travel schedule. In the end it was plain that, even if they compromised on the size and speed of the boats, confined themselves to the regular ports of call, and cut out South America completely, the trip would still take at least two months. If they did not want to spend all the time traveling, it would take three.

Greg had some very capable men working for him, but, at the management level, Nilsen Die-Casting and Tools was very much a one-man business. A three-month vacation could not be embarked upon just when he felt like it; and although he had for some time been planning a reorganization that would enable him to delegate more responsibility, it involved changes that could only be made gradually. He had allowed two years—one in which to make the changes, and one in which to see that they worked—but, even so, it had still not been easy to get away. There had been some moments in the month before they had sailed when difficulties over a new government contract had made it look as if the trip would have to be called off. However, the difficulties had been ironed out in time and they had left Wilmington early in October. Because of the amount of baggage they were taking, they had gone by train to San Francisco. They had sailed on the seventh.

Neither of them had traveled much by ship before. During the war Greg had gone to Europe on a troopship. Together they had been to England and France and back on the *United States* and the *America*. That was all. They had received much advice from more experienced friends. One of them, Greg remembered later, had had a solemn warning to deliver.

"It's the first two or three days you want to be careful of," this man had said, "and especially the first day just after you sail. You're going to be with those people for weeks. But you'll be feeling strange and want to be friendly. You'll go into the bar and have a drink to celebrate the start of the trip. Watch it. Don't start getting friendly with anyone. Wait. You start talking to someone, and before you know it, bingo, you're stuck with the ship's bore. It can ruin a trip."

Arlene Drecker was not the ship's bore, but, as far as Greg was concerned, she became an even more maddening affliction.

After the ship had sailed, he and Dorothy had stayed on deck until they had cleared the Golden Gate. They had promised the boys to make a complete photographic record of the trip, and Greg had been up on the boat deck with the 16 mm. Bell and Howell for the best part of an hour. It had been a sunny day, but with a cool breeze. They had been glad, when there was no more to see aloft, to get down into the warmth of the bar for a pre-lunch drink.

Arlene had been sitting by herself at a small table about six feet away from them. She had been writing radio telegrams and sipping a Martini. Then the pen she had borrowed from the writing room had run out of ink, and she had looked round in exasperation. Greg had politely offered her his. She had accepted. Later, when she returned his pen, she had asked them to have a drink.

"No, no. You join us," Dorothy had said.

Arlene had smiled. "You know, a gal traveling alone has one big problem—how to persuade people to sometimes let her buy a drink."

Nevertheless, she had joined them and had another Martini. They had gone down to lunch together. Later that day the chief steward had approached Greg with the permanent seating plan for the dining room and asked if he and Mrs. Nilsen minded having Miss Drecker sit at their table. There were no single tables, he had explained, and Miss Drecker did not want to be with a crowd. Greg had had little choice but to agree.

That night, when they went down to dinner, there had

been a bottle of champagne on the table—to thank them, Arlene had explained, for letting her sit with them, and to drink a toast to the voyage.

Later, in their cabin, Greg had grumbled about this. He did not care for champagne, which always gave him indigestion; but Dorothy had not been sympathetic. It showed, she had said, that Arlene did not intend to impose on them. The champagne had been a very nice way of telling them that. The fact that it gave him indigestion was beside the point. Dorothy had taken a liking to Arlene.

She was a tall, angular blonde with large white teeth, a beige complexion, and very thin legs. Dorothy deduced from things said that she was probably in her late forties, but she certainly looked younger. She dressed smartly and in a vaguely masculine style that suited her, although she was inclined sometimes to overload herself with chunky gold bracelets and wear earrings which accentuated the narrowness of her head. She talked freely, and not unamusingly, about herself in a carefully mellifluous voice which creaked slightly on each change of register. Her father had been a Los Angeles real-estate man. During the war she had been in the American Red Cross and had stayed on with that organization in France and Germany until '47. Then her father had died and she had gone back to California. She had a house in Palm Springs now, which she rented when she went away on her trips. She had never had any great desire to get married, although she liked married people and was crazy about kids. But things had to work out right, or it was no good. She had a sister who had been married four times, and what a mess and misery all that had been. Her attitude toward men was one of sardonic camaraderie tinged with disdain.

By the fourth day out, Greg's dislike of her had become intense. The bottle of champagne had been a minor irritant; but when at dinner on the second night a bottle of claret had appeared, he had objected.

"It was very thoughtful of you, Miss Drecker," he had said, "but Dorothy and I don't drink wine as a regular thing. So if you don't mind . . ."

"But the steward's already opened it. Oh, come on, Mr. Nilsen. Live dangerously."

Dorothy had giggled. The steward had smiled and poured the wine.

"Now, look, Dorothy," Greg had said when they were alone, "Arlene Drecker can drink all the wine she wants and so can you, for that matter. But I'm not having her tell me what I'm going to drink."

"She didn't mean it that way."

"I don't care what way she meant it. The way it worked out was that I had to drink something I didn't want or seem boorish. Dammit, she's not our hostess on this ship. I wish she'd stop behaving as if she were."

"She's only trying to be friendly."

"Listen. If you want wine or we want wine, *I'll* order it."

The following night Arlene had ordered burgundy; but Greg had taken the precaution of ordering in advance a bottle of *rosé* and the two wines arrived together.

"Too bad," Greg had said blandly. "What about joining us and having rosé, Arlene?"

"Rosé with roast beef?" Arlene had raised her eyebrows. "Thanks, I prefer burgundy."

But the next night, when the steward had produced the partly consumed bottle of burgundy, Arlene had not pressed them to share it with her. Greg had succeeded in making his point. It had not been until later in the evening that he had discovered that she had paid his bar bill for the day. Dorothy had not been able to help laughing.

Two days before they had reached Yokohama, a notice had gone up announcing that, during the ship's stay in port, conducted sightseeing tours ashore had been arranged. Those passengers wishing to take advantage of the special rates offered should inform the purser's office within the next twenty-four hours.

Greg had put his and Dorothy's names down. At lunch Dorothy had mentioned the fact.

Arlene had stared at her incredulously. "Sightseeing tours! Honey, you must be out of your mind."

"What's wrong with sightseeing tours?" Greg had asked. "After all, that's what we're making the trip for—to see sights."

"Oh, Greg!" Arlene had laughed tolerantly. "Have you ever been on a Japanese sightseeing tour?"

"Have you?"

"Yes, and I can tell you it's the end. They just cram you into a bus, give you a box lunch, and then drive you from one clip joint to another. They don't want to show you what you want to see. They just want you to buy things—cameras, fans, bits of fake jewelry."

"That's not what it says on the notice board."

"Naturally. Look, if you want to go rubber-necking, let me take you. I've been before. All you do is hire a car and have the man drive you around. You're on your own. You can stop when you want and go on when you want."

Dorothy had turned to him uncertainly. "What do you think, Greg?"

"Well, we've put our names down now."

Arlene had sighed. "Well, take them off again. Why not? If you want to be tourists, you may as well do it properly. This is not the best time of the year to come to Japan, but, since you are here, at least make yourselves comfortable."

Unhappily, she had been right. Those who had gone on the sightseeing tour had returned exhausted, ill-tempered, and late for dinner. Dorothy had had a fascinating day and bought a pair of carved soapstone hairpins which the barman said were worth at least three times what she had paid for them.

The following day, and then later at Kobe, the performance had been repeated. It could have been his fancy, but Greg suspected that both Dorothy and Arlene had a tacit agreement to ignore his leadership and run things their own way. When the table steward had reported that Miss Drecker was staying in her cabin, seasick, it had required an effort of will to utter the appropriate words of regret.

The bad weather lasted for two days and Greg thoroughly enjoyed them both. When on the third day Arlene made a wan appearance at lunch, he was almost as solicitous as Dorothy.

Then came the misunderstanding over the ship's shuffleboard tournament. The doctor had wanted Greg and Dorothy on his team, and Greg, without consulting Dorothy, had accepted. When the first round was announced over the ship's loudspeakers, Dorothy was missing. Greg found her eventually in Arlene's cabin playing Scrabble. By the time he had explained what had happened and they had reached the deck, the teams had been rearranged and they were out of the tournament.

Greg was annoyed. He did not mind about the shuffleboard, which he thought an old man's game, but he did mind having to apologize to the doctor.

Dorothy was very reasonable about it. "I'm sorry, dear, but you didn't tell me, did you?"

"I thought you were around on deck."

"Well, you were reading and Arlene suggested Scrabble. I know how you hate that, so I didn't bother you."

"Did you have to play down in the cabin?"

"She's got a very comfortable cabin. You haven't seen it. It's twice the size of ours. Look, dear, I'm sure the doctor didn't mind a bit. He understood."

"Yes, I know. But all the same . . ."

All the same, he was annoyed. That evening, when Arlene and Dorothy began to talk about the shopping they were going to do in Hong Kong, his annoyance returned.

"The big stores are in Victoria," Arlene was saying. "That's on Hong Kong island itself. But for us gals the best places are over in Kowloon. That's on the mainland. There's one called Star of Siam in the Peninsular Hotel that's a must."

"Shops in a hotel?" asked Dorothy.

"That's right. There are two whole floors of them."

"Sounds like a tourist trap to me," said Greg.

Arlene smiled at him. "What would you say to a suit in the best English tropical worsted, made to order, for twenty-five dollars?"

"Oh, sure, I know all about that. They just copy a suit you have and it falls to pieces the first time you wear it."

Arlene smiled again, very gently. "Is that what happens? I've never heard that, not from anyone who's really been there and bought one."

"Why don't you try, dear?" said Dorothy. "I mean, twenty-five dollars for a suit is cheap. And you do need some more summer outfits."

"Brooks Brothers is good enough for me." He knew it was a dull, foolish remark even as he said it.

"Well, it's not important." Dorothy spoke a trifle grimly. Arlene's silence was monumentally tactful.

It was a Sunday night and there was no dancing after

dinner. When Arlene had gone to her cabin, Dorothy suggested a walk around the deck before they went to bed.

After a while she said: "Darling, I'm worried. I'm having a good time, a wonderful time. You don't seem to be."

"Because I don't happen to want to buy a suit in Hong Kong?"

"Now you're being tiresome."

"All right. That woman gets on my nerves."

"Arlene? But she's really a very nice person."

"Well, I don't like her and I wish she'd get out of our hair."

"She's not in *my* hair. I think she's being very sweet and helpful. Can you imagine what it would have been like in Tokyo if we hadn't been lucky enough to have her to show us around? It couldn't have been very exciting for her. She'd seen it all before. She went to a lot of trouble for us."

"Well, I wish she'd go to a lot of trouble for somebody else. Anyway, if she's seen it all before, why does she come on the trip?"

"Greg, dear, you're usually more understanding and tolerant. She's a very lonely woman."

"And for some very good reasons."

"That's an unkind thing to say. It doesn't sound like you."

"Well, it is me. I told you, I don't like the woman. The chief steward told me she didn't want to sit with a crowd. Why not, if she's so lonely? Why did she have to pick on us?"

Dorothy did not reply immediately, and they walked once around the deck in silence.

"Look, darling," she said finally, "we didn't come on this trip just for a vacation, but because we wanted to travel and because we wanted to see something of the world outside America. If we were multimillionaires, maybe we could have done it in our own private yacht. As it is, we have to go with other people. We're not in a position to choose our traveling companions, any more than they're in a position to choose us. So, we've all got to make the best of one another. Isn't that common sense?"

Greg chuckled. "It's a poem, and beautifully delivered."

"Greg, I'm serious."

"I know you are, dear." He drew her arm through his. "That's why you're so cute."

He had recovered his good humor. Dorothy's homilies usually had that effect on him. Before they were married, she had taught at a kindergarten school, and in moments of stress traces of the old Montessori manner were still discernible.

"You're maddening," she said.

"I know it." He stopped and kissed her cheek. "All right, darling, we'll be nice, well-behaved American tourists spreading sweetness and light and hard currency wherever we go."

"If you'll just spread a little of that sweetness in Arlene's direction, that's all I ask."

"You said make the best of one another. Okay, I'll make the best of her, whatever that is."

"Thank you, dear."

He sighed. "Anyway, I'll try."

And, for some days, try he did.

ii

The *Silver Isle* was to be in Hong Kong for forty-eight hours, discharging and taking on cargo, and she docked on the Kowloon side of the harbor by the wharfs on the Canton Road.

This was convenient for the passengers. They could go ashore any time they wanted, and were within easy walking distance of both the ferry to Victoria and the Peninsular Hotel.

Left to themselves, Greg and Dorothy would probably have taken the ferry straightaway and gone across to see Hong Kong itself; but Arlene led them first to the hotel.

"There'll be plenty of time for sightseeing later," she told them. "Let's get organized first. I suppose you've heard that these Chinese can make anything from a pair of earrings to a man's tuxedo overnight. Well, it just is not true. If you want anything properly made, you have to give them at least thirty-six hours. So let's do our shopping first, and then we don't have to worry."

They window-shopped for a while in the hotel, and then the girls left Greg with a tailor named Mr. Yu and went back to the Star of Siam to order Thai silk skirts. They had arranged to meet in the hotel lobby. When Greg had chosen his suit materials and had his measurements taken, he made his way down there.

He knew that he had at least half an hour to wait. It was too early for a drink. There was a row of travel agents' booths in the lobby, most of them offering sightseeing tours. It might be a good idea, he thought, to see about renting a car and driver.

The moment that thought came into his head another one followed it: "Maybe I'd better check with Arlene first." It was enough. He said "God dammit" between his teeth, and went over to the nearest booth.

A Chinese in a black business suit came forward.

"Good morning, sir. What can I do for you?"

"I want to rent a limousine with a driver to take us around. Do you have cars?"

"We do not have our own cars, but we can arrange that for you, sir. An American car, if you wish. When and for how long would you want it?"

"Well, we only have two days. We'd like to see as much as we can. We could start right after lunch from here."

"Then I would suggest, sir, that this afternoon you go across on the car ferry to Hong Kong and drive up to the Peak. There is a magnificent view from there. After that I would suggest a drive to Deep Water Bay and Repulse Bay, with tea at the hotel there. Tomorrow you could tour Kowloon and the New Territories."

"Would that take us as far as the Red Chinese border?"

"Certainly, sir. And you could lunch at Shatin. But I will get you a good driver who will know all these things and make helpful suggestions."

"How much would it cost?"

By the time Arlene and Dorothy arrived it was all settled.

Arlene clearly resented having the arrangements taken out of her hands in this fashion, but had difficulty in finding anything in them to criticize. She did the best she could, however.

"We didn't have to have a car this afternoon," she said. "We could have gone across to the island by the Star ferry and taken a cab on the other side."

"In all this humidity?" said Dorothy. "It's worse than August in New York."

"Humidity?" Arlene smiled knowingly. "You wait until we get to Singapore."

Greg congratulated himself on this small rift in the female alliance; but his satisfaction was short-lived. They went to a Chinese restaurant for lunch and Arlene insisted on their all using chopsticks. It was considered discourteous, she said, to use a fork. Dorothy thought it great fun; but Greg, who liked Chinese food and was hungry, became impatient and dropped some egg on his tie.

After lunch they went back to the Peninsular Hotel to pick up the car and driver.

The car proved to be a three-year-old Chevrolet Bel-Air, and Arlene looked at it disdainfully. The driver was a young Chinese wearing gray flannel trousers, a dark blue blazer, and a chauffeur's cap. He took off the cap and stood respectfully at attention as he held the rear door open for the ladies.

"Want me to go in front with you?" Greg asked him.

"If you do not object, sir, I think you will be more comfortable."

"Okay."

When they were in the car the driver turned to him.

"I see you have a camera, sir. There are certain places on the road up to the Peak where particularly good shots can be obtained. Would you like me to stop at those places?"

"That'd be fine. By the way, what's your name?"

"My Chinese name is Khoo Ah Au, sir." The driver smiled. "American clients find it easier to call me Jimmy."

iii

Khoo Ah Au liked American tourists. He found them, on the whole, generous, easygoing, and completely predictable. They were rarely ill-tempereed, as the British often were, or eccentric in their demands, as were the French. They did not harass him with questions he had not been asked before, and listened politely, if sometimes inattentively, to the information he had to impart. They used their light meters conscientiously before taking photographs and bought their souvenirs dutifully at the shops which paid him commission. Above all, he found their personal relationships very easy to read. It was probably a matter of race, he thought. His own people were always very careful not to give themselves away, to expose crude feelings about one another. Americans seemed not to care how much was understood by strangers. It was almost as if they enjoyed being transparent.

This American and these two women, for example. You had only to listen for a few minutes to what they said and how they said it, and everything was clear. The woman called Arlene was attracted to the wife, and the husband was jealous. Possibly he had no cause; possibly the two women had done no more than exchange confidences or touch each other's hands; but he was jealous. And the hungry woman was jealous of him. Only the wife, personable but middle-aged, seemed unconcerned. She did not appear flattered by the situation, or even aware of it. Perhaps she was more subtle than she sounded. When he had listened a little more, he would be able to decide.

They were on the car ferry when he heard something that interested him keenly. "If we'd gone across by the passenger ferry," the Arlene woman was saying, "you'd have been able to get a beautiful shot of the boat in dock."

"Well, maybe I'll do that tomorrow," the American said. "Anyway, there'll be plenty of chances of seeing her in dock."

It was the word "boat" that had interested him. He had assumed that the trio were staying at the Peninsular Hotel because he had been engaged from there. The possibility of their being transit passengers off a boat had not occurred to him.

"You've come by boat, sir?" he inquired diffidently.

"Yes, the *Silver Isle*. Know her?"

"Oh, yes, sir. And are you staying here?"

"No, we're going on in her. Manila, Saigon, Singapore, Rangoon, Calcutta. My wife and I are on a world trip."

"Ah, that is very nice."

They were coming in to the landing ramp now, and his passengers had plenty to engage their attention. It gave him time to think.

Almost two months had elapsed since his wife's uncle had visited them; and, so far, all his attempts to find an American who would meet Mr. Tan's specifications had failed.

Moreover, his last attempt had been a frightening failure. The American, a department-store executive from Cleveland, had accused him of trying to work a confidence trick and threatened to go to the police. After that, he had made up his mind to do nothing further in the matter. Unfortunately, Mr. Tan was a highly respected member of his wife's family, and she had begun nagging him about it—not in an angry way, but reproachfully, intimating that his failure to do what her uncle wanted would cause her to lose face. There was also the money to be considered. With the five hundred dollars (Hong Kong) that Mr. Tan had offered for the service, he could go to Cheong Ming and Co. and buy a hi-fi set. But was it worth the risk?

He began to study the American beside him.

He was tall and thin with loose-fitting clothes and short, graying hair. He spoke quietly and with a slight smile in one corner of his mouth. His eyes were watchful and shrewd; but there might be innocence there, too. Not an easy man to deceive; but one who might sometimes deceive himself.

Ah Au drove up toward the Peak. Near the lower cable-car station he stopped so that they could admire the view of the port from the road. The American took his camera and got out of the car.

The Arlene woman said: "There's a much better view from the top."

She and the wife stayed in the car.

Ah Au went over to the American and began pointing out various landmarks in the panorama below them.

"Yes, it's a great place," the American said. "By the way, Jimmy, *is* the view better from up top?"

"There is a fine view there, too, sir, which I will show you in a minute, but this is better for photography. From the Peak there is more haze."

"I see." He was winding the camera.

"Are you using Kodachrome, sir?"

"Yes. Why?"

"From here, sir, at f. eight with a haze filter you will get a very good picture."

"Thanks. You take many pictures?"

"No, sir, but I have such information for my clients."

The camera whirred. As they were walking back to the

car, the American said: "Is this your car or do you just drive for someone else?"

"It is my car, sir. I like to give personal service to clients."

"I expect you make more money working for yourself, too."

Ah Au smiled. "There is also that, sir."

The American smiled back.

Ah Au drove on up to the Peak. Some progress had been made, he thought. They had established a personal relationship.

The tour continued. His passengers had tea at the Repulse Bay Hotel. Then he drove them on to the fishing village of Aberdeen and showed them the floating Chinese restaurants. At the Arlene woman's suggestion, it was decided that he should drive them out there to dine the following night. It was on the way back to the ferry that Jimmy had the glimpse of his client's mind for which he had been hoping.

He was driving along Connaught Road, by the long quay where the junks tied up for unloading, when the American turned to him.

"Jimmy, what are all those barges lined up along there? I mean the green painted ones with the yellow stars on them."

"They are junks from Canton, sir."

"But that's in Red China."

"Yes, sir. Canton is only ninety miles away."

"Stop the car. I've got to have some shots of this."

Ah Au parked the car and, leaving the women sitting in it, walked back along the quay with the American. The man seemed curiously excited and was almost tripping over himself in his eagerness to get a closer look at the junks.

"What are they doing here?" he asked.

"They come and go all the time, sir."

"Doing what?"

"Carrying cargo." Ah Au was puzzled. He could not understand why the man was so interested.

"What sort of cargo?"

"Any sort of cargo, sir. That is rattan cane they are unloading. It is made into chairs and baskets here."

"But I don't see any police about. Do you mean they're allowed just to come and go as they please?"

"They are ordinary people. They make no trouble, sir."

"Well, I'll be . . ."

He began to take pictures. When they got back to the car, Ah Au listened thoughtfully as the American told his wife and her friend what he had found out.

The women were interested, and the Arlene one said that it showed what the British had come to when they didn't worry about Communists going in and out of one of their Colonies; but they were not interested the way the man was. As they drove on toward the ferry, Ah Au saw him looking about him intently, as if he were discovering a new meaning in everything he saw.

By the time they reached the mainland Ah Au had decided to take matters a stage further. As he drove them back along the Canton Road to the ship, he asked a question.

"Tomorrow morning, sir, for your tour of the New Territories, do you wish me to go to the Peninsular Hotel, or shall I take the car to the ship?"

"Can you do that?"

"Oh, yes, sir. If I have your name to give at the dock gate."

"My name's Nilsen. Would ten o'clock be okay?"

"Perfectly, sir." He frowned as if making an effort of memory. "Mr. Nilsen, there was another Mr. Nilsen here last year. He was in the textile business. He had a big plant at a place called Dayton, I think. Perhaps you know him."

Mr. Nilsen smiled tolerantly. "No, Jimmy, I don't. I'm an engineer and I have a small die-casting plant at a place called Wilmington. Nilsen's a pretty common name in the United States."

"I beg your pardon. I did not know that. Someday, perhaps, I will be able to go to America."

He congratulated himself. The chances of his being caught out in the lie about a textile man named Nilsen from Dayton had been small. The information gained had been reassuring. Mr. Nilsen was neither a government official, who might consider it his duty to notify the authorities, nor a newspaperman, who might become indiscreet in other ways. He was a respectable businessman of just the type that Mr. Tan had described, and traveling by just the specified route. The problem now was to find a way of putting Mr. Tan's proposition in an attractive light without being either compromised or misunderstood.

When he returned home, Ah Au said nothing to his wife about Mr. Nilsen. He had already decided to make this further attempt to oblige Mr. Tan; but only if a favorable opportunity presented itself. The pressure of her expectations could distort his judgment.

During the night he lay awake for an hour, going over every moment of the afternoon and re-examining his image of Mr. Nilsen. When he was sure that nothing had escaped his attention, he went back to sleep.

The Arlene woman was late, and they did not leave the dock until nearly ten-thirty. Mr. Nilsen controlled his impatience too obviously. It was an inauspicious beginning. Ah Au wanted Mr. Nilsen in as relaxed a mood as possible, and took an early opportunity of suggesting that, as they had plenty of time in hand, they might like to stop at the Castle Peak Hotel for coffee. It was about four miles out on the Tai Po Road, and they would be passing it anyway.

Mrs. Nilsen thought this a good idea, and the tension seemed to slacken. By the time they left Castle Peak and were heading for the frontier, the atmosphere had improved still further. Soon, as they began to pass farms and paddy fields, Ah Au was hearing the familiar exclamations—*Look at that wooden plow! This is really old China! What about those hats with curtains! My God, the smell!*—which told him that his passengers were enjoying themselves.

He drove absently, answering the questions put to him promptly and fully, but not elaborating on his answers. He was waiting for a British army truck to come along. Presently they overtook one, and he slowed to stay behind it. It was, happily, full of troops.

He glanced at Mr. Nilsen and smiled. "We are getting near Red China," he said. "This is the beginning of the military zone."

Mr. Nilsen was leaning forward, staring at the truck. "Are those British troops?"

"Yes, sir, a Scottish regiment. There is a camp farther along this road."

"How many do they have to guard this frontier?"

"One or two battalions, I think."

"One or two battalions!" He turned around. "Did you hear that, Dorothy? Only one or two battalions to guard this frontier. My God, the Reds could walk in here any time they wanted. Isn't that right, Jimmy?"

Ah Au smiled. "Oh, yes, sir. But I think they could do that even if there were two divisions to guard the frontier."

Mr. Nilsen nodded grimly. "You could be right at that. How near to the frontier can we get?"

"About a mile, sir. It is dangerous, you see."

"How dangerous?"

"Sometimes they shoot from the other side at persons moving too close to the frontier line."

"Nice people."

The army truck turned off the road into the camp entrance, and Ah Au put on speed again. He could feel the mounting excitement of the man beside him and wanted to satisfy it.

About a mile and a half from the frontier the road turned sharply to the right and ran parallel to it. However, there was a narrow cart track heading straight on, and Ah Au drove down it until they reached a small farmhouse. The track continued, but a few yards past the house there was a large signboard prohibiting movement beyond that point. Ah Au stopped the car, took a pair of binoculars from the glove compartment, and they all got out.

For about a mile ahead the landscape was flat. Then there was a line of low hills, the sides of which were dotted with groups of burial urns, and a ridge. Along the ridge and near the top of it ran a thin black line.

"That is the frontier, sir." Ah Au handed Mr. Nilsen the binoculars.

"That black line?"

"Yes, it is a barbed-wire fence. There are machine-gun towers, too, but you cannot see them well from here."

Mr. Nilsen scanned the line of the fence from side to side, then handed the binoculars to his wife and got out his camera.

"F. eleven with the haze filter," Ah Au murmured.

Mr. Nilsen nodded and went to work. He did a panning shot first, beginning close on his wife as she looked through the binoculars, then going on to the signboard, then moving into an extreme long shot of the frontier. Then he switched the turret onto the telephoto lens. He used two magazines of film before he was finished.

The Arlene woman became bored and went back to the car. Small children from the farmhouse came out to peer at her through the car windows and hold out their hands for money. Ah Au had to chase them away.

Mr. Nilsen returned to the car reluctantly, and insisted on taking some shots of the farmhouse and the giggling children before he could be persuaded to leave. Even as they bumped along the track back to the road, he kept looking over his shoulder toward the frontier. Ah Au was pleased with the impression it had made.

When they passed the Kowloon-Canton Railway where it curved toward the frontier station, there were more questions.

"Is there a lot of railroad traffic between Kowloon and Canton?"

"Oh, yes, sir. People go to see friends and family in Canton."

"I don't get it. You mean they just go?"

"They must get a permit from the Chinese government office in Hong Kong, but it is quite easy."

"Hear that, Dorothy? So that's the bamboo curtain!"

"You wish to go to Canton, sir?"

"Me? No, thanks!" He laughed. "I have United States government contracts to think about."

They stopped at Tai Po market so that the two women could look at the small shops there and buy coolie hats. Ah Au bargained for the hats and, when they had been paid for, took them back to the car.

He was about to return and render further assistance when Mr. Nilsen joined him.

"They've gone into a silk shop," he said. "They're not going to buy, but they'll be there an age. You smoke?"

"Not when driving, sir. But now, thank you."

They sat in the car and smoked. A ring of children collected to stare at them, but Mr. Nilsen took no notice.

"Have you ever been to Canton?" he asked.

"No, sir. I have been to Macao, where my wife has some relatives, but my family is in Manila."

"Is that so? Don't you like the Philippines?"

"My family went there from here, sir. But I was born here and I am British. There are more opportunities here, I think."

"I don't get it. I should have thought this was the last place where you could look forward to any sort of security for your family. This section, for instance. You call it the New Territories. But it's leased, isn't it, from the government of China?"

"Yes, sir, in eighteen ninety-eight. It was leased for ninety-nine years.

"So in nineteen ninety-seven you'll have to give it back to the Reds, if they're still in business."

"That is so."

"Or if they don't walk in and take it back before?"

"There is always that possibility, sir, but I do not think the risk is great. Hong Kong is no danger to them and it is a useful outlet to the West. That is why, too, the Portuguese are allowed to stay in Macao."

Ah Au spoke almost without thinking. He had planned to wait until after lunch at Shatin before attempting to broach the subject of Mr. Tan's proposition. Now, he was being offered an opening of a kind he could not possibly have contrived. His heart began to beat faster. Then, he made up his mind.

"All that could change overnight," Mr. Nilsen was saying. "Some shift in the Cold War or another Korea over the Formosa situation, and I wouldn't give you a nickel for the Peninsular Hotel."

Ah Au smiled. "You are probably right, sir. But, meanwhile, there are advantages to both sides, and not only for the big bankers and trading companies here."

"That so?"

"In fact, I can tell you a story that may amuse you, sir."

"What's that?"

"Well, sir, it is a little confidential, but you are not a policeman or a newspaperman, so I can tell you." He paused.

"Sure, go ahead."

"You see, sir, we Chinese are all pirates at heart." He shrugged. "Chinese piracy is as old as history. When the Reds began sending arms and ammunition down by sea in junks to the terrorists in Malaya, there were naturally some men, both here and in Macao, who thought it a pity that such valuable cargoes should arrive at their destinations. It was a great temptation. So as often as they could, they . . ." He spread his hands deprecatingly.

"They hijacked them?" Mr. Nilsen smiled.

"Yes, though that was not the best part of the joke, sir. You know that arms and ammunition are very valuable in this part of the world."

"They are in most places."

"Particularly in the Far East, sir. But the trouble is that there are government regulations and embargoes that make it difficult to sell equipment. It was not easy to seize these cargoes, and although the Reds could not make international complaints without admitting openly that they were supplying the terrorists, these pirates, these hijackers you would call them, they ran great risks. There had to be profit." He paused again. He could see that he had Mr. Nilsen's whole attention.

"Well, how did they get rid of the stuff?"

"It was very simple, sir. They took the Communist arms down to Indonesia and sold them to the *anti*-Communist rebels."

Mr. Nilsen stared and then began to laugh.

Ah Au sighed inwardly with relief. He saw the holes in his own story so clearly that he had been afraid Mr. Nilsen would see them, too.

He did see one an instant later. When he had stopped laughing, he said: "What I don't see is why the Reds sent the stuff down by sea at all. What about the British navy? Couldn't they intercept the shipments to Malaya?"

"They intercepted many, sir, but, you know, there are a lot of junks in the China Seas. Last year there were over twenty-five thousand of them using Hong Kong alone. You cannot intercept and search every junk at sea between here and Singapore."

"I suppose not."

"Though you are right, sir. The illegal arms traffic was stopped in the end. A friend of mine in Manila was very sad about that."

"Yes?"

"Some time ago he took a shipment of arms and ammunition out of a Red junk off Hainan. It was modern equipment —rifles, machine guns, bazookas—worth sixty thousand dollars. And it is still in Manila."

"Why? Aren't there any more anti-Communists in Indonesia?"

"Plenty, sir, but it is not as simple as it was before. This is no longer a small business. The buying agents for the rebels are in Singapore, and they must be careful. They will not buy illegal arms any more. My friend has tried to sell. Now he says he must try to make the arms legal."

"How does he propose to do that?"

But Ah Au had seen the two women approaching and was already getting out of the car to open the door for them. Mr. Nilsen's forecast that they would buy nothing had proved incorrect. His wife had a Shantung dress length and the Arlene woman had some jade earrings. They got into the car, showing their purchases and chattering about the other things that the shop had for sale.

Ah Au drove on toward Shatin.

The interruption of his conversation with Mr. Nilsen had not dismayed him. On the contrary, he was glad of it. He was quite sure that Mr. Nilsen was sufficiently intrigued to want an answer to his last question, and it was much better that he should be the one to return to the subject.

Ah Au did not have to wait long. When the three Americans had had lunch at the Shatin Hotel, the women went for a walk in the gardens overlooking the valley. Mr. Nilsen had gone to the toilet, but when he came out, he did not join the women in the garden. Instead, he came out to Ah Au, who was sitting in the car.

Ah Au got out to open the door, but Mr. Nilsen waved him back.

"I've seen enough sights for the moment," he said with a smile. "I want to hear more about your friend in Manila."

"Yes, sir?"

"What did you mean about making that shipment of arms legal?"

"You understand, sir, this is very confidential."

"Sure, I understand."

"For arms to be legal, sir, they have to have a legal owner and a legal place of origin. What my friend needs is a nominee."

"How do you mean?"

"What my friend would like to do is ship the arms to be held in bond at Singapore, and then sell them."

"Why can't he do that?"

"Sir, the authorities at Singapore would not accept the consignment in bond without a proper certified bill of lading from a reputable shipper at the port of origin. Unfortunately, residents of Manila cannot trade in arms without a government permit. That is difficult and expensive to obtain. So, he must have a foreign nominee."

"Why? I don't get it."

"After the war in Manila, sir, a lot of surplus American war material was sold to dealers who exported it. The regulations about permits do not apply to non-resident foreigners exporting arms."

"I see."

"Also, sir, the nominee would have to go to Singapore to sign clearance papers. My friend has tried to find the right person, but although he is willing to pay as much as five per cent for the service, he has been unsuccessful. He will not deal with crooks."

"Hijackers aren't usually so particular."

"A crook would cheat him, sir. Once the papers are signed, what is to prevent the nominee from claiming the goods are his and keeping all the money? Sixty thousand Straits dollars is a lot. Twenty-one thousand dollars American."

"And five per cent of that is a thousand and fifty." Mr. Nilsen grinned amiably. "Jimmy, you couldn't be telling me all this for a reason, could you?"

Ah Au's heart missed a beat. Was Mr. Nilsen going to be like the man from Cleveland after all?

"A reason, sir? But you asked me."

"I know it. But you sort of raised the question in the first place, didn't you? Come on, now, Jimmy. Didn't you have some idea that I might be suckered into acting as your friend's nominee?"

Ah Au looked amazed. "You, sir? I had not thought of it."

"All right. Never mind." He started to turn away.

Ah Au spoke quickly. "But would you consider such a proposition, sir?"

Mr. Nilsen looked at him coldly. "What's the angle, Jimmy?"

"Angle, sir?"

"What's your friend in Manila trying to smuggle? Opium?"

"Sir, that is not a good thing to say. You asked me questions. I answered the truth."

"All right. Let me ask you some more questions. What's your friend's name?"

"Sir, if you believe that he is smuggling opium, you will go to the police. How can I tell you?"

"All right, I promise not to go to the police. What's his name?"

Ah Au hesitated, then bowed slightly. "As you promise, I must accept your promise. Please note that, sir. His name is Mr. Tan Tack Chee."

"Right, then why does Mr. Tan Tack Chee have you touting for him? Why doesn't he find a nominee himself?"

"Because he has no contacts, sir, with passengers off boats. He cannot go up to strangers and make his request. And it has to be someone who is going to Singapore. How would he know?"

"Why doesn't he get hold of an officer on one of the ships and ask him to do it?"

"A ship's officer dealing in arms would be an object of suspicion to the authorities in Singapore, sir."

"So would I."

"No, sir. Many of the dealers in war material are American businessmen. You are an engineer with a business in America. You would be perfectly acceptable."

"Don't you mean innocent-looking? Don't you mean I'd be a good cover? You say no opium. Okay, but there are other kinds of contraband. How do I know what'd be in that shipment."

Ah Au smiled. "Mr. Nilsen, sir, no person who wished to make an illegal shipment of any kind would describe it on a bill of lading and a ship's manifest as arms and ammunition. That is asking for it to be examined by port authorities."

"Is that how it would be described?"

"Of course, sir." Ah Au spread out his hands. "That is my friend's need, to be able to have the shipment legally bonded in Singapore. I explained this."

Mr. Nilsen thought for a moment, then nodded. "Yes, you did. This Mr. Tan, now. You say he's a friend of yours. How did you get to know him?"

Ah Au drew himself up a trifle stiffly. "He is my wife's father, sir," he said.

Mr. Nilsen began to laugh, then checked himself. "Sorry, Jimmy, I was just amused at the idea of a man calling his father-in-law his friend."

"You are not friendly with Mrs. Nilsen's father, sir?"

"Oh, sure, but . . . no, skip it. I'd better go and see where those women have got to."

He had started to go. Ah Au followed him.

"Then you will consider the proposition, sir?"

Mr. Nilsen grinned affably. "Oh, sure, I'll consider it."

"When will you decide, sir?"

"I'll let you know tonight. Now back the car up, Jimmy, will you? I have to stop off at the Peninsular Hotel for a fitting at the tailor's."

iv

Greg was feeling good that evening. The idea of his having been asked, in all seriousness, to act as front man for a Chinese pirate had appealed to his sense of humor.

At least, that is how he chose to explain the sudden lightness of heart that had come to him as he was changing for dinner. He regarded himself, not without reason, as a mature and level-headed man. If anyone had suggested that somewhere in the back streets of his mind another Greg Nilsen—a roistering, romantic, ten-year-old swashbuckler—had escaped from custody and was out enjoying a game of cops and robbers, he would have been angrily incredulous. It had not yet occurred to him to ask himself why, if the whole thing were simply a good joke, he had not told Dorothy about it.

Jimmy Khoo brought the car to the boat at seven o'clock and drove them across to Aberdeen.

The trouble with Arlene started in the sampan which took them out from the quayside to the floating restaurant. Halfway out across the harbor, she suddenly jumped up out of her seat.

"I've been bitten," she said to Dorothy.

"Oh, no!"

"I've been bitten."

"Where?"

The light sampan rocked dangerously.

"Better sit down," Greg cautioned them. "You're rocking the boat."

Dorothy sat down, but Arlene ignored him. "I've been bitten," she repeated maddeningly and, pulling up one side of her skirt, began examining the back of her leg.

The sampan lurched over in the other direction. The Chinese girl, standing on the stern counter with the oar, was thrown off balance. The old woman who owned the sampan screamed. Greg felt the wicker chair he was sitting on start to slide. He grabbed at the side of the boat.

"For God's sake, sit down!" he shouted.

Arlene sat down, the Chinese girl giggled, and a minute later they were at the restaurant steps. Greg paid off the sampan and joined Dorothy and Arlene on the veranda. They appeared to be having some sort of argument.

He heard Dorothy saying: "I'm sure Greg didn't mean to . . ." And then Arlene turned to face him. Her nose and mouth were pinched and white with anger.

"I'm not used to being yelled at like that," she said.

"Arlene, I only asked you to sit down. That sort of boat upsets pretty easily."

"There was no need to yell at me like that."

"I yelled because I didn't want to have to swim the rest of the way."

"Oh, really, Greg!" This was Dorothy. "I do think you ought to apologize to Arlene. I know you meant well, but it wasn't very polite."

"All right, I'm sorry. Now, for goodness' sake, let's go eat."

It was not a gracious apology and nobody attempted to

pretend it was. The situation was not improved when they found that the desirable tables on the upper deck were all reserved, and that they would have to sit down below surrounded by very noisy mah-jong players. Arlene had said that it was unnecessary to make table reservations. Greg pointedly refrained from reminding her of the fact. The critical moment came, however, when they went with the waiter to the big traps moored alongside the vessel to choose the fish they would eat.

There was a man with a long-handled landing net standing by the traps. As the customers pointed to the fish they wanted, he would scoop them dextrously out of the water and fling them on to a long tiled slab which led to the kitchen.

One of the fish he pulled out was some kind of grouper. It was a heavy fish and it landed on the slab with a force that stunned it. For a moment or two it lay there almost still, its eyes staring vacuously, its big slack mouth gaping in an expression of the deepest gloom.

Arlene glanced at Dorothy. "Isn't that someone we know?" she asked slyly.

She did not look at Greg; but Dorothy did, and then burst out laughing.

"Oh, really, Arlene," she said, "he's not looking as miserable as all that."

Then she squeezed Greg's arm in affectionate apology; and, of course, he had to laugh, too.

But there was murder in his heart, and at that moment a resolution was born. Somewhere, somehow, their plans, his and Dorothy's, would have to be changed. He was not going to go all the way to Calcutta in the *Silver Isle* with Arlene Drecker.

When they arrived back at the ship, the two women went on board while Greg stayed to settle the account with Jimmy. He added a generous tip.

"Thank you very much indeed, sir." Jimmy took off his cap and bowed, but made no move to leave. He was looking at Greg expectantly.

Greg smiled. "Oh, yes. You want to know about that proposition."

"I hope you can accept, sir."

"Well, I don't know, Jimmy."

"Sir, all that is necessary is that you sign some papers in Manila and Singapore."

"People have been hanged before now just for signing papers, Jimmy."

"In this case, sir . . ."

"No. I tell you what I will do. When we get to Manila I'll see your Mr. Tan, if you'll have him contact me on the ship. And *then* I'll decide. Okay?"

Jimmy beamed. "Certainly, sir. That will be entirely satisfactory. Thank you very much indeed, sir."

"There's nothing to thank me for. And mind you explain the exact position to him. I don't want any misunderstandings."

"There will be none. And may I say what a pleasure it has been to serve you, sir?"

"The pleasure's mutual. Be seeing you again someday, maybe."

"I sincerely hope so, sir."

When Greg got back on board, he found that some mail had been sent up to the cabin from the purser's office. Among it was a progress report from his vice-president in charge of production. Everything at the plant was running smoothly. He didn't have to worry about a thing; just enjoy the trip.

v

The following morning Khoo Ah Au dispatched two cables: one to his wife's father in Manila, the other to his wife's uncle in Kuala Pangkalan.

The cable to Mr. Tan Tack Chee read:

CONTACT POSSIBLE PROSPECT MR. G. NILSEN PASSENGER S. S. SILVER ISLE ARRIVING MANILA 14TH RESPECTFUL AFFECTION WIFE AND SELF. KHOO.

The cable to Mr. Tan Siow Mong read:

HAVE ADVISED MANILA SUITABLE PROSPECT ARRIVING S. S. SILVER ISLE 14TH RESPECTFUL AFFECTION WIFE AND SELF. KHOO.

That night Mrs. Khoo had the unusual and elevating experience of receiving an overseas telephone call from her father in Manila. The only disappointing thing about it was that more time was devoted to the business talk with her husband than to the discussion of her possible pregnancy.

CHAPTER IV

TWO DAYS later the *Silver Isle* docked in Manila, and hordes of scarlet-shirted Filipino stevedores swarmed on board. They seemed to penetrate into every corner of the ship. Some even found their way into the writing room, where they lounged with their feet up on the tables until indignant stewards shooed them away.

The passengers had been warned that Manila was one of the worst ports in the Far East for pilfering. Greg was depositing a package containing Dorothy's jewelry in the purser's safe, when a steward came up with the message that Mr. Tan Tack Chee would like to see him. The gentleman was in the bar.

Dorothy was waiting for him by the notice board. They— or, rather, they and Arlene—had decided not to go ashore immediately, but wait until after lunch. When the purser's clerk had made out the receipt, Greg went over to her.

"Darling, I meant to tell you before. There's a man here who wants to see me on business. It'll only take a few minutes. I'll see you up on the sports deck."

Dorothy pulled a face. "Business? I thought we'd left that behind."

"It's nothing important."

"I didn't know you did any business here."

"It's just a man I promised to see." There was nothing untrue about the statement; nevertheless, he did not feel quite easy about it. "I'll tell you the story later," he added. "Look, darling, do you mind holding on to the camera for me?"

He went up to the bar. It was crowded with dock police, customs officials, and the usual collection of "business" visitors thirsty for free drinks. The steward who had brought him the message pointed to a table in the corner of the bar. Greg made his way over.

Seated at the table with an open briefcase in front of him was a middle-aged Chinese. He wore a well-pressed light gray suit and thick tortoise-shell glasses. He was writing busily in a loose-leaf notebook. As Greg approached, he glanced up.

"Mr. Tan?"

"Mr. Nilsen?" As he spoke he rose and they shook hands.

Mr. Tan's voice and manner were subdued, and his hand was like a soft bag of chicken bones. It would have been difficult to conceive of anyone less piratical. Greg, whose imagination had had three days to prepare for the encounter, was disconcerted.

"My son-in-law in Hong Kong cabled me that you would be passing through Manila," Mr. Tan said easily. "He hoped that I might perhaps be of some service to you and Mrs. Nilsen."

"Well, that's very kind of you, Mr. Tan. But I rather understood that there was a matter of business you wanted . . ."

"Do you or Mrs. Nilsen know Manila?" Mr. Tan's interruption was so gentle in tone that Greg scarcely noticed the firmness of it.

"No, we don't."

"Then, may I make a suggestion? I have my car on the wharf. It would be a favor if you would allow me to place it at your disposal."

"Mr. Tan, I don't think . . ."

Mr. Tan held up a slender hand. "And an additional favor if you would allow me to be your host at lunch. You understand, I do not have the professional skills of my son-in-law, but my driver knows Manila well and can show you what there is to see."

"As a matter of fact, Mr. Tan, we've sort of committed ourselves to taking another passenger along with us. A lady."

"She is included in the invitation," Mr. Tan said promptly.

"I think . . ."

"I understand perfectly, Mr. Nilsen. Please feel free to consult with your wife before you accept."

Greg hesitated. "Mr. Tan, I think I had better explain that I have not mentioned to my wife the business we might have to discuss."

"Naturally, Mr. Nilsen, one does not trouble ladies with business." He smiled. "I am in the so-called import-export market. That is a very loose term covering everything from powdered milk to earth-moving equipment."

Greg nodded uncertainly. "I guess so. If you'll excuse me, I'll go and find my wife."

Half an hour later the four of them left the ship and walked along the quay to the car park. As they approached, a pink Cadillac swung out of the parking line and pulled up alongside them. A Filipino driver sprang out to open the doors and they all got in.

Mr. Tan took them to his house for lunch. It was in the Spanish style and built on a hillside overlooking the bay. Mrs. Tan, obviously a second wife, proved to be young, very attractive, and a graduate of the University of Southern California. She wore toreador pants, and barbecued steaks for them on the patio. Arlene was enchanted. Mr. Tan talked about Philippine politics, skin diving, and the amusing misfortunes of an American motion-picture company who were trying to shoot on location up in the hills. He did not once mention business.

After lunch the car dropped him back at his office, which was in a modern, American-style building, and then the Filipino driver took them on a tour of the city. When they returned to the office Mr. Tan's secretary informed them that he had had to go out, but that he hoped Mr. and Mrs. Nilsen and Miss Drecker would dine with him that evening. The car would call for them at seven. Mr. Tan would wear a white tuxedo.

Dorothy glanced at Arlene with a smile of triumph. "We're certainly getting the full treatment," she said. "He must want those die-castings pretty badly, eh, darling?"

Even Arlene was looking at him with approval.

Greg mumbled something noncommittal. He was feeling thoroughly confused. His neglecting to tell Dorothy about

the conversation with Jimmy Khoo in Hong Kong had been
natural enough, he assured himself. The commercial techni-
calities about nominees, manifests, and shipping in bond
would only have bored her; and, besides, they had agreed
from the start that business talk was to be taboo on the
trip. The last thing he had been prepared for was having
to account for Mr. Tan in the role of a generous host.
When he had first reported the invitation to lunch, Arlene
had been there, and it had been impossible to go into long
explanations. "He's in the import-export business," had been
all that he had said; but Dorothy had jumped to the conclusion that the man wanted to buy die-castings.

He had not realized it until later, or he could have said
something to her in time. As it was, the first he had heard
about it had been during the afternoon's sightseeing. He had
been listening to the driver talking about the village he came
from, when a fragment of conversation from the back seat
had caught his attention.

"You see," Dorothy had been saying, "Greg's plant only
does this special precision work. Most of his contracts are
with the government, or people like airplane manufacturers,
or those other people who develop the missiles. He's never
had much time for export business before."

"Well, you ought to encourage it."

"Why?"

"Won't it make part of your trip tax-deductible?"

Dorothy had laughed. "I'd never thought of that."

"I'll bet Greg has."

Greg had pretended not to hear. An explanation at that
moment would merely have made his wife look foolish and
gratified Arlene's appetite for discord.

Now he was almost sorry that he had not taken the risk.
He had maneuvered himself into one false position where
Dorothy was concerned; and it looked very much as if Mr.
Tan had maneuvered him into another. It was going to be
embarrassing now to say "no" to Mr. Tan, or even to question him closely, when the questions could only imply doubt
of his good faith. The fact that Mr. Tan's hospitality had a
clear purpose was beside the point. Wisely or unwisely, the
hospitality had been accepted; and so, an obligation, of
courtesy at least, had been incurred.

Dinner was at a country club just outside the city, and had been specially ordered by Mr. Tan. The rum drinks were innocent-tasting but very potent. Toward the end of the evening Arlene became emotional and, in trying to express her gratitude for the wonderful day she had had, was moved to tears of joy. Her mascara ran and she was forced to retire to the powder room. Mrs. Tan and Dorothy decided to join her there. Greg and Mr. Tan were alone.

There was a pause.

"This has been a very enjoyable day," Greg said.

Mr. Tan smiled. "For me, too, Mr. Nilsen. Although—" he smiled again—"it would have been more enjoyable if you had not been so troubled by your suspicions."

"Suspicions?"

"My son-in-law in Hong Kong is a very praiseworthy young man. He is not a man of great substance as yet, but he is honest and hard-working. Otherwise, I would not have allowed my daughter to marry him. But he has a weakness."

"Oh, yes?"

"A taste for melodrama. Did he mention piracy, Mr. Nilsen?"

"He did, yes."

"I was afraid so. He lives in the richly flavored past of lions and dragons. It is an engaging weakness, but embarrassing in business."

"I guess it would be."

"You know, Mr. Nilsen, this small parcel of arms was acquired by accident, but, as far as I am concerned, perfectly legally. I will confess to you that its existence is inconvenient, and I would like to disembarrass myself. A technicality makes this difficult. You, as you know, are in a position to overcome the technicality. That is the length and breadth of the problem."

Greg pushed his drink away. "Mr. Tan, are you on the level?"

"Sir?"

"I want to get this straight. These are arms from Red China originally intended for Red terrorists in Malaya. Is that correct?"

"Perfectly correct. As I said, they fell into my hands by accident."

"What sort of accident?"

"The man who seized them off Hainan left them with me as a pledge for a loan. Later, I am afraid, he went bankrupt."

"And now you want to sell them to the *anti*-Red people in Indonesia. Is that correct?"

"Entirely correct, Mr. Nilsen."

Greg considered for a moment and then nodded. "Okay, it's a deal."

Mr. Tan stroked his chin thoughtfully before he said: "Very well. I will bring the papers to you to sign in the morning." He hesitated and then went on. "I will be frank with you, Mr. Nilsen. I am not entirely happy with this arrangement."

Greg stared at him. "You mean you've changed your mind?"

"Indeed no. On the contrary, I am quite satisfied with the arrangement as far as it goes. My regret is that it does not go further."

"How do you mean?"

"My brother in Singapore is capable of handling the shipping and delivery arrangements, but when it comes to dealing with the buyers, I am not sure that he is the best man. An American can always drive a harder bargain in that business. How long will you be in Singapore, Mr. Nilsen?"

"Two days."

"Not very long. I had hoped you might consider conducting the negotiations personally. For an additional consideration, of course."

Greg shook his head. "I don't think I'm qualified to do that, Mr. Tan. And, as you say, I won't be there long enough."

"I quite understand. Ah, here are the ladies."

The ship was sailing at midday. At ten-thirty Mr. Tan arrived with the papers for signature.

The first was a consignor's note requesting the Anglo-Malay Transport Company of Kuala Pangkalan to ship the goods listed from the Tak Wah Godown and Storage Corporation, Manila, to the Chen Warehouse Company, Singapore, to be held in bond there pending further instructions. The second was an export license giving Greg's name and address in the United States and a list of the goods to be xported. This required his countersignature and passport umber to become effective.

When Greg had signed, Mr. Tan gave him copies of the ocuments. "As soon as you arrive in Singapore, Mr. Nil-en," he said, "my brother, Tan Yam Heng, will contact you. have written his name down here. He will have copies of he bill of lading, and go with you to make the proper cus-oms declaration. He will then ask you to sign a paper trans-erring the ownership of the goods in bond to a company r person to be designated later. When you have signed that aper, he will hand you a check for one thousand and fifty ollars U.S."

"Not going to have any trouble with the customs people, m I?"

"No. The goods are being held in bond. It is merely a for-nality." Mr. Tan stood up. "It has been a pleasure to meet nd do business with you, Mr. Nilsen."

Dorothy was ashore with Arlene, doing some last-minute hopping and arranging for flowers to be sent with their note f thanks to Mrs. Tan. She did not get back until half an our before the ship sailed. By that time Mr. Tan had left.

"What a pity," she said when Greg told her. "I think he's ice. I hope you decided to let him have his castings after ll."

Greg hesitated and then side-stepped the question. "As a natter of fact, he wanted to see me about something else, omething he wants me to do for him in Singapore."

"Are you going to do it?"

"I think so."

Dorothy nodded approvingly. "After all, they did put them-elves out for us, didn't they?"

ii

That afternoon a cable went from Manila to Kuala angkalan:

DOCUMENTS SIGNED AIRMAILED YOU TODAY. TACK CHEE

That evening Girija was in the estate office when the tele-

phone rang. As he lifted it off the cradle he heard the op
erator telling Kuala Pangkalan to go ahead.

"Mr. Krishnan?" said a voice a moment later.

"Yes."

"I am speaking for Mr. Lee."

"Yes?" He did not recognize the voice, which was that o
Mr. Tan Siow Mong's eldest son.

"Mr. Lee wishes for delivery three days from now of th
goods previously discussed."

"Very well."

"Mr. Lee will be at the rest house on Thursday evenin
at eight o'clock, if you will meet him there."

"Very well."

The caller hung up.

Girija sat down again at his desk. His heart was pound
ing, but whether from excitement at the prospect of havin
a long-cherished dream realized, or from fear of the thing
he would now have to do, he did not know. He sat ther
for a while until he felt himself calmer. Then he looked a
his watch.

It was half past six. He had three nights in which to mov
the arms and ammunition to the pick-up point near the road
If everything went according to plan, that was only jus
sufficient time. His instinct was to lock the office and se
out at once for Awang; but he restrained himself. The firs
thing to remember was that his behavior must not appear i
any way unusual.

At seven o'clock he left the office and went to his house
There were the remains of some food which he had prepare
at midday, and he forced himself to eat it. At eight o'cloc
he took his bicycle and left the compound.

His first care was to see that he was not followed. Th
possibility of Mr. Lee's attempting to discover where th
arms were hidden, so that he could remove them withou
payment, had to be considered. All appeared to be well
however, and he reached the tin workings without encounter
ing anyone he knew on the way.

He had been up to the camp site at night only once before
That had been months ago, when he had been planning th
operation; but he still remembered the panic that had seize
him when he left the open ground by the tin workings an

entered the terrifying blackness of the jungle. The track to the lower end of the dried stream bed was the worst part. It was too near the village for him to risk using a flashlight, except intermittently, and, well as he knew it in daylight, at night there was always the danger of his getting lost. Above all, there was his fear of leopards. It was at night that they raided villages on the edge of the jungle, carried off chickens and goats, and killed men. He knew the fear to be largely irrational—there had been no reports of leopards in the area for some time—but still it haunted every step he took. He plunged on desperately along the track, living for the moment when he would reach the stream bed and be able to keep the flashlight on all the time.

His plan for moving the boxes of arms and ammunition fell into three parts.

On the first night he would move them from the shelter to the cane thicket at the edge of the stream bed. On the second night he would move them to the foot of the stream bed where it met the track. On the third night he would move them to the pick-up dump that he had contrived in one of the derelict mining-company buildings.

It had taken a long time to prepare the dump. The building he had selected for it was a windowless Nissen hut that had formerly been used as a store for drums of diesel oil. The corrugated-iron sections were so badly rusted that it was possible to put a fist through them in most places; and there were several big holes near the ground where the rusting process was more advanced and the metal had simply disintegrated. From Girija's point of view, it had three things to recommend it. There was still enough metal there to prevent a casual passer-by seeing inside; it contained some empty oil drums which had been punctured for some reason, and so had not been stolen for use as waterbutts by the villagers; and it had a door with a hasp on it to take a padlock.

Once the arms and ammunition were out of the shelter, the risk of their being discovered increased as they were moved nearer the road. While they were in the cane thicket, the risk was small. The second stage at the foot of the stream bed was a greater risk, but, for twenty-four hours, an acceptable one. For the third stage, however, there had to be an effective hiding place. Girija had never read *The Purloined*

Letter, but the technique he employed was similar in principle to that used in Poe's story: concealment by familiarity.

The first thing he had done was to buy a padlock, grease the interior mechanism carefully, and leave it in the underbrush for the exterior to rust. Then, one day he had gone to the oil store and padlocked the door. A gleaming new padlock would have excited too much interest in a passer-by. The rusty one, if noticed at all, would only arouse mild curiosity. When he had returned a week later, the padlock had still been there; but there had been signs that someone had crawled through one of the holes near the ground to find out what was behind the locked door. As there had still been nothing inside but the useless oil drums, nothing had been touched. Girija's next move had been to move the oil drums about inside, so as to cover the bigger holes in the corrugated iron, and draw a series of squares and circles on the dirt floor with a stick, to make it seem as if children had been playing there. The following week he had found that one of the drums had been pushed aside. He had replaced it. He had considered defecating on the floor as an additional discouragement to the curious, but had finally decided that it would require too many visits to make that form of deterrent completely effective. In the event, additional measures had not been needed. That had been the last time the drums had been touched. The former oil store with the padlocked door had become accepted as a place where children sometimes played, containing nothing worth stealing and nothing of interest. It would look no different during the twenty-four hours it held the arms and ammunition.

By the time he reached the camp site, it was after nine thirty; but he rested a few minutes before starting work. He had calculated that it would take him less than two hours to move all the boxes to the cane thicket, and was determined to reserve his strength as much as possible. The hardest part of the job would come on the third night, and he must be prepared for that.

The problem of handling the boxes, he had solved almost by accident. At intervals Mr. Wright received catalogues from a mail-order house in Singapore, and in one of them Girija had seen a device that had interested him. It was a gadget for those with heavy suitcases who could not afford porters,

ᵃnd consisted of a strap attached to a bracket with two small
ᵗrolley wheels mounted on it. The strap was fastened length-
ʷise around the suitcase, with the wheels at one corner.
There was a handle on the strap. The owner of the suitcase
ˢimply grasped this handle and walked along, trailing the
ᶜase behind him, with half the weight of it carried on the
ᵗrolley wheels. The price was six dollars.

Girija had sent for one and experimented. The thing
worked on firm ground; but up at the camp site, and with a
ʰeavy box of rifles, the small wheels sank into the spongy
ˢurface of the hillside and were useless. Larger wheels with
broader tires were needed. He had found them eventually
ᵒn the estate. Before the Wright children had been sent away
to school in England, one of them had had a scooter. It
ʰad been left in Mr. Wright's garage, and Girija had had
ⁿo difficulty in removing the wheels. Mounted on an axle
made out of a spare jack handle, they worked quite well.

The transfer to the cane thicket was completed by mid-
night, and Girija began the journey back. In spite of his
ʳesolve to conserve his energies, he was very tired, and real-
ⁱzed that he could no longer rely upon his wits to see him
ᵗhrough. Now it would be a question of stamina.

There was a compensation. As his weariness increased, his
ᶠears seemed to diminish. By the time he had completed the
ⁿext night's work, he had forgotten about leopards, and
ᶠeared the dark track from the stream bed to the tin work-
ⁱngs only because it threatened his powers of endurance.

The nine boxes containing the rifles were the most awkward
ᵗo handle, and only one could be moved at a time. It required
ᵗwenty stumbling journeys each way to shift all the boxes and
ᵃmmunition containers, and the final move from the stream
ᵇed to the oil store took five and a half hours. When he had
ˢecured the padlock he sank down onto the ground in a state
ᵒf collapse. It was another hour before he could summon the
ˢtrength to get on his bicycle and ride back to the estate;
ᵃnd only his fear of being seen returning to the estate com-
ᵖound at daybreak, and before he had had time to wash and
ᵖut on clean clothes, drove him to make that final effort.

He was in the office that morning on time, as usual, but he
ᵏnew that unless he could get some rest during the day, he
ʷould be unable or unfit to keep his appointment with Mr.

Lee in the evening. If he pleaded sickness, Mrs. Wright, a
keen amateur physician, would dose him with pills and order
him to bed; and she would see that he stayed there, too. In
the end, on the pretext of looking into some minor pay dispute among the tappers, he left the compound, walked to a
part of the estate which he knew was not being worked, and
went to sleep under the trees. He awoke at sundown and
hurried back to the office. His body ached almost intolerably,
but he was no longer stupid with fatigue. When Mr. Wright
looked in at the office on his way to the bungalow, Girija
was able to report, with his usual air of efficiency, that the
pay dispute had been satisfactorily settled.

Girija's business arrangements with Mr. Lee were somewhat complex.

When they met at the rest house, Mr. Lee would give him
a draft on the Hong Kong and Shanghai Bank for twenty-five
thousand Straits dollars, postdated thirty days and guaranteed by Mr. Tan. He would also give him a receipt for the
arms and ammunition. Girija would, in return, give Mr. Lee
a promissory note for twenty-five thousand dollars, acknowl-
edging the sum as a loan repayable within thirty days. Then,
Girija would return alone to the estate compound, put the
check in an envelope marked "To be opened in the event of
my death," and leave it in a safe place of his own choosing.

An hour later he would meet Mr. Lee at a rendezvous on
the Awang Road. Mr. Lee would have a truck. Guided by
Girija, they would then drive to the dump, where Mr. Lee
would be allowed to inspect what he was buying.

This would be a critical moment for both of them; but both
would feel reasonably secure. If there were no arms and
Girija had brought Mr. Lee there merely in order to kill him
and keep the check, Mr. Tan would know and be in a position
to inform on Girija. If, on the other hand, Mr. Lee contemplated killing Girija and making off with the arms, there
would be the telltale check to accuse Mr. Lee. The promissory
note and the receipt were safeguards of a more genteel nature.
The promissory note was Mr. Lee's insurance against Girija's
making off with the check and failing to deliver the goods.
The receipt for the arms was Girija's insurance against Mr.
Lee's declining to return the promissory note when the arms
had been delivered. These two documents would be formally

xchanged at the conclusion of the transaction.

Girija reviewed the procedure once more as he cycled out o the rest house. He knew that Mr. Lee could trust him; he was quite certain that he could not trust Mr. Lee. His tired mind began to imagine new ways in which he could be betrayed. Supposing Mr. Lee had henchmen hiding in the truck. What was there to prevent their pouncing on him, retrieving the receipt for the arms, and then seizing the whole consignment? Mr. Lee could still use the promissory note, and Girija would be in no position to complain to the police of what had happened. Or supposing Mr. Lee had a confederate in the estate compound who would watch where he put the check, and then steal it while he was away delivering the arms. There were countless opportunities for treachery remaining in the situation. Only one possibility did he refuse to consider: that the check guaranteed by Mr. Tan might not in the end be honored.

Mr. Lee was already at the rest house when he arrived. His attitude was wary but businesslike. He merely grunted a greeting and handed Girija the promissory note to sign. He then produced the check and the receipt. When the documents had changed hands, he nodded.

"That is satisfactory. Now, where do we meet?"

"At the twenty-one-mile post near Awang."

"Where is that?"

Girija told him how to get there, and then stood up to go. His whole body was aching, and a spasm of pain shot up his spine as he moved.

Mr. Lee was eying him thoughtfully. "Are you sick?" he asked.

"No, I am tired."

"Will your friend be there?"

"No, but I will help you load the boxes."

"Then I will meet you in one hour's time."

The whole transaction had taken no more than five minutes. Girija cycled back to the estate compound and went to his house. When he had written the inscription on the envelope, he put the check inside and locked it in his tin trunk. If he did not return, Mr. Wright would probably take charge of the trunk and ultimately hand it over to the authorities. It was not an ideal arrangement, but it was the best Girija could think of. As long as Mr. Lee did not know how he had disposed of the check, that was all that mattered.

He had ten minutes to wait before setting out for the rendezvous. He considered opening up the tin trunk again and passing the time with his bus catalogues, but made no move to do so. Through his weariness, he knew that the time for dreams was over. The next time he looked at the catalogues, if there were to be a next time, he would be seeing them through different eyes. There was half a tin of butterscotch on the table by his charpoy. He sat and ate that until it was time to go.

The truck was already at the rendezvous when he arrived. About a hundred yards short of it, he dismounted, switched off his bicycle lamp, and walked along the edge of the road. As he approached, he saw that the canvases above the tailboard of the truck were drawn and tied. He did not like this, and made up his mind to see that the truck was empty before they moved off.

Mr. Lee looked out of the driver's cab window as Girija came up.

"You are late," he said.

"I am two minutes early," Girija replied evenly. "Would you open the back of the truck, please?"

"Why?"

"I wish to put my bicycle inside."

"Why can't you leave it among the trees there? No one will steal it. We have to come back this way."

"I prefer to have it with me."

Mr. Lee got down impatiently and went to the rear of the truck. Girija joined him. In silence they unfastened the tailboard. Girija knew the truck. It belonged to a copra dealer in Kuala Pangkalan. The Anglo-Malay Transport Company hired it sometimes when their own trucks were busy. Mr. Lee must have learned of it from Mr. Tan.

The back of the truck was empty. Girija put his bicycle inside and they set off. Mr. Lee was a fast and bad driver. Luckily, they met little traffic on the way. After ten minutes they reached the road leading to the tin workings.

"You turn off here," said Girija; "and I must ask you to put your lights out."

"On this cart track? We shall run into a tree."

"If you drive slowly, you will be all right. If you keep your lights on, we may be seen from the kampong and someone will come to see what is happening."

Mr. Lee grumbled, but submitted. The truck ground along the road as far as the derelict pump shed.

"We stop here," said Girija.

They got down from the cab and Mr. Lee looked around. "What is this place?"

Girija told him. "We go this way," he added.

"One moment. Are the cases open?"

"Of course not."

Mr. Lee took a case opener and a hammer from the cab of the truck. In his hands they looked like weapons. Girija's scalp crawled as he led the way to the oil store. However, Mr. Lee's main concern at that moment seemed to be to avoid tripping on the uneven ground beneath the scrub. He muttered a complaint about the darkness.

Girija took no notice. Not until they were inside the oil store with the door firmly shut did he switch on his flashlight.

Mr. Lee looked at the stacked boxes. "Is this all of it?"

"Everything on the list is there."

Mr. Lee produced the list from his pocket. "Which are the rifles?"

"Those long boxes there."

Mr. Lee began opening them. He opened every one. When Girija suggested that this was a waste of time, Mr. Lee straightened up.

"Cases full of stones have been sold before now," he said. "I am buying only what I see. If you want to save time, you can refasten the cases after I have examined them."

When he had finished with the rifles, he went on in the same methodical way with the rest—the machine pistols, the bazookas, the grenades, the land mines. Only when he approached the ammunition did Girija protest again.

"If you open those, Mr. Lee, you will not be able to reseal them. You will reduce their market value."

Mr. Lee looked at the ammunition boxes. They were airtight metal containers with soft inner lids which had to be cut or torn open with a tool. He nodded reluctantly.

"Okay. I will accept them unseen. Now we can start loading."

He grabbed the rope handle of one of the rifle boxes and looked up at Girija.

Girija smiled, but made no move to take the other handle. Once the boxes were in the truck, there was nothing to prevent Mr. Lee's hitting him on the head with the case opener and taking the receipt from him while he was unconscious. He had a feeling that Mr. Lee was aware of the fact.

"Do you not think, Mr. Lee," he said, "that we should complete our business first?"

"There is plenty of time for that."

Girija held up the flashlight. "By the time we have finished the loading, this battery will be very weak. Let us complete our business now, Mr. Lee, while there is light."

Mr. Lee stared at him resentfully, then shrugged. "As long as you help with the loading, I do not care."

"I will certainly help you." Girija produced Mr. Lee's receipt from his pocket and held it up.

Mr. Lee shrugged again and got out the promissory note. The two pieces of paper changed hands. The moment he had his note, Girija lit a match and burned it. Mr. Lee did the same with his receipt. The transaction was complete.

It took an hour to load the truck, and Mr. Lee became abusive over Girija's refusal to use the flashlight to guide them across the scrub. When the job was finished, Girija went back alone to the oil store to replace the padlock on the door. As he did so, he heard the truck start up and drive off. Mr. Lee had not had the elementary courtesy to wait and say good-by.

Girija went back to the track, picked up his bicycle, and started for home. When he had gone about a mile, he remembered that he had left the trolley with the scooter wheels in the oil store. For a moment or two he wondered if he should go back and get rid of it; then the absurdity of the notion struck him. What could a pair of wheels and a strap tell anybody? He had nothing to hide any more; nothing, that is, except a check for twenty-five thousand dollars.

When he reached his house he examined the tin trunk to see that the lock had not been tampered with. He did not open it. He did not even wait to undress before he lay down on the charpoy and went to sleep.

iii

It was one in the morning when Tan Yam Heng drove the truck up to the gate of the Anglo-Malay Transport Company's compound. The Sikh night watchman came out of his hut and opened the gate. Yam Heng told him to remain at the gate and then drove through to the unloading bay of number-two godown.

The unloading platform was level with the tailboard of the truck. It did not take him long to drag the boxes out and stack them inside the two large machinery crates he had brought in some hours earlier. He had only been able to guess at the various dimensions of the boxes, and they had to be wedged and braced inside the crates; but he had anticipated this, and had provided himself with the wood and tools he would need to do the job. By two thirty both crates were ready to ship. He left them on the platform and drove himself in the truck back to his brother's house. Tan Siow Mong had waited up for him.

"Was everything in order?" he asked.

"Yes."

"Were the goods according to specification?"

"I opened and counted everything except the ammunition. Those boxes are sealed."

"And he has the check."

"Of course."

"You do not seem pleased. Has anything gone wrong?"

"That Indian clerk is insufferable. He treated me as if I were a crook."

His brother nodded calmly. "I warned you he was no fool," he said.

The following morning Tan Siow Mong had a brief interview with Kwong Kee, master of the Anglo-Malay Transport Company's motor junk *Glowing Dawn*, just back from her weekly run to Manila.

Kwong Kee was a square, pot-bellied man with a cheerful disposition and a veneral appetite that bordered on satyriasis. He was not greatly interested in the commercial reasons Mr. Tan gave him for switching the *Glowing Dawn* temporarily to the Singapore run. Nor was he interested in the cargo she carried. And if Mr. Tan's young brother were fool enough to want to go home by sea instead of comfortably by train, that was no business of his either. He was quite content to do as he was told. It was some time since he had sampled the Singapore brothels.

The *Glowing Dawn* sailed that afternoon with a cargo of latex and two machinery crates. When she was well out to sea, Yam Heng went down into the hold and stenciled the consignee's name and address on the crates: "G. NILSEN, C/O CHEN WAREHOUSE CO. SINGAPORE. IN BOND."

iv

The night before the *Silver Isle* reached Saigon, there was a ship's gala dance. The notice had said: "Fancy Dress Optional."

On the advice of his cabin steward, who had lived through many of these occasions, Greg went as a Spanish hidalgo. It was easy. All he had to do was wear the black pants belonging to his tuxedo, an evening dress shirt with a black string tie, and two cummerbunds instead of one to raise the waist line. The steward provided the extra cummerbund and also a flat-topped black hat with a wide brim. He always carried them in his baggage. They had earned him many an extra tip. As he explained to Greg, the advantage of the costume was that a gentleman did not have to wear a jacket with it, and in the steamy heat of the South China Sea that was a real blessing. Dorothy painted on the long sideburns he needed with her eyebrow pencil.

She herself had been undecided what to wear. She had discussed the problem with Arlene; but Arlene had been curiously unhelpful, and had even refused to say what she was going to wear herself; she wanted it to be a surprise. Finally, with the aid of the stewardess, Dorothy had settled for a German doll costume. The stewardess happened to have the dirndl skirt and the blouse with embroidered smocking. Dorothy made herself a coif with two white napkins from the dining room, and put big dabs of rouge on her cheeks.

Both she and Greg were ready early, but lurked in their cabin with the door on the hook until, by watching their fellow passengers passing along the alleyway outside and listening to their conversation, they had assured themselves that they were not going to be the only ones who had opted for fancy dress. Then they went up to the bar.

Most of the passengers had decided on some form of fancy costume for the evening, and, although many had contented themselves with funny hats, false noses, and other easily discarded fripperies, a few had allowed their enthusiasm to run away with them. In the bar, the pirates, Al Jolsons, hoboes, and Indian maharajahs were already drenched with sweat and in difficulty with their burnt-cork make-ups. Over their Martinis, Greg and Dorothy congratulated themselves on having hit it off just right; they had taken trouble, but not too much trouble; and they were comfortable.

Arlene did not appear until just before the ship's speakers announced dinner. Then she made a slow, regal entrance through the double doors leading to the lounge. She was wearing a *cheong sam,* the silk formal dress with the high collar and split skirt that Chinese women wear, and long jade earrings. Just inside the door, she stopped and smiled as if expecting a round of applause.

The *cheong sam* can be an attractive and becoming garment; but it makes certain demands on the wearer. She must be small-boned and very slender, with invisible hips and near-to-invisible buttocks, a flat stomach, and minute breasts. Her arms and neck must appear fragile, and her face must be round with high cheekbones. She must, in other words, be Chinese. On Arlene's shapely but large and well-padded body, and surmounted by her equine head, it looked grotesque.

Greg said: "My God!"

"She bought it in Hong Kong," muttered Dorothy. "It's the most lovely material."

"It still looks ridiculous."

"I didn't see it on her at the fitting."

"She must be out of her mind."

Arlene's entrance created a minor sensation, and there were one or two uncertain whoops of gallantry as she swayed over to the Nilsens' table. If she were kidding, everyone was prepared to laugh. If she were serious, they were ready to be polite. Meanwhile, they were embarrassed.

Arlene sat down beside Dorothy and the splits in her skirt gaped to reveal, on Greg's side, a large area of thigh and one pink suspender. She smiled archly.

"Well, what do you think of Chinee laundly girl?"

"It's a lovely dress," said Dorothy eagerly.

"It certainly is," said Greg. "Martini?"

"No." Her smile was challenging now. "Tonight I am drinking champagne."

They went down to dinner twenty minutes late, and had to run a gauntlet of eyes as they crossed to their table. Arlene's half-bottle of champagne seemed to have gone to her head, and she began calling Greg "Don Gregorio" and Dorothy "Gretchen." She was thoroughly pleased with herself, looking about her with the calm assurance of a woman who knows that she is the most attractive in the room.

When the dancing began, she became skittish, breaking away from her partners to execute little hip-waggling solos in the middle of the deck. Greg and Dorothy, dancing sedately on the outskirts, glanced at one another.

Dorothy was worried. "I don't understand it," she muttered; "she usually has such good taste in clothes."

"Yes."

"Well, you must admit she *has*."

"If you ask me," said Greg, "she had a few belts in her cabin before she came up."

"Now, darling, that's a nasty thing to say."

"Well, look at her."

Arlene, with her arms stretched out wide, her head turned over her right shoulder, and her chin tilted imperiously, was now dancing a flamenco. Her partner, one of the ship's officers, was rotating around her somewhat helplessly. He had an uneasy grin on his face.

"She's just a little excited," said Dorothy defensively. "Anyway, she's having a good time."

"In my opinion, she's making a horse's ass of herself."

"Really, Greg!"

Arlene did not return to their table. When a "Leap Year" dance was announced, she made a beeline for the Captain. After that dance she returned with him to his table; whether by invitation or not it was impossible to determine.

The following morning, when they were going up the river

to Saigon, she did not appear at her usual time; but Greg and Dorothy were too busy shooting with their movie camera and watching the sampans and the riverbanks go by to give her much thought. They found her, immaculate but a trifle pensive, sitting in the bar after the ship had docked.

"What happened to you last night?" she asked Dorothy as they joined her.

"We went down around eleven thirty."

"Four o'clock, me," Arlene said grimly. "The barman opened up a can of wienies. He's got an electric grill back there. That was after I'd switched to Scotch."

"Who else was there?" Dorothy asked.

"Nobody. Just the barman and me. He comes from L.A. and he's a Dodger fan," she added sourly.

But after lunch she felt fine again and they all went ashore. At Arlene's suggestion, they crushed into a small Renault taxi for a tour of the city.

It was insufferably humid, and the driver, a handsome young Vietnamese, smelled peculiarly of rotting fish. Arlene explained that the smell came from a sauce used in all Vietnamese cooking and was no reflection on the driver's personal cleanliness.

The driver grinned. "Is made from fish," he said suddenly in English. "You like me show where make it?"

Up to that moment he had spoken nothing but French, and Arlene had been the interpreter. Nobody had troubled to ask him if he understood English, Greg remembered. Arlene, proud of the French she had acquired in her Red Cross days, had just gone ahead and spoken for them. As a result, they had unwittingly hurt the man's feelings. That was precisely the sort of stupid incident, Greg thought, that made Americans unpopular abroad.

However, the driver did not seem offended. "I show you on way back ship," he went on. "Make bad smell, but many vitamins."

"That so?"

They were traveling along a broad, tree-lined street that reminded Arlene and Dorothy of Paris, when the driver turned to Greg.

"Now I show you where Quiet American made bomb explosion," he said.

"How's that?"

"That café there." The driver pointed. "That was where Quiet American made bomb explosion. Many killed."

They were crossing a square now. Greg looked from the café to the driver.

"But *The Quiet American* was a novel," he said.

"Yes, sir. That is café back there. I was near at time of explosion. Was very bad."

"But it was fiction," Dorothy said. "It didn't actually happen."

"Apparently there was a bomb explosion there," Arlene explained. "I had this when I was here before. Somebody told me Graham Greene was in the city at the time."

"Graham Greene, yes." The driver nodded emphatically. "Presently I will show you bridge where Fowler found dead body of correspondent, and place where there was restaurant where they talk. Real restaurant now gone, pulled down."

"You mean people here believe that story?"

"Is true, sir. I show you the place."

"But it was just a novel."

"Look," said Arlene impatiently, "if you go to Marseille, they take you out to the Chateau d'If and show you the hole in the wall that the Count of Monte Cristo made when he scratched his way through to the Abbé Faria. They show you the dungeon occupied by the Man in the Iron Mask. It doesn't mean anything. It's just to make the tourists feel they're getting their money's worth."

"But that was an anti-American novel. If they believe all that stuff, my God! We're giving these people millions in aid."

"That's right," said Dorothy.

Arlene smiled. "I can see you two have got a few surprises coming to you on this trip."

They returned to the ship hot, tired, and out of temper. On their way down to shower and change, Greg and Dorothy had to squeeze their way past a pile of baggage in the alleyway. Their steward told them that three new passengers had come on board. When they went up on deck, they saw Arlene sitting talking animatedly to a florid, thick-set man in a khaki bush shirt. They were drinking Pernod.

At cocktail time Greg and Dorothy were sitting in their usual corner when Arlene appeared with the same man. He

had changed into a white sharkskin suit. Evidently he was one
of the new passengers. They came over.

"Ces sont mes amis Greg et Dorothy Nilsen," said Arlene.
"Je veux vous présenter Monsieur Seguin."

"How do you do?" said Monsieur Seguin.

They shook hands. Greg said: "Will you join us?"

"Thank you." With a courteous bow to Dorothy, Monsieur
Seguin sat down.

He had small blue eyes, a merry smile, and large pudgy
hands with little mats of gleaming blond hair on the backs of
them.

"Monsieur Seguin est ingénieur civil," Arlene explained.
"Il va nous accompagner jusqu'à Calcutta. Monsieur Nilsen
est ingénieur aussi."

"Indeed?" Monsieur Seguin looked interested. "In what
branch of our profession, sir?" His English was excellent.

"How do you say die-casting in French?" Arlene asked.

Greg shrugged helplessly.

"Oh, but I understand," said Monsieur Seguin affably. "Mr.
Nilsen makes the small pieces of all those things that the
world thinks of when it hears an American use the phrase
'standard of living.'"

Arlene laughed heartily. Greg and Dorothy smiled. More
Pernods were arriving.

"Isn't it lucky?" Arlene said. "I had a word with the chief
steward and he's fixed it for Monsieur Seguin to sit at our
table."

The *Silver Isle* was an American ship and most of her passengers were Americans. Not unnaturally, the cooking was
American, and served in the American style.

Monsieur Seguin did not like it. He did not like the shrimp
cocktail and tried to remove all the sauce from it. He asked
for his steak *bleu* and, when it came rare, regretted that it
had been overcooked. He did not want his salad on the side,
but as a separate course, and requested that the slices of
avocado pear be removed. He ignored the baked Idaho potato,
and refused the ice cream. He took one mouthful of the Wis-
consin Brie, made a face, and ate no more. However, he remained, apparently, good-humored. His only comment seemed
mild enough for a Frenchman who had not enjoyed his dinner.

"I needed to lose some weight," he said with a smile. "This ship will be very good for me. Here it will be easy to maintain a regime."

"I don't know what they think they're doing," Arlene burst out angrily. "You could get better food at a drugstore."

Dorothy chuckled. "The other day you were saying you thought the food was great."

"Great is a relative term, dear. Even an American chef must be able to cook eatable food *one* day in thirty." She was sharing a bottle of wine with Monsieur Seguin, and now she drained her glass.

Monsieur Seguin refilled it. "Mademoiselle, I think you are being very unfair to America," he said. "She has made some very important contributions to world civilization. Let us see—" he pretended to search his memory—"she has given us chewing gum, and Coca-Cola, and gangster films, and she has given us atomic bombs." He smiled slyly at Greg. "As well as a lot of advice."

Greg raised his eyebrows. "Aren't you forgetting popcorn?"

"Ah, yes. Pardon. And I was forgetting democracy also. McCarthy style, of course."

Arlene laughed. "That's telling 'em!"

Dorothy's face froze.

Greg smiled placidly at Monsieur Seguin. "I expect you have a lot of jokes about American tourists, too. And foreign aid."

Monsieur Seguin shrugged. "It is sad," he said. "You Americans give away billions of dollars to defend yourselves against Communism, but you ask everyone to believe that you give it because you are good and kind. Why?"

"Because big daddy-o wants to be loved," said Arlene promptly.

"America," said Monsieur Seguin, "is rich, and behaves like the rich always behave. When they begin to fear death, they become philanthropists."

"Well, most Americans aren't rich," said Greg, "and they certainly don't feel particularly philanthropic when they're paying their taxes."

"That's just childish," snapped Arlene. "Monsieur Seguin was talking about us as a nation."

Dorothy's face went pink. "I don't think Greg's the one who's being childish," she said.

"What I meant to say," Monsieur Seguin went on evenly, "was simply that American foreign policy has always, from the first, been made by men who saw the world through the eyes of money, of riches."

"If you don't mind my saying so, Monsieur Seguin," said Greg, "that is one of the stupidest remarks I've ever heard."

Monsieur Seguin smiled. "You know, Mr. Nilsen, there was an American who owned fifteen thousand acres of some of the best land in America. He owned land in New York and Pennsylvania and Virginia and Maryland and the city of Washington. When he died he was one of the richest men in your country."

"Who was that, Rockefeller?"

"His name was George Washington," said Monsieur Seguin quietly; "but, of course, you knew that."

Arlene laughed so much that she had the whole dining room looking at their table.

Dorothy sat with a face like stone.

After dinner she and Greg went straight to their cabin.

"I think Arlene behaved disgustingly," Dorothy said; "and as for that ghastly little Frenchman . . . Was it right what he said—about Washington, I mean?"

Greg shrugged. "Probably. He's the sort of man who collects facts of that kind. Of course, they weren't relevant to the point he was trying to make, but that wouldn't interest him. He's a debater."

"It's Arlene I don't understand. Encouraging him to go on talking all that anti-American nonsense. And on an American ship, too. I mean, it's such bad taste. And how dared she ask the steward to put him at our table, without even consulting us?"

"I tell you one thing, dear," said Greg, "and you'd better be ready for it. The next time that guy starts any anti-American stuff, I'm going to take a poke at him."

"You mean we have to go on eating with him?" Dorothy demanded.

Greg stared at her, a wild hope surging through him. "Darling, the ship's full. You know that. They can't rearrange the seating now."

"You mean we're stuck with them all the way to Calcutta?"

"Unless we complain to the purser and make a personal issue of it, I'm afraid we are."

"Oh, Greg!" She sat down miserably on her bed. "Our lovely trip!"

He sat down beside her and put his arm around her waist. "You said it yourself, darling. We're not in a position to choose our traveling companions."

Dorothy stuck out her chin. "Maybe not. But we *are* in a position to choose the way we travel."

"Darling, we're booked through on this ship to Calcutta."

"Maybe we are, but we can change our minds. We could stop over at Singapore, take a side trip or two, and then go on by air to Calcutta. You said you were going to do something for Mr. Tan in Singapore. All right! It's business. If you explained that, I know we could get a refund on the passage."

Greg had never loved her more. "That's right. Pan-Am and B.O.A.C. go via Bangkok. Maybe we could stop over there instead of Rangoon before we go on to Calcutta."

"Bangkok! That would be wonderful!"

"As a matter of fact, it wouldn't cost us any extra, even allowing for side trips. I didn't tell you, but this business that Mr. Tan asked me to do will net me a thousand dollars."

"Hong Kong?"

"No, real American dollars. And I could make a thousand more if we spent a day or two extra in Singapore."

"How?"

"Signing papers. Anyway, I'll tell you about that later. The main thing is that we enjoy ourselves. We don't have to worry about the extra expense. If we decide we want to get off at Singapore, then that's all there is to it."

Dorothy was silent for a moment. Then she said: "I know you never liked Arlene. I suppose she's not really a very likable person. I think that's why I felt sorry for her."

Later that evening Greg had a talk with the purser and then sent a radiogram to Mr. Tan Tack Chee in Manila.

CHAPTER V

AT THE upper social levels of the British community in Singapore, Colonel Soames was known as "The Policeman."

There was nothing derogatory about the name. It had been applied originally to distinguish him from another Colonel Soames, who had been a retired Ghurka officer and a prominent member of the Turf Club. The fact that its use had continued after "Ghurka" Soames' death, however, had been only partly the result of habit. Although Colonel Soames' status as a senior police official was well known, the nature of his duties was not. He never discussed them, and any attempt to draw him out on the subject was met by him with a frosty silence. It was generally assumed that he was not, strictly speaking, a policeman at all, but something to do with Intelligence. To go on calling him "The Policeman" was a mildly sardonic way of underlining that assumption.

It was, in a sense, correct. Singapore was a naval, military, and air base of crucial importance to the British Commonwealth; but it was also a free port and a trading post, largely dependent for its economic existence on international commerce. In the latter capacity it was obliged to receive many strange guests. Colonel Soames' job was to detect the undesirables among them, and to see that their interests and those of Singapore as a whole did not seriously conflict. He worked in collaboration with the immigration department, the service intelligence organizations, the port and airport authorities, and the customs. He never ordered arrests. If any major criminal activity came to his attention, he either turned the facts over to an appropriate colleague for action, or, if, in his judgment, inaction would be more productive, he merely watched and waited. Occasionally he might suggest a deportation or the refusal of an entry permit; but most of his results were obtained simply by contriving to let the objects of his attentions know that they were observed and understood. Officially, he was in charge of a branch of the internal security forces. His own definition of his function was "discouraging the bad boys."

His second-in-command was a plain-clothes inspector named Chow Soo Kee. Every morning at ten they met to discuss the reports of the previous day. It was at one of these meetings that the name "Nilsen" first came to Colonel Soames' attention.

They had reviewed the current activities of a Belgian who was attempting to set up a central distribution agency for "blue" films from Bangkok, an Austrian who was buying girls for a new brothel in Brunei, and an Australian couple who seemed to be doing too well at the badger game. They has discussed the steps to be taken in the case of the consul of a Central American republic who, comfortably shielded by his diplomatic immunity, was making money in the opium market. It had been decided to advise a man posing as a theatrical booking agent that his record had been forwarded by Scotland Yard. Inspector Chow was getting up to leave, when he remembered something.

"By the way, Colonel," he said, "we have another arms dealer."

"Not that Italian again?"

"No, sir, a new one. Customs told me about him. There was a parcel of arms consigned in bond to a G. Nilsen from Manila."

"How big?"

Inspector Chow told him. "Probably Korean war surplus," he added. "They could be samples."

"Rather a lot for samples, don't you think? Sounds more like a small man trying to get his toe in."

"Well, that's the funny thing, sir. He isn't the usual type. Full name is Gregory Hull Nilsen. American citizen. Engineer. Comes from Wilmington, Delaware, where he has his own light-engineering business. Traveling with his wife. They arrived on the *Silver Isle* two days ago. Staying at the Raffles Hotel. They have an air-conditioned suite. Highly respectable sort of people, apparently."

"Well, that's a comfort."

"Yes, sir." Inspector Chow paused. "Except for two things. He made a false statement to the immigration people. Said he and his wife were here just as tourists. Made no mention of the arms business."

"How long did he ask for?"

"Two weeks. Immigration visa'd them for thirty days. The other thing was that he was brought to the hotel by Tan Yam Heng."

"You mean that union thug who's always losing his shirt on the pickle market?"

"Yes, sir. Apparently on friendly terms with him. That's what I didn't like. Tan's a member of the Democratic Action Party."

"Who else has this man seen?"

"Nobody, as far as I can gather. Yesterday he and his wife hired a car and drove round the island—to see the sights, they said. The driver says that's all they did do."

"Could be establishing their cover. I wonder why he lied, though. Stupid thing to do, if he's just a dealer. Who'd be in the market now for what he's got to sell?"

Inspector Chow thought for a moment. He knew that what he had to say would not please Colonel Soames, and he wanted to phrase it as delicately as possible.

Indonesia, the young republic which claimed sovereignty over the three thousand islands of the former Dutch East Indies, was an uneasy neighbor. The Central Government in Java was weak, unstable, and hag-ridden by Communism. In the big outer islands, especially Sumatra and Celebes, there were powerful revolutionary movements demanding secession and independence. The political thinking of these movements was religious in tone and strongly anti-Communist; and they had made fighting alliances. For three years or more, parts of Sumatra and Celebes had been virtually in a state of civil war, with insurgent forces in control of large areas and Central Government troops having in some places to defend even the big towns. With the long coastline of Sumatra only thirty miles away across the Straits of Malacca, Singapore was, whether it liked it or not, the natural supply base for the Sumatran insurgents. Their "liaison officers" and purchasing agents were the bane of Colonel Soames' existence.

"As you pointed out, sir," Inspector Chow said finally, "it is a small consignment. I don't think the Darul Islam people would be interested at present. You know they had a shipment of eighty machine guns and fifty three-inch mortars three weeks ago."

"Not through here, I hope."

"No, sir. Direct from Macao."

"That Dutchman handle it?"

"Yes. But he shipped the ammunition separately—over three tons, apparently—and an Indonesian Government destroyer intercepted it. They'll be wanting to replace that ammunition first. I don't think they'll bother about a few more rifles. I would say that at the moment the most interested buyer would be Captain Lukey."

He was careful to say the last two words very casually. Captain Lukey was the liaison officer and representative in Singapore of a small insurgent force that had recently begun to operate in Northern Sumatra. Colonel Soames's dislike of him was personal and intense.

Herbert Henry Lukey had been a regular soldier in a British county regiment, and commissioned as a lieutenant quartermaster during World War II. He had served, without distinction, until 1950, when the final period for which he had signed on had expired. His regiment had been stationed in Egypt at the time, and much of his last six months of service had been spent answering questions at Courts of Inquiry appointed to investigate the virtual disappearance of a number of emergency gasoline storage dumps of which he had been in charge. His answers had revealed qualities of imagination and ingenuity not hitherto apparent in his military career; and a secret, though unauthorized, investigation of his bank balance had shown him to be in the possession of funds far exceeding his total army pay for the previous five years. However, the smoke screen of confusion which he had succeeded in creating had, in the end, led to the inquiries being abandoned for lack of evidence. The gasoline losses had been written off, in the way he had originally advocated, as "due to evaporation." He could, and frequently did, claim that his army record was as clean as a whistle.

His subsequent record, as a civilian in North Borneo, Malaya, and Singapore, was not. He had worked in minor executive posts for several big trading concerns, most of which had, like the army, suffered some evaporation of assets before dispensing with his services. Eventually one of them had thought forthrightly and unconfusedly enough about its loses to go to the police. There had been talk, too, of forged references. He had left Singapore hurriedly, and after a while the charges against him had been dropped. Occasional inquiries over the next three years from police authorities in Colombo, Cape Town, Mombassa, and Bombay had made it possible to chart his subsequent progress. The report of his return to Singapore had been referred immediately to Colonel Soames.

"The Policeman" was not an intolerant man. He disapproved of the crooked and the *louche*, but he did not generally dislike them. Admittedly, his attitude was not as objective as he thought it was, and had a paternalistic, schoolmasterish quality about it; but that was largely a result of his training. He had come late to police work, and was inclined to treat most of the adult transgressors who came his way as if they were delinquent members of a regiment of which he was in command, and to which both he and they owed a common loyalty.

However, with Captain Lukey it was different; and the difference resided in the word "captain."

The day after Lukey had returned, Colonel Soames had summoned him to his office for an interview.

"According to your statement to the immigration authorities," Colonel Soames had begun, "you are here as a liaison officer and purchasing agent for the armed forces of the Independent Party of the Faithful of North Sumatra. Is that correct?"

"Perfectly correct."

"You say you are a liaison officer. What is the liaison between, may I ask?"

"The army of the Party of the Faithful and other forces in Sumatra hostile to those Commies in Djakarta, sir."

"I see. And in your role as purchasing agent, what are you intending to purchase?"

"Supplies, Colonel."

"Arms?"

"Supplies of various kinds, Colonel."

"Do you have funds for these purchases?"

"Naturally, Colonel."

"And where do these funds come from?"

"They are subscribed by loyal Sumatrans and certain friendly parties."

"Have you a banking account?"

"Yes, Colonel. Hong Kong and Shanghai, Orchard Road. All perfectly respectable."

"Are you empowered to sign checks?"

"With a counter-signature, yes."

"Whose counter-signature?"

"A member of the Executive Committee of the Party of the Faithful."

"Is the Committee aware of your previous record?"

"My British army record, Colonel? Certainly."

"I was thinking more of your record here, and in Borneo."

"I wasn't aware that I had one, sir."

"Weren't you?"

"I don't think I understand you, Colonel. Are you suggesting I have a criminal record in Singapore?"

That had been just what Colonel Soames had been suggesting, but he knew better than to say so. There had been no convictions recorded against the man in that area.

"All I am suggesting is that while you are in Singapore you are careful to respect the law. Do you understand, Mr. Lukey?"

"*Captain* Lukey if you don't mind, Colonel."

Colonel Soames had smiled unpleasantly. "And that brings me to another point. I don't think that there is much sense in my pointing out that the use of a military title to which one is not entitled is bad form and caddish. Perhaps I should simply remind you that it is an offense in law."

Captain Lukey had smiled back, equally unpleasantly. "And perhaps I should simply tell you, Colonel, that the British army isn't the only army in the world. Here, take a look at this."

He had handed over a paper. It had been a commission
from the Commander in Chief of the army of the Independent
Party of the Faithful of North Sumatra, appointing his loyal
servant Herbert Henry Lukey a staff captain.

It had touched Colonel Soames in a very sensitive place.
He had lost his temper.

"This is meaningless. You cannot accept such a commission."

"Why not, Colonel?"

"In the first place, you are a British subject. In the second
place, you are, unhappily, an officer in the armed forces of
Her Majesty the Queen."

"Not any more, Colonel."

"You may not be a serving officer, but you are on the
reserve. You could be recalled to active duty if necessary."

Captain Lukey had grinned. "Do you take me for a fool,
Colonel? I came off the reserve two years ago. I'm over age."

"Well, that's something to be thankful for, but don't expect me to recognize this rubbish." Colonel Soames had
tossed the paper contemptuously back across the desk.

Captain Lukey had picked it up, folded it carefully, and
put it back in his pocket before speaking. Then he had said:
"Is that your considered opinion, Colonel?"

"It is."

"Then you won't have any objection, I take it, if I report
back to my commanding officer in Sumatra as the official
British view."

Colonel Soames had hesitated. The Independent Party of
the Faithful was probably little more than a gang of dissident
Sumatran officers greedy for the spoils of local political
power. But in Sumatra anything might happen. Within a few
months those same officers could be members of a lawfully
constituted government. A senior Singapore police official who
had gratuitously insulted its leaders would find himself
most unpopular with the British Foreign Office, to say
nothing of Government House. The fact that H. H. Lukey
was, in his opinion, a cad would not excuse the indiscretion.

He had swallowed his annoyance. "No, it's not an official
British view. It merely represents my personal opinion of
you."

Captain Lukey had not been deceived by the evasion. He

had grinned infuriatingly. "Good show, Colonel. I'll tell my masters I'm getting full co-operation and all proper respect."

"You can also tell them that if there's any hanky-panky here you'll be out on your ear, and pretty damn quick."

It had been a feeble threat and Captain Lukey had known it. He had still been grinning when he left.

Colonel Soames had not forgotten the humiliation. He looked up sharply at Inspector Chow. "Why Lukey?"

"He doesn't seem to have much money to spend, sir. I should think he could just about manage this deal, though. Another thing: he's been trying to buy three-oh-three ammunition. They must have rifles of that caliber already. It would make sense to buy more. Most of the stuff going about at present is three-oh-oh."

"I see." The Colonel was thoughtful for a moment, then he nodded. "Put a man on to Tan Yam Heng. See if he tries to contact Lukey. Keep me posted."

"Very good, sir."

"What did you say that American's name was? Nilsen?"

"Yes, sir. Do you want me to . . . ?"

"No. I think I may look into that myself."

ii

Greg and Dorothy were enjoying Singapore. They had made two tours of the island and also crossed the causeway into Johore; and although they had had to admit to themselves that there was not really all that much to see, they were so glad to be on their own again that it did not seem to matter. In any case, they were having fun arranging side trips. There was a Garuda Indonesian Airways flight that could take them down to Bali, and they had made provisional reservations for early the following week. The only snag was that they would have to have an Indonesian tourist visa, and that took several days to get. Until it came through they would not know for certain what their plans were. So they had applied for the visa and decided that, if it did not come through in time, they would console themselves with a trip up to Penang. The man in Thos. Cook's had shown them some pictures of the island that made it look almost as enchanting as Bali.

The only area of dissension between them was that surrounding the Tan arms deal.

When Greg had, finally, explained it to her in detail, Dorothy had stared at him almost incredulously.

"But, darling, it sounds to me completely crooked."

"What's crooked about it? It's just a question of helping Mr. Tan to avoid a technicality in the Philippine law. Nothing more."

"Well, that's something, isn't it? It's their law."

"It wasn't made to cover this sort of eventuality."

"What sort is that?"

"Well, I think the idea of selling Communist arms to the anti-Communists is a pretty good idea."

"Maybe. But how do you know they *are* Communist arms? Who told you they were? How do you know he's telling the truth?"

It had been a long, inconclusive, and uncomfortable discussion. One passage of it had stayed in his mind to trouble him later.

"Supposing someone back home had come to you with a proposition like this," she had said.

"How could they?"

"But supposing they did. You know what? I think you'd call the police or the FBI."

"Well, this isn't America, and the circumstances and the people are all entirely different."

She had nodded calmly. "That's just my point."

"I don't get it."

"Maybe we don't know *how* different they are."

Their first encounter with Mr. Tan Yam Heng in Singapore had not improved the situation. They had found his appearance unprepossessing and his manner furtive. Indeed, when he had contacted them on the boat, Greg had at first mistaken him for some sort of tout. Then he had tried to hustle them through the immigration and customs before they had had a chance to say good-by to anyone on the ship. Greg had had to be very firm.

Later, at the hotel, Tan had produced an airmail letter from Manila confirming that Greg would act as sole selling agent for Mr. Tan Tack Chee, and revising their financial arrangements accordingly. That had been all right; but, although the letter had been addressed to Greg personally, Tan Yam Heng had already opened it and read the contents.

When he had gone, Dorothy had raised her eyebrows. "Not much like his brother, is he?"

"No."

"Do you think opening other people's letters is an old Chinese custom?"

"Well, I don't suppose it matters. By the way, Mr. Tan sends you and Arlene his best wishes."

The meeting at the Customs House the following morning had been no more propitious. After Greg had signed the appropriate papers, they had gone outside.

"The next thing, Mr. Nilsen," Tan Yam Heng had said briskly, "is for me to arrange meetings with buyers."

Greg had smiled and shaken his head. "No, Mr. Tan. The next thing is for you to give me a check for one thousand and fifty dollars."

"But that is not until you sign the papers transferring ownership of the goods. That is the arrangement."

"That *was* the arrangement. You read your brother's letter. The arrangement is changed. The first five per cent is to be paid over on signature of the customs documents. The *second* five per cent will be paid when ownership is transferred to the actual buyer."

It had been at that moment that Greg had understood why Mr. Tan in Manila had been so anxious for him to act as his agent. Under the earlier arrangement, there would have been nothing to stop Mr. Tan in Singapore from completing the blank transfer of ownership in his own favor. Under the new arrangement, ownership would only be transferred to the buyer. The explanation was simple: Mr. Tan in Manila did not trust Mr. Tan in Singapore, and probably for very good reasons.

Tan Yam Heng had scowled almost threateningly. "Between associates in business enterprise," he had said, "there must be trust and personal dignity in all negotiations."

"I couldn't agree more. And I think the best way of keeping that trust and personal dignity, Mr. Tan, is for everyone to do just what they've agreed to do right along the line. No more, no less."

Mr. Tan Yam Heng had had the check, drawn on the Manila office of an American bank, ready in his pocket, and had handed it over in the end, but with a bad grace. He had left, saying that he would telephone when he had arranged the meetings.

Since then, two days had elapsed and Greg had heard nothing. He had not told Dorothy about the argument over the check; nor had he thought it necessary to discuss with her his other misgivings. He was on the point of cabling to Mr. Tan in Manila to remind him of the time limit they had agreed on, when Tan Yam Heng called.

"Mr. Nilsen," he said, "I have an interested buyer."

"Oh."

"He would like to meet with you and discuss the proposition."

"Who is he?"

"A British army captain, now acting for a group in Indonesia."

"What sort of group?"

"I think it is religious."

"What do you mean, religious?"

"Does it matter? We wish to sell, he wishes to buy."

"It matters a great deal. Anyway, what's the man's name? How do I meet him?"

"His name is Captain Lukey, and, if convenient, I will bring him to your hotel this afternoon at five."

"Okay."

"And the price is agreed?"

"We ask seventy-five thousand, accept anything over sixty."

"Yes. This is very confidential."

"I'll see you at five."

He told Dorothy.

"What's a religious group want with rifles and machine guns?" she asked.

"How should I know? I don't think Tan knew what he was talking about. Anyway, there's a British officer acting for them, so they must be fairly respectable."

"I suppose you'll have to see him alone."

"You can stay in the bedroom and listen through the door, if you want."

Tan Yam Heng arrived ten minutes early, looking more furtive than ever.

"I wished," he explained, "to find the best route from the courtyard entrance to your suite. As soon as he arrives I will bring him straight here without telephoning from the reception desk first, if you agree."

"It's all right with me."

"The fewer people who see us together, the better."

"Why all the cloak-and-dagger stuff?"

"In such negotiations it is important to be secret. If some spy of the Indonesian Government got to know of this, it would be dangerous."

Greg avoided looking at Dorothy. "I see."

"Captain Lukey may wish to search the suite before discussions begin."

"Well, he can't. My wife's going to be in the bedroom."

"These are serious matters. I am sure Mrs. Nilsen understands."

"Look, there's not going to be any searching, and if the gallant captain doesn't like it, he can lump it. How well do you know him?"

"I have talked to him."

"Did he say he wanted to search the place?"

"No, but . . ."

"Then supposing we let him speak for himself. He'll be here in a minute. Now, why don't you just go down and wait for him, Mr. Tan?"

Tan Yam Heng went, sullenly. Twenty minutes later he returned with Captain Lukey.

The Captain was a tall man in the late forties with a slight paunch, a florid complexion, graying brown hair, and a large handlebar mustache stained on one side by nicotine. He wore the Singapore business uniform—white duck slacks, white long-sleeved shirt with breast pockets, and a regimental tie. He had a reverberating voice and a hearty manner. He came into the room with hand outstretched.

"How do you do, Mr. Nilsen? Sorry I'm late. Got held up in a spot of traffic."

"Glad to know you, Captain," said Greg. "Won't you sit down?"

Captain Lukey seemed not to have heard the invitation. He smiled broadly, put his hands on his hips, and looked around the room. "Well, now," he said, "the last time I was in this suite, General Blacklock had it. That was before he became C. in C. of course. I was his A.D.C. for a time. Rum bird, old Blackie."

"Can I get you a drink?" Greg asked.

"Very handsome of you. I'll have a stengah, if you don't mind."

"That's Scotch and soda, isn't it?"

"Little Scotch, lot of soda. Got to keep the old waterworks going in this climate."

"Oh, yes, I see." Greg was having trouble placing Captain Lukey's accent. Behind the stage British there was another intonation that he could not identify. Colonel Soames could have told him that it came from Liverpool.

"You know," said Captain Lukey, "lots of people say business before pleasure." He sat down heavily. "Never been able to understand it myself. But then people say all sorts of things they've never thought about. They've got rule-of-thumb minds. The shortest distance between two points is a straight line. Agreed?"

"Agreed."

"Is the hypotenuse of a right-angled triangle a straight line?"

"It is."

"And the sum of the lengths of the other two sides is greater?"

"Yes."

Captain Lukey gave him a cunning leer. "Yet the *square* of the hypotenuse is *equal* to the sum of the squares of the other two sides. How do you account for that?"

"Euclid accounted for it quite satisfactorily." Greg put some more soda in the Captain's drink. He was wondering if the man were as sober as he had at first appeared to be.

"Euclid!" The Captain laughed shortly, as if Greg had mentioned some long-discredited mutual acquaintance, and glanced over his shoulder at Tan Yam Heng. "You never bothered your head about that sort of thing, eh, Tan?"

"I do not understand." Tan Yam Heng had stationed himself in front of the door like a character in a trench-coat melodrama.

The Captain eyed him sourly. "I'll bet you don't. Shortest distances, maybe. Straight lines? Don't make me laugh."

"Are you meaning to insult me, Captain?"

"Me? Perish the thought."

Greg finished mixing the drinks and crossed over to them.

"Shall we talk business?" he said. There was a touch of impatience in his voice that he could not quite conceal.

Captain Lukey chuckled. "That's what I like," he said. "American hustle. Okay, brother, where do we go from here? You name it."

He was speaking now with what he evidently imagined to be an American accent.

Greg smiled. "All right. I understand you're in the market for small arms and ammunition. Did Mr. Tan show you a list of the stuff I have in bond here?"

"Yup," said Captain Lukey sportively.

"He's told you the price?"

"Yup."

"And I gather you're interested."

"Nope."

Greg stared at him coldly. "Then, why are you here?"

"Because I just *might* become interested." He had abandoned his American accent.

"In what circumstances?"

"Well, if the stuff were really new and not re-conditioned, for instance."

"You can inspect it."

"And if you cut your asking price by fifty per cent, so that I could make a reasonable offer at something like the current market price."

"There is no current market price."

"Mr. Nilsen, I'm just a simple soldier, but even I know better than that. I can buy rifles at twenty dollars apiece."

"Then you should."

"I'm not all that interested in rifles. Now, if you were to put a fair price on the machine pistols, we might talk. As it is . . ." He broke off, swallowed the rest of his drink, and got to his feet. "Tell you what. You think it over and we'll be in touch tomorrow. What do you say?"

"I might come down a little, but the price'll still be in the same range."

Captain Lukey nodded, almost appreciatively. "Well," he said, "there's no taste in nothing."

Greg found the statement obscure, but he, too, nodded. The Captain wrung his hand and went, exuding good will.

The moment the door had shut, Tan Yam Heng went to it, listened, and then flung it open suddenly.

The corridor outside was empty.

Tan shut the door again and turned to Greg. "Of course, he is bluffing," he said.

"How far? You did check the going prices thoroughly, I suppose?"

"Oh, yes. If he does not come back to us, it will only be because he does not have the money to pay."

"What happens in that case?"

Tan looked shifty. "There is another buyer, but he is away in Macao at present."

"When's he coming back?"

"Next week, perhaps."

"Well, he won't find me here. All right, Mr. Tan, we'll check in the morning."

When he had gone Dorothy came out of the bedroom.

"What a curious man," she said. "Do you think he really is a British officer?"

"Why not? I've met some pretty curious American officers in my time. Why shouldn't the British army have some dogs, too?"

The telephone rang. Greg answered it.

"Mr. Nilsen?" It was Captain Lukey.

"Yes."

"I'm speaking from downstairs. I wonder if I could slip up and see you again for a tick."

"Very well."

"Be up in a brace of shakes."

Greg looked at Dorothy. "Lukey again."

"I'll go back into the bedroom."

"No, you stay here."

Captain Lukey returned looking bland and businesslike.

When he saw Dorothy, however, he became stickily gallant.

"Well, this is a delightful surprise. I'd no idea."

Dorothy said: "How do you do, Captain?"

The Captain did not miss the lack of warmth in her tone. "Terribly sorry to butt in like this, Mrs. Nilsen. Frightfully bad form, but I did want another word with your good husband. Ghastly shop talk, I'm afraid."

Dorothy sat down. "That's quite all right, Captain."

"I'm afraid Tan's not here," said Greg.

"I know. Saw him go." The Captain smiled boyishly. "As a matter of fact, I waited downstairs until he did."

"Oh?"

"Mind if I sit down?"

"Do."

"You see, it was a bit awkward."

"What was?"

The Captain smoothed his mustache. "Well, it's a funny sort of game, this. I didn't know quite what to expect here. No offense meant, of course. As soon as I met you, I knew that you were a good type." He hesitated.

"But . . . ?" said Greg encouragingly.

"Well, as I say, it's awkward." Captain Lukey gave the impression of a simple man wrestling with an unfamiliar problem in ethics. "I'm no saint myself, and if you tell me to run along and mind my own confounded business, I'll understand, but I do think white men ought to stick together a bit. Nothing against Asians, mind you, but, well, sometimes . . ." He broke off, his pale, anxious eyes searching Greg's face for understanding.

"Captain, if you'll just tell me what you're talking about."

The Captain turned apologetically to Dorothy. "So sorry about all this, Mrs. Nilsen."

Dorothy smiled sweetly. "Oh, I'm just as interested as my husband."

The Captain did not seem reassured. He went on with knitted brow. "Well, it's awkward, you see," he said again, and then appeared to make up his mind. "Look, Nilsen, man to man, how long have you known this fellow Tan?"

"Three days. Why?"

"I see. Thought it might be like that."

"Like what?"

"Nilsen, I'm not asking you how you came to meet him or who put him in touch with you or who recommended him as a contact man." He paused and then added somewhat unexpectedly: "Ask no questions and you'll be told no lies, I always say."

Greg shrugged. "I may not answer your questions, Captain, but I'm certainly not going to lie to you."

"Very decent of you to put it that way." Captain Lukey seemed genuinely pleased.

"Is it?"

"Frankness begets frankness, Nilsen. So I'll be frank with you. How much do you know about Tan?"

"Very little."

"Do you know what he does for a living?"

"Import, export—at least, that's what I gathered."

"Did he tell you that?"

"Not in so many words, no."

"What would you say if I told you that he ran a labor protection racket down at the docks?"

"How do you know?"

"Made inquiries about him. You see, I know most of the people in this business. Part of my job. I didn't know you and I didn't know him. Could have been a trap."

"A what?"

The Captain looked surprised. "Well, of course. Naturally the Indonesian Government knows what's going on. You know as well as I do that they've only got a few old destroyers and gunboats to patrol a huge area. They can't stop more than a fraction of the stuff getting through. So, naturally, they go for our weak spot."

"What's that?"

"Money. If they can get me tied up in a phony deal, they will."

"I'm afraid I don't get it. Are you suggesting I'm operating a phony deal?"

"Good God, no! Please don't misunderstand. This is nothing personal."

"Then, what's the problem? You inspect the stuff first. You don't pay until you take delivery, do you?"

"No. But I take delivery in bond. As soon as I start to move it, things happen. First some cheap lawyer comes along and claims that the goods have been obtained by trickery and gets a court order holding them. By the time that's straightened out, there's some other stooge claiming that all the ammunition is phony, and that instead of having cordite inside them the cartridges are loaded with morphine. So then the narcotics people have a go. And so on."

"But the stuff gets there in the end."

"If you're lucky."

"But you said yourself that the Indonesian Government can't maintain an effective patrol."

"If they know exactly when the stuff is going, the size of the consignment, and the approximate delivery area, they've got at least a fifty-fifty chance of intercepting it. It stands to reason."

"You said money was the weak spot."

"You don't know these people, Nilsen."

"What people?"

"The people I work for. Oh, they're good types in lots of ways, but when they pay out money, that's something special."

"Who are they? Tan said something about their being a religious group."

"They're devout Moslems, if that's what you mean. Most of the anti-Communists are. That doesn't mean they're not tough, though. Life and death don't mean much to them. They'd kill a man or be killed themselves without turning a hair. But they're funny when it comes to money. If things go badly, they give up."

"And you think Tan's working for the Indonesian Government?"

"I don't know. In my opinion, he's the type who'd work for anyone who paid enough. Anyway, I don't want to risk it."

"Then you don't want to deal?"

"I didn't say that. I said I don't want to deal with Tan."

"But Tan already knows about all this. If what you say is true, he can cause just as much trouble, whoever deals."

"Not if you're the principal. Are these goods bonded in your name?"

"They are."

"Then we don't need Tan at all."

Greg was silent. He was inclined to believe what the Captain had said, or some of it, anyway; and his own instincts were against having business dealings of any kind with Mr. Tan. Unfortunately, they were almost equally against having dealings with Captain Lukey. And there was the overriding complication of the fact that he was not in reality a principal at all, but an agent. To some extent he was deceiving Captain Lukey. He temporized.

"I'll have to think about that, Captain."

"Sure. Don't get me wrong—" the Captain was Americanizing again—"I'm not trying to pressure you, old boy."

The sudden lapse into British made Greg smile. "Oh, I didn't think you were, Captain," he said hastily.

His smile and his tone of voice combined to create an effect he had not intended.

"No need to apologize," said Captain Lukey cheerfully. He suddenly snapped his fingers. "I tell you what. Have you and Madame made any plans for the evening?"

Greg looked quickly at Dorothy. "Well, we . . ."

But it was too late. The Captain swept on enthusiastically. "I tell you what. Why don't we stop talking shop now and all go out to dinner, the four of us?"

"Four?" For one wild moment Greg thought that the Captain was proposing to include Tan in the invitation.

"I know my good lady will be dying to meet you. She's mad about America. Do you like Indian food? I mean the real stuff, not those ghastly Madras curries the planters ruin their livers on. There's a little restaurant we found where it's absolutely the real thing. You know India, of course?"

"Well, no. But I'm sure you don't want to . . ."

"Then that's settled, then." The Captain smiled broadly at them both. "Sorry to butt in again like this. Supposing I pick you up at seven. No jackets. Just a tie. We might have a spot of the cup that cheers first."

He gave them a mock salute and left.

Greg looked at Dorothy. "Sorry, darling," he said, "I didn't think fast enough."

But Dorothy did not seem unduly put out. "Well, at least we'll go somewhere we wouldn't have been to on our own," she said. "I wonder what Mrs. Lukey's like."

Promptly at seven Captain Lukey called up from the lobby and they went downstairs. He was alone.

"Left my good lady outside in the taxi," he explained.

It was dark, and Mrs. Lukey was sitting in the shadows at the back of the taxi; but even in the brief glimpse Greg had of her as they were introduced, he saw that she was strikingly beautiful. Her husband got in beside the driver and told him to go to the Cathay Hotel. On the way there he talked almost continuously, identifying buildings which they could not see, and having rapid conversations in Malay with the driver which they did not understand. Dorothy, sitting next to Mrs. Lukey, exchanged one or two brief courtesies with her. From her English, which was fluent but overprecise, Greg deduced that Mrs. Lukey was not British. It was not until they were in the elevator which took them up to the Cathay Hotel bar that he saw her clearly.

She had dark hair, cut short, and a long face with a delicate, high-cheeked bone structure that reminded him of a bust of Queen Nefertiti which he had seen illustrated in *Life*. Her skin was pale without being pallid. She wore no powder and very little lipstick. Her figure was slender, with a small waist that the flared silk skirt she was wearing made seem even smaller. Only her legs were disappointing. Greg thought them too straight and shapeless. Nevertheless, she was an exquisite creature, and it was difficult to understand how she had been captivated by Captain Lukey. Beside her, he looked oafish and gross. She smiled readily, revealing excellent teeth. However, the smile did not reach her eyes, and at those moments she became less beautiful. It was possible, Greg thought, that she had a dull mind.

Her husband was an overpowering host. He drank deeply and talked incessantly, mostly about people whom he had known in South Africa and Egypt. Many of the stories he told seemed pointless to Greg until he realized that, in deference to Dorothy, and possibly also to his own wife, the Captain was censoring his tongue. He was the kind of man who has a stock of anecdotes packed away in his mind like the contents of a kit bag. He cannot rummage about and select what he wants; everything must be pulled out as it comes to hand, dirty clothes as well as clean. It was noticeable, too, as the evening progressed, that the social pretensions of those who peopled his memories became more and more modest. Brother army officers, generals, senior civil

servants, important businessmen, and embassy attachés gradually gave way to sergeant majors, canteen managers, stewards, bartenders, and seedy men encountered in pubs. Captain
Lukey's accent also deteriorated, or at least changed, earthier
tones and racier speech rhythms replacing the plummy affec-
tations of the afternoon. Greg and Dorothy found him easier
to understand and, as some of his stories were quite funny,
even began to warm to him. Captain Lukey the officer and
gentleman might verge on the odious, but Lukey the soldier
of fortune was not unengaging.

The Indian restaurant was in a street off Orchard Road. It
was small and squalid. The waiters were Indians wearing
dhotis and striped shirts with the tails hanging out. They
spread sheets of white wrapping paper on the table instead
of a cloth. A single fan stirred the warm, curry-laden air.
There were a great many flies. Greg made up his mind that
the first thing he and Dorothy would do when they got back
to the hotel would be to take full doses of the Entero-Vioforme which they had bought in Saigon.

Mrs. Lukey ordered dinner in a language which she told
Dorothy was Urdu. The food took a long time to prepare,
and Captain Lukey had drunk four more stengahs and paid
two visits to the toilet before it arrived. There were four
dishes, two of them curries, and a bowl of boiled Patna rice.
To Greg's surprise, it was all delicious. He often ate curried
dishes—the University Club in Wilmington always had curried shrimps or curried turkey on the lunch menu—but he
had never tasted curries like these. They were hot but not
harsh, and there were undertones of flavor that he could not
begin to identify.

"In the West you use curry powder already made," Mrs.
Lukey explained. "Here the spices are ground fresh and
mixed according to the needs of the dish. In this case, for
instance, there is less turmeric and more cumin. That is
what you taste."

A plate of Indian condiments was put on the table.
Among the seeds and sauces and shredded coconut there
were sliced bananas.

"If a curry is too hot," said Mrs. Lukey, "you add sliced
banana and it becomes milder."

"You mean it seems milder?"

"No. It *is* milder. I do not understand why. Some say it is the juice of the banana. Try."

Dorothy tried and was impressed.

Mrs. Lukey smiled. "Some curries are so hot," she said, "that even I could not eat them without banana, even though I have lived many years in India."

The Captain, returning from yet another visit to the toilet, overheard her.

"If you think this is a good curry," he said, "you wait until you taste Betty's. She's a wonderful cook."

This was the first time they had heard Mrs. Lukey's first name. The Captain's endearments, which had ranged from "darling" through "the memsahib" to "old girl," had not hitherto included it.

Suddenly the Captain slapped the table. "I tell you what. One night you must come over to our place and have a binge. The old girl will cook, and if we can still move afterwards we'll have a rubber of bridge. You play bridge?"

Greg admitted that they did.

"Then, it's a date. As a matter of fact, why don't we go back now and have a drink? It's only a furnished place we've taken while we look around, but it's not all that bad, and at least we'll be able to drink some decent whisky."

Greg had opened his mouth to hedge, but Dorothy spoke first. "I think that would be a lovely idea," she said.

The Lukeys' apartment was a few minutes' walk from the restaurant. It was over an electrical-appliance showroom and was approached by a long steep stairway at the side. The living room had pale green walls and contained a polished teak table and some bamboo-framed lounge chairs. In one corner there was a card table with some papers and a desk pad on it. Light came from a frosted-glass ceiling fitting. The effect was bleak.

"Make yourselves at home," said the Captain. Going to a wardrobe in the small hallway, he got out bottles and glasses.

Dorothy and Mrs. Lukey retired to the bedroom. Greg sat down in one of the lounge chairs.

"You know," Captain Lukey continued as he made the drinks, "the trouble with my job is that you never know where you're going to be next. Can't put down any roots."

"I suppose not." Greg had not thought of the Captain's

occupation as one about which it was possible to generalize in such terms. Acting as purchasing agent for Sumatran insurgent forces scarcely seemed the basis of a career. Whether the insurgents won or lost, their need for a foreign representative with Captain Lukey's special qualifications seemed bound eventually to disappear; and, while there might be other insurgent forces in other parts of the world who could use his services when available, the business of contacting them would be hazardous as well as difficult. The Captain did not strike him as being a particularly robust type of adventurer. "How did you come to get into the job?" he asked.

"Oh, I don't know. Friends, influence." The Captain grinned. "Never could stand the ordinary desk job. 'Sing ho for the open road,' that's me." He reached for the soda siphon. "Say when."

"That's enough, thanks." Greg went over and took the drink.

"Yes, always on the go." The Captain shook his head ruefully. "Take next week, now. I'll probably have to go off to Macao for a few days."

"On business?"

"You can bet your sweet life I wouldn't go for pleasure."

Greg was beginning to understand the Captain. When dissembling he had the too artless look of a boy telling a lie.

"I shouldn't have thought there'd be much for you there at the moment," he said casually. "My information is that the buyers are all moving in here."

The Captain looked at him quickly. "The Dutchman's still there."

"I'm only telling you what I heard."

The Captain stared at him gloomily for a moment and then, with a visible effort, relaxed. "No shop in the mess," he said. "Cost you drinks all round in the old days. All the same, I'd like to know where we stand pretty soon. About Tan, for instance, you said you'd think it over. How long do you want?"

"Twenty-four hours."

"Cards on the table, Nilsen. Got another buyer on ice?"

"Could be." Greg was enjoying this.

"Is he dealing with Tan?"

"Look, I said I want twenty-four hours to think it over.

Until tomorrow evening. I'd like to deal with you, Captain, and as long as there's no misunderstanding about price range, I'm sure we can work something out. If you want to save time, you can arrange with Tan to inspect the stuff at the warehouse in the morning."

"I told you, I don't want to deal with Tan."

"He's merely holding the customs documents at present. You wouldn't be committing yourself to anything."

"All right. As long as we understand one another."

The women came out of the bedroom and the Captain returned to his reminiscences. Soon Greg and Dorothy left.

As they were walking to the taxi rank by the Cathay Hotel, Greg told her about his brief business discussion.

"You know," he added, "I'm a bit sorry for that man."

Dorothy laughed.

"Oh, I know he's a phony," Greg said. "All that gobbledygook he talks, all those stories, all that false bonhomie."

"And all those trips to the men's room."

"It's not his fault if he has a weak bladder."

"He shouldn't drink so much."

"I think he's a pretty depressed character. I think he has to have a few drinks to stay in one piece. You know, he wants those arms badly and tried to pretend that he didn't. It was pathetic, bush-league stuff. It made me feel like a con man."

"Famous last words."

"All right. We'll see."

They walked on in silence for a moment or two. "I liked her," said Dorothy.

"Yes, what about that! How in the world did he do it? She looks like something out of *Vogue*. Do you think she really likes him?"

"Oh, yes."

"Attraction of opposites, I suppose. What nationality is she? 'Betty' sounds British enough, but she's got a funny sort of accent."

Dorothy glanced at him wonderingly. "You mean you didn't get it?"

"Get what?"

"She's Eurasian."

"She's what?"

"Well, Anglo-Indian, she called it. Her mother came from

Bombay. She didn't say much, but I think it must have been very important to her to marry an Englishman."

"Even that one?"

"I told you, she's very fond of him."

He drew her arm through his. "I'm glad we came on this trip together," he said.

Dorothy smiled.

When they got back to the hotel, there was a message for Greg. Mr. Lane Harvey of the American Syndicated Wire Service had telephoned, and would call again in the morning.

Before he went to sleep that night, Greg booked a person-to-person call to Mr. Tan Tack Chee in Manila.

iii

While they were at breakfast the following morning, the Singapore overseas operator called to say that Mr. Tan was not then in Manila but was expected back that afternoon. Greg placed a call for 4:00 p.m. Manila time.

Just as he put the telephone down, it rang again.

"Mr. Nilsen? This is Lane Harvey, American Syndicated Wire Service."

"Yes?"

"You're from Wilmington, Delaware, I believe."

"That's right."

"And you have a die-casting business there?"

"Yes. What's all this about? The plant hasn't burned down, has it?"

Mr. Harvey chuckled. "No, nothing like that. It's just that I'd like to send back a story on you, if you could spare me half an hour sometime today."

"Well, yes, of course. But, Mr. Harvey, it's not a very big plant, you know, and I'm not an important man. Mrs. Nilsen and I are just tourists stopping over for a few days. I don't want to waste your time."

"Mr. Nilsen, you wouldn't be wasting my time. That's the very reason I want to talk to you. More Americans are traveling now than ever before. New York's doing a survey on the problems they run into, what they don't like, what they do like, and so on. We don't get many stopping over here in Singapore, so if you could spare the time I'd be grateful."

"Okay, if you think it's worth it. When do you suggest?"

"Well, let's see. Are you doing anything for lunch?"

"I don't think so."

"Then why don't you and Mrs. Nilsen come along to the American Club?"

"Well, that's very kind of you, but . . ."

"Mr. Nilsen, I've got to try and justify my expense account sometimes."

Greg laughed. "All right, Mr. Harvey."

"Twelve thirty, then? I'll send the office car for you."

"We can take a cab."

"No trouble. The car'll pick you up at twelve thirty."

Greg gave Dorothy the gist of the conversation.

"Isn't it a bit unusual?" she said. "Why doesn't he just come over here?"

"I don't know. Perhaps that's the way they like to do things in Singapore."

Lane Harvey was a balding man of about forty with an unhealthy complexion and sleepy eyes. He spoke slowly and carefully, as if he were under some emotional pressure that he was striving to ignore, or as if he were listening all the time to the voice of a doctor telling him to relax or suffer the consequences.

"For a wire-service man," he said, "this place is Siberia. Politically, Southeast Asia is one of the most important areas in the world. In Vietnam, Laos, Cambodia, Thailand, Sumatra, Java, the Islands, everywhere around, there's history being made. But all around. Not in Singapore. We're in the eye of the storm here."

"So all you have to do is interview American tourists," said Dorothy. "It's a shame."

Lane Harvey smiled. "I'll tell you a secret, Mrs. Nilsen. It's more comfortable here than those other places, and I like being comfortable. But an American correspondent who doesn't wail for the dangers and discomforts of the battle-front is guilty of unprofessional conduct." He signaled to the waiter for another round of drinks. "Now tell me about your trip."

Greg began to do so. Lane Harvey listened attentively, nodding understandingly now and then, but asking no questions. After a few minutes Greg, beginning to hear the sound of his own voice droning on, broke off.

"Look, Mr. Harvey, this must be very boring for you."

"No, no."

"Isn't there something else we can talk about?"

"You've given me just what I wanted." He looked across the ranch-style patio. "By the way, I hope you don't mind. I asked someone else to join us for lunch. He's very British, pukka sahib and all that, but he knows a lot about Singapore. You might find him interesting."

A lean, gray-haired man with a long, narrow head and a receding chin was advancing across the patio toward them. He was one of the few men there wearing a jacket. He came up to the table.

"Hallo, Harvey. Hope I'm not late."

"Not a bit. Sit down and have a drink. Mr. and Mrs. Nilsen, this is Colonel Soames."

Over lunch, Lane Harvey insisted on telling the Colonel all about their trip, the details of which he recalled with remarkable accuracy. Greg became embarrassed.

"Now, wait a minute," he said. "Thousands of Americans must do this trip every year. There's nothing special about it."

"Yes, but we ought to do more about them in Singapore," said the Colonel. "All we get as a rule are the transient passengers off the boats. They buy a few batik sarongs and that's the end of it. Now, you, for instance—what made you decide to stay in Singapore? It would be interesting to know."

Greg glanced at Dorothy and grinned. "We were escaping," he said.

The Colonel looked startled. "Indeed?"

"From the ship's bore."

"Oh, now, that isn't fair," Dorothy protested. "Arlene may have been difficult, but she wasn't a bore." She turned to the Colonel. "You see, we were going on to Calcutta, but—well, we thought it might be better to get off here and take a side trip. Anyway, there was some business Greg wanted to attend to here, so it fitted in quite well."

The waiter came over and said something to Lane Harvey. He got up apologetically. "Call from New York," he said. "I'll only be a few minutes, but don't you wait for me, please." He left them.

The Colonel nodded genially. "Nothing like combining business with pleasure," he remarked.

"Harvey was saying that you knew a lot about Singapore," Greg said. "Are you in the tourist business here?"

The Colonel began eating his steak. "I suppose you might call it that," he replied.

"Then I expect you know quite a lot of the local people."

The Colonel shrugged. "Big place, Singapore," he said. "Over a million now. Mostly Chinese, of course."

"I suppose you don't happen to know of a Chinese named Tan Yam Heng?"

Dorothy said: "Oh, darling, I don't think you ought to bother the Colonel with all that."

"No bother, Mrs. Nilsen," the Colonel said cheerfully. "As a matter of fact, I do happen to know the chap. Trade-union organizer. That the one you mean?"

"Well, I heard it put a little more crudely," Greg said.

"Labor thug?"

"Something like that."

"Who told you?"

"A Captain Lukey. Perhaps you know him, too?"

"Met him, yes. Having trouble with Tan?"

"It's a long story. I won't bother you with it. Captain Lukey doesn't want to deal with Tan. I wondered why. You confirm what Lukey said. That answers the question. I'm much obliged to you."

The Colonel gave him a toothy grin. "Could be another answer though, couldn't there?"

"How do you mean?"

"You're selling something?"

"Yes."

"Lukey wants to buy?"

"Yes."

"And Tan Yam Heng's the contact man?"

"Yes."

"Could be that Tan's trying to get a commission out of Lukey as well as you, couldn't it?" The Colonel smeared English mustard on a large piece of steak and popped it into his mouth.

Greg stared. "But . . ." he began, then stopped. The possibility had simply not occurred to him.

The Colonel chewed for a moment or two and then swallowed. "Squeeze," he said. "Old Chinese custom."

"But why didn't Lukey tell me that?"

"Might think you already knew. Might think you didn't want to know. Might think a lot of things. What's your impression of Lukey?"

"I only met him yesterday. We had dinner. Do you happen to know anything about these people he represents?"

The Colonel shrugged. "They're called the Army of the Independent Party of the Faithful," he said. "All I know about them is that their Committee seems to have some sense of self-preservation."

"Oh?"

"They don't allow Lukey to sign checks on his own. One of them has to countersign. Met that chichi wife of his?"

"Chichi, Colonel?" Dorothy said. "What does that mean?"

"Indian slang for Eurasian, Mrs. Nilsen." He grinned. " 'Anglo-Indians,' as they like to call themselves nowadays."

The diversion had given Greg time to think. "Colonel," he said, "you told us that your business was with tourists. You didn't mean that quite literally, did you?"

"I said you could call it that."

"What are you really? Police of some kind?"

"I work for the government, yes."

"And this little party was prearranged, I take it." Greg's smile was wide but hostile.

The Colonel nodded. "We try to do these things in a friendly fashion."

"What things? Is there something wrong, Colonel?"

"Wrong?" He appeared to consider the adjective. "That rather depends upon your point of view, doesn't it? Of course, three are some cranks who think that gun running and the arms traffic are evil things in themselves, ethically indefensible. I think that's a lot of nonsense myself. In your country and mine the people can change their governments, if they want to, by voting. But there are a lot of places where it takes a revolution to do that. Look at Cuba. If somebody hadn't supplied that fellow Castro with arms, Batista would still be a dictator. Some people might say that those gun runners deserved a vote of thanks. Take Sumatra. The people there are afraid that Java's going to go Communist. They want to

secede from Indonesia before that happens. Maybe they're
right. Sumatra could be a self-supporting country. There are
quite a few people here who think that she might one day join
the Federation of Malaya. But, whatever they do, they'll have
to win their independence first. They won't do that with
words. Mind you, these are only my personal views."

"Do they conflict with your official views, Colonel?"

The Colonel shook his head. "No, Mr. Nilsen, they don't.
And for a very simple reason. I have no official views. I am
not entitled to any. My job is to obey orders. The British
government recognizes the Indonesian government, and is in
normal, friendly, diplomatic relations with it. That means
that we don't like to add to its difficulties by helping its
enemies. At the moment, that means you."

"Well, that's certainly laying it on the line, Colonel."

"I'll go farther." The Colonel took a cigar case from his
pocket and offered it to Greg.

Greg shook his head. "No, thanks."

The Colonel took a cigar for himself and glanced inquiringly at Dorothy. "Do you mind, Mrs. Nilsen?"

"Not in the least." Dorothy's tone was icy.

"You were going farther, Colonel," said Greg.

"Yes. I should tell you that I was considering having you
deported."

"I beg your pardon."

"Making false statements to the immigration authorities
is a serious offense."

"False statements? What the hell are you talking about?"

"Steady, darling," Dorothy said quietly.

Greg took no notice. He was glaring across the table at
the Colonel.

The Colonel stared back coldly. "Nature of visit—tourism.
Isn't that what you told the immigration inspector?"

"Of course. It happened to be the truth."

"No. Only part of the truth. You are also here dealing in
arms."

"Oh, for God's sake! Look, I also had a letter from the
man I left in charge of my plant back in America. I even
replied to it. So I'm in the die-casting business here, too."

"There's no point in losing your temper, Mr. Nilsen, and

it's bad for the digestion. I said I had considered deporting you. Of course, now that I have met you and Mrs. Nilsen, I have no doubt of your good faith."

"Is that intended as a compliment, Colonel?"

"No, reassurance."

"The American consul will be glad to hear that."

The Colonel smiled. "You can't threaten me with your consul. I know him very well, and he doesn't have much patience with empty indignation."

"How does he feel about petty officiousness?"

"If I'd wanted to be officious, Mr. Nilsen, we would not be sitting at this table, but in my office. I don't expect you to like what I'm saying, but I think you might try to understand the political reasons for it. Singapore is a free port and a center of international trade. I admit that, legally, there is nothing to stop you or anyone else using its warehouse facilities as you are using them. But we don't like it, and you can't expect us to welcome your presence here." He smiled at Dorothy. "I'm speaking officially, of course, Mrs. Nilsen."

"But you don't disapprove of selling arms to anti-Communists?" demanded Greg.

"Personally, not in the least."

Greg laughed shortly. "You change hats rather easily, don't you, Colonel?" he said, and had the satisfaction of seeing the Colonel redden.

"I'm sorry you think that," he said stiffly. He looked at his watch. "I think it's time I was getting back to my office."

The look at the watch was evidently some sort of signal, for almost immediately Lane Harvey returned to the table.

"Sorry to have to leave you like that," he said when the Colonel had gone. "You know how it is."

"Yes," said Greg acidly. "The Colonel explained."

Lane Harvey was unembarrassed. He even grinned. "Funny old guy, isn't he?" he said. "I thought you'd like him."

iv

Late that afternoon Inspector Chow interviewed the driver of the American Syndicated Wire Service car. Then he reported to Colonel Soames.

"They went straight back from the American Club to the Raffles Hotel. The man was expecting a telephone call from Manila. The driver had no difficulty in hearing their conversation."

"Well?"

"The man was very angry, sir."

"I imagine he was."

"With Mr. Harvey, mainly. He used strong language and talked of reporting the incident to Mr. Harvey's superiors in New York, with a view to having him dismissed."

"He'll think better of that."

"Yes, sir. He spoke of humiliation and feeling ridiculous. He also apologized to the woman and talked of forgetting the whole deal. That was a reference to the arms, I take it."

"Pulling out, eh? Good show. I was pretty sure he was an amateur."

"Later, sir, he changed his mind."

"Oh?"

"The woman said that he had a business obligation to Captain Lukey."

Colonel Soames stared. "Mrs. Nilsen said that? Are you sure?"

"That is what the driver reports, sir."

"But she was on my side right from the start. I could see it."

"According to the driver, sir, Mrs. Nilsen made some highly unfavorable remarks about you. She appeared to think that you had insulted Mrs. Lukey."

"I?" Colonel Soames was genuinely bewildered. "I only asked her if she'd met the woman."

"Yes, sir." Inspector Chow's face was quite expressionless. "It appeared that you used the word 'chichi.' "

"What about it? She asked what it meant. I told her."

"She appeared to think that it was equivalent to using the word 'jigaboo' in America."

"What the hell does that mean?"

"I don't know, sir, but I assume that it must be something to do with the race question." Inspector Chow hesitated. "The woman used one very unladylike phrase."

"Well?"

Colonel Soames could not be quite certain, but he thought he detected a hint of relish in Inspector Chow's tone as he answered.

"She said you were a bigoted old bastard, sir."

CHAPTER VI

THE CALL to Manila came through on time.

Greg was still out of temper, and cut through Mr. Tan's preliminary courtesies almost brusquely.

"Mr. Tan, I'll come to the point. The prospective buyer doesn't want to deal through your brother."

"Oh. Does he give a reason?"

"He says he doesn't trust him, but I have an idea that that's not the real reason."

"I see. And what do you think the real reason is, Mr. Nilsen?"

"Are you paying your brother a commission?"

"Of course."

"Well, I think he's trying to make the buyer pay him a commission for the introduction as well."

There was a pause. "What do you propose, Mr. Nilsen?"

"That I negotiate on my own with the buyer, and that you tell your brother to behave himself."

"Leaving everything in your hands, Mr. Nilsen?"

"You're covered. Your brother has the customs documents. He can hold on to those as security."

There was another pause before Mr. Tan said: "Very well. I will cable to my brother."

"Today?"

"At once. It is a pleasure to do business with you, Mr. Nilsen."

At five o'clock there was a call from Captain Lukey.

128

"Did you inspect the stuff?" Greg asked him.

"Yes. It seemed pretty fair. What about Tan?"

"He's taken care of."

"Good show."

"Do you want to talk business?"

"Be over in a jiffy."

Despite his admitted eagerness to buy, the Captain proved to be a stubborn bargainer. It took an hour and three stengahs to force his price up to fifty thousand dollars. His method of haggling was to isolate two items, the machine pistols and the bazookas, admit their worth, and then insist on putting a nominal valuation on the remaining items. He wore a tortured expression throughout, gnawed steadily at his mustache as if it were hurting him, and covered sheets of hotel stationery with pointless calculations. In the end Greg became impatient.

"Captain, we're not getting anywhere. Sixty-five thousand is rock bottom. If you don't want the stuff, just say so."

"But if we disregard the rifles . . ."

"Well, let's not disregard them. They're there, and that's the price."

Eventually, at sixty-two thousand five hundred, there was a meeting of the minds. When they had shaken hands on the deal, the Captain grinned.

"I'd have paid sixty-five if you'd stuck out."

"Well, I'd have gone down to sixty if you'd stuck out," Greg replied, "so we're both happy. Now, about terms. Cash on delivery, of course. Okay?"

"Okay."

"Good. If you'll get a certified check made out and meet me at the Customs House tomorrow morning, we'll square it all away."

The Captain stared at him indignantly. "I'm afraid I can't do that, old boy."

"Why not?"

"Well, I'm only the liaison officer, the agent. I have to follow the drill."

"What drill?"

"Well, I told you. Those people are funny about money. They like to do the paying out themselves."

"As long as it's clearly understood that the stuff stays

where it is until I have sixty-two thousand five hundred dollars in my hand, I don't care who does the paying."

"You needn't worry about that, old boy. They want that stuff and the sooner the better. This is how we handle it. I give you a draft on the Hong Kong and Shanghai Bank, made out but unsigned. It requires two signatures, mine and a member of the Central Committee's. When you present that check to him, he knows that I've inspected the stuff and agreed to the price. He signs. Then you and I go down to the Customs House, you sign the transfer, I countersign the check, and Bob's your uncle."

"Will the check be certified?"

"We can go to the Bank and cash it first, if you like."

"Well, it sounds unnecessarily complicated to me, but if that's the way they want it, okay. Where do I see this Committee man?"

"In Labuanga."

"Where's that?"

"Oh, it's only half an hour or so by air. Anyway, my good lady will arrange all that side of it." He spoke rather too airily.

Greg was suddenly suspicious. "Where is it?"

"Just across the other side of the straits, opposite Penang."

"In Sumatra?"

"Well, naturally."

Greg took a deep breath. "Now, wait a minute. Why didn't you say something about this before? I'm not going gallivanting off into the wilds of Sumatra in order to get a check signed."

"Labuanga isn't in the wilds, old boy," the Captain said patiently. "It's a coast town with its own airport and a hotel. Pretty little place, as a matter of fact."

"I don't care how pretty it is."

"But that's the drill. There's nothing to it, really. It's always worked out fine. Don't misunderstand, old boy. I'm not asking you to pay your own expenses."

"I tell you, it's out of the question. Quite apart from anything else, I don't have an Indonesian visa."

"Well, that's easily fixed."

"Is it? I understood it took a week."

The Captain threw up his hands in exasperation. "Old boy,

this isn't my idea. You want cash on delivery, Singapore. All right. Cash it is. I'm not arguing about that. But you've got to look at things from their point of view. They've been let down before now, and they like to know who they're dealing with. You only have to go the first time. After that it's plain sailing."

"Don't they trust you?"

"Of course they trust me. I tell them what to buy and what they ought to pay. They just finalize the first deal."

"Well, I don't like it. If you can't produce the money here without this drill, as you call it, the deal's off."

The Captain drew himself up. "I'm sorry, old boy, but I can't accept that. I thought we shook hands on it."

"We didn't shake hands on a trip to Sumatra."

"Old boy," the Captain said wearily, "there's a plane every day. You can be there and back in twenty-four hours. It's perfectly simple. Betty goes along with you, calls up when you get there, arranges the meeting, and takes you to it. You don't have to bother about a thing. Take Dorothy along with you for the ride, if you like."

"I don't get this. Why does your wife have to go? Why don't you go yourself?"

"I would, but the Indonesians won't give me a visa any more."

"Why not?"

"Naturally, they know what I'm up to."

"But they let your wife in?"

"She's got her passport in her maiden name. As a matter of fact, she looks forward to these little trips. Makes a change for her. Look, old boy," he went on persuasively, "you admit the deal's a good one for you. All I'm asking you to do is finalize it."

"You could have said something about this before."

"It never occurred to me that you'd object, old boy. Most of you chaps are popping in and out all the time."

"Well, I'm not."

"A half-hour plane trip, that's all. Surely, old boy . . ."

"All right, all right," Greg snapped irritably, "I'll think about it."

"I'll have to know tomorrow. They're waiting to hear about this stuff." He was looking tortured again.

"I understand."

The Captain smiled bitterly, shook his head, sighed, finished his stengah, and went.

Dorothy came out of the bedroom.

"You heard?" Greg asked.

"Yes. Do you think he meant that if I went with you he'd pay my expenses too?"

Greg chuckled. "I wonder. That colonel was certainly right about his needing a counter-signature on checks. What a way to do business!"

"What will you do?"

"I'm darned if I know. The trouble is that, as Mr. Tan's appointed agent, I'm virtually the legal owner, as far as Singapore customs are concerned. If I don't sell it to Lukey, what happens? After all, I do have an obligation to Tan. I can't just do nothing at this stage. As for that crooked brother of his, I'd be crazy if I expected him to find another buyer while I'm around to stop him picking up two commissions. It's got to be Lukey."

Dorothy shrugged. "Well, we'll never get another chance to see Sumatra."

"Are you serious?"

"Why not? Why shouldn't we both go? You know, while you two were arguing about money, the Cook's man called up. He said our Indonesian visa has come through. All we have to do is take our passport around in the morning."

ii

Mrs. Lukey, or, as her British passport somewhat incongruously proclaimed her, Miss Elizabeth O'Toole, met them at Singapore Airport with the tickets. The plane, a Garuda Indonesian Airways Convair with an Australian pilot, was reassuring. The discovery that the flying time to Labuanga was not thirty minutes, as the Captain had claimed, but a full two hours seemed a matter for amusement rather than annoyance. They were getting off the beaten track—and not merely as tourists, but in order to sell arms to a band of freedom-loving anti-Communists. Moreover, they were traveling at someone else's expense. The spirit of high adventure tingled in their veins.

Mrs. Lukey had explained the whole thing to them while hey had been waiting in the departure lounge. The Captain's contact man in Labuanga was a Sumatran oil-company employee who had legitimate reasons for cabling regularly o Singapore. This man also had access to a clandestine radio, through which he kept in touch with insurgent headquarters n the hills. On these check-signing occasions he notified headquarters and arranged the rendezvous three days in advance. This gave the Committee member time to make the journey to the coast without running the risk of traveling by day.

"What sort of people are they?" Greg had asked her. 'The Committee members, I mean."

"I've only seen two of them. One is a lawyer from Medan, the other is an army officer. I think those two are sent because they both speak English. A European comes with them, but only as a guard, I think. All the Committee members are Moslems."

"What sort of European?"

"He is Polish. Hamid, who is our contact, said that he had been in the French Foreign Legion in Indochina and was training them to use the arms."

The plane reached its crusing altitude and headed north along the coast of Sumatra. The Malacca Strait moved slowly beneath them, green among the shoals of the offshore islands, brown where the river mouths discharged the silt carried down from the hills, slate blue where the colder currents flowed down from the Bay of Bengal. Then, as the Strait widened, they altered course and began to fly over land. Soon, from their seats on the port side, all they could see below was something that looked like a vast sand dune covered with green moss.

"Jungle," said Mrs. Lukey.

The Indonesian stewardess began to serve bottled lemonade and stale cheese sandwiches. Twenty minutes before they were due at Labuanga they ran into a local storm and had to fasten their seat belts. The plane bucketed about wildly for a time, and they came in to land under a huge black cloud and in a deluge of rain. A sheet of spray went up as the plane touched down; but by the time it had taxied in to the arrival apron, the rain had stopped and the sun was out

again. Their first impression of Labuanga airport was th
smell of steaming mud.

It was the most favorable impression they received.

Mrs. Lukey had warned them about the immigration an
customs officials. "They are appointed from Djakarta," sh
had said, "and they are not friendly to anyone here. Euro
peans especially they do not like. The last time I was here
they made two Europeans undress to be searched; but th
papers in Singapore were very angry about it, and I do no
think we shall be troubled in that way if we are careful. I
is better not to smile or look impatient."

Greg and Dorothy did their best to remain impassive
but it was difficult. One immigration official took their pass
ports away for examination and did not return. A secon
official then demanded the production of the passports. Whe
Mrs. Lukey had explained to him what had happened
they were told to wait. It took an hour to recover the pass
ports. Next the currency-control official ordered Greg t
turn out his pockets and, for some unexplained reason, de
cided to confiscate his Diners' Club Credit Card. Finally
the customs inspector insisted on taking the lens number
of his camera and impounding the exposed film in it.

Mrs. Lukey seemed to be as shaken as Greg and Doroth
by the experience. "I am sorry," she said. "They have neve
been so bad before."

"What the hell were they trying to prove?" demanded Greg
"Why take a credit card? I don't particularly mind. I ca
replace that. But what's the idea?"

"Darling, at least they didn't make us undress."

Greg, whose cotton and Dacron shirt was clinging wetl
to his body, muttered that he wished they had. The loss o
the film had particularly annoyed him.

The airport was three miles from the town, and the ai
line bus had already gone. There were no taxis. The
found that they had to wait for another bus. There was
painful silence.

Mrs. Lukey made an unfortunate attempt to dispel th
gloom. "Well, anyway," she said, "I don't suppose the sam
men will be on duty tomorrow when we leave."

"You mean we have to go through all that again?" aske
Dorothy.

"If we are careful about our exit visas, it will be all right."

Greg swung around. "What exit visas?"

"We have to get those tomorrow morning at the police office. As long as we give the man who makes them out a good tip, there will be no trouble." She gave them an anxious smile.

There was another silence.

As the mud dried, other, more human smells were beginning to emerge from the vicinity of the airport. The heat was stupefying. Dorothy could feel the sweat trickling down her legs. She made a determined effort to be objective.

"Well," she said lightly, "it's their country."

Mrs. Lukey turned to her eagerly. "Yes, they are really gay, laughing, happy people, but they are not always understood. It is the same in India. Because a European coming to Bombay cannot buy alcoholic drinks without a permit, he thinks that the Indians are not friendly people. That is not true. One must live in a country to know it. One should not judge a country from the airport. Nor from its customs officials."

She had spoken quickly and vehemently, and, in doing so, had suddenly become more Asian than European. It was a disconcerting transformation.

Dorothy started to make some sort of reply. Fortunately, a bus drew into the yard at that moment and she did not have to complete it.

Almost as soon as the bus left the airport they passed through a village. The houses were of the small teak-framed atap kind with which they were becoming familiar, but on most of them the atap was faded and torn or patched. Only one house looked new and cared for. There was a signboard across the veranda. On it, painted in Malay and English, were the words: LABUANGA DISTRICT COMMUNIST PARTY.

Dorothy and Mrs. Lukey were on the other side of the bus. Greg did not draw their attention to it.

iii

Labuanga was a port, and the terminal point of a system of pipelines connecting the oil fields in the area. The town sprawled over a broad alluvial tongue of land jutting out

into the sea beside a river delta. It had been built by the
Dutch, and the tree-lined streets and public gardens of the
civic center had been laid out like those of a provincial town
in Holland. The effect was bizarre. The trees were not lindens
or sycamores, but casuarinas. Flower beds which should have
contained orderly rows of tulips, narcissi, and hyacinths
were lush with crotons, wild orchids, and scarlet lilies.
Hibiscus rioted over the iron railings surrounding a plinth
which had supported a statue of Queen Wilhelmina. The
portico of the Stadhuis looked raffish under the burden of a
monstrous bougainvillaea. The center of Labuanga was like a
respectable Dutch matron seduced by the jungle and gone
native.

Radiating out from it were the wide roads and bungalow
compounds of the former European quarter. There were still
a number of Europeans living there, mostly oil-company em-
ployees; but many of the buildings had been taken over by the
security forces and other agencies of the Central Government.
It was now called the "Inner Zone."

The change had a military as well as a social significance.
The District of Labuanga covered an area of several hundred
square miles and included oil fields, pipelines, copra planta-
tions, over fifty villages, and substantial tracts of virgin jungle
in addition to the city and port. An effective system of
defenses against the insurgents operating from the hills
would have absorbed at least three divisions of reliable and
well-equipped troops. Major General Iskaq, the military governor of Labuanga, had at his disposal a garrison consisting
of two demoralized infantry battalions, with three small
field guns, ten decrepit armored cars, and sixty policemen.
So far, the insurgents had confined themselves to night
raids on outlying oil-storage installations, the dynamiting of
bridges, and harassing reconnaissances in force. But the
General knew that the day must come when the Party of
the Faithful would feel itself strong enough to mount an all-
out assault on the city, capture it, defend it against counter-
attack, and proclaim an autonomous regional government.
When that day (or night) did come, the Inner Zone would
become a fortress within which the garrison could hold out
until help came from Medan. The problem had been to
guard against surprise. At every road junction on the

erimeter of the zone, concrete defense positions had been
uilt. Now, at the first sign of any insurgent activity at all
a the vicinity of the city, an alarm button was pressed, the
efense positions were manned, and the rest of the garrison
ithdrew behind them. Only a small mobile column was
ft outside the zone to deal with the raiding party which
ad been the cause of the trouble.

The Inner Zone plan was one of those dreamlike pieces of
ilitary thinking which even their authors know to be un-
ound, but which are solemnly acted upon, nevertheless, be-
ause any plan is preferable to none. The General was well
ware of the illusory nature of this one. The zone contained
ne police headquarters, the Stadhuis, and a number of office
uildings and houses. From a tactical point of view, it was
mere geographical location, no easier to defend than any
ther part of the city. The power station, the water-pumping
ation, the port installations, and the telephone exchange
ere all outside it, together with the bulk of the population.
ut there were similar disadvantages to every other area
aat had been considered. The truth was that, with only two in-
antry battalions, ten armored cars, and three field guns,
ere was no right way of defending a place the size of
abuanga against superior forces.

General Iskaq was a cunning and ambitious man with a
eep contempt for Djakarta politicians and a sensitive regard
or his own interests. He knew that many of his officers were
a sympathy with the insurgents and that he had only to hint
t such a sympathy himself to initiate secret negotiations with
ne committee. He had a reputation as a patriot, and the
rice they would pay for his defection would be high. He had
ever heard the axiom "if you can't lick 'em, join 'em" ex-
ressed in just those terms, but it exactly described his own
leas about power. Only one thing secured his allegiance to
ne Central Government.

His father had been a Javanese coolie. All through his
hildhood the General had seen his father kicked, shouted at,
nd bullied by white men, or *mandurs* working for white men.
'here had been nothing strange about this. His friends' fathers
ad been treated in the same way. That white men should
rive Javanese coolies to work, coolies who would other-
vise have idled in the shade, had been in the natural order of

things, just as it had been natural to stop work when a whit
man drove by in his car or carriage, and turn toward him, an
bow. Then, one day, a white man who had drunk too muc
gin had accused the General's father of smiling at him. Whe
the General's father had denied it, the white man had starte
to beat him about the head and shoulders with a thick can
The General's father had been strong, but the cane had bee
stronger, and, as his face had become covered with blood, h
had fallen to his knees crying like a child.

From that moment, and for many years after, the Genera
had found nothing natural in a relationship with white me
but hatred. It was not until the Japanese army had surren
dered and the white men had tried to reclaim Java as a colon
that he had been able to assuage much of his hatred by killing
What was left of it had in time been transformed into th
irrational but unshakable belief that white men and Asian
could have no interests in common, and that what was goo
for one must be bad for the other. The Party of the Faithfu
was financed by white men, its forces were trained by whit
men, and, if it came to power, it would be friendly wit
white men. For the General, the idea of coming to term
with such an organization was totally unacceptable.

His repeated requests to the area commander for reinforce
ments had been refused—and for a good reason. The are
commander had no reinforcements to send. The General ha
been in a mood of bitter desperation when his new intell
gence officer, Captain Gani, had come to him with an in
teresting proposal.

According to the Captain's estimates, the insurgents ha
roughly three thousand men in the hills and many unarme
sympathizers in the city, ready to help them when the tim
came. The General had only two thousand men at presen
Yet, did he but know it, he could have a powerful ally wit
over fifteen hundred men to throw in on his side. That all
was the local Communist party. If the General were prepare
to arm the Party men, he would have a disciplined auxiliar
force at his side and superior fire power.

The General had stared at him angrily. "Are you mad?

"Far from it, sir. What I am proposing is the creation of
loyal militia to meet an emergency."

The General had laughed harshly. "You know the are

commander. He is one of Dr. Hatta's men. Are you fool enough to imagine that he would give me permission to arm the Labuanga Communists? He would have me arrested for suggesting it."

"You are responsible for the defenses here, sir, not the area commander. You are entitled to take emergency measures without consulting him. Besides, until it is equipped, the militia should remain a secret force."

"Only the area commander can authorize the issue of arms and ammunition. What is your militia to be equipped with? Stones?"

Captain Gani had had an answer for that, too.

Two months later the General had promoted him to major and made him his personal aide.

iv

The Harmonie Hotel was in the Inner Zone and consisted of a number of porticoed colonial bungalows built inside a rectangular, wire-fenced compound. The reception clerk, a handsome young Indonesian in European dress, was courteous but firm. The only accommodation he could offer them was a bungalow with three beds in it. All other bungalows in the hotel were occupied by permanent residents. This was by Government order.

Greg and Dorothy stared at one another in dismay, but Mrs. Lukey nodded as if she had anticipated the difficulty. "There is a sitting room," she said. "I can sleep in there."

The clerk took them along to the bungalow. The sitting room was an unscreened veranda with a tiled floor. The bedroom beyond contained three cubicles completely enclosed by perforated zinc screens and looking rather like old-fashioned meat safes. As the clerk turned on the ceiling fan, a thing like a soft-shelled crab with black fur on it flopped onto the floor at their feet and began scuttling toward the wardrobe.

Dorothy let out a yelp of fear. Giggling, the boy who had brought their bags in picked the creature up by one of its hairy legs and tossed it out through the sitting room.

"My God!" said Greg. "What was that?"

"They are quite harmless," Mrs. Lukey said. "It is better to leave them. They eat the insects."

But the thing had unnerved Dorothy. While Mrs. Lukey
was away telephoning the contact man, she insisted on Greg
searching every inch of the bungalow. He found some lizards
and a mildewed slipper, but no more of the black creatures.

He did make the discovery that the bungalow contained no
bathroom.

When Mrs. Lukey returned, she showed them the row of
bathhouses, separated, for hygienic reasons, from the living
quarters. One of those gloomy cement caverns had the number of their bungalow on it. Inside, there was a toilet, a large
urn full of water, and a metal scoop.

"It is a Siamese bath," Mrs. Lukey explained. "You throw
the cold water over you. It is very refreshing."

The rendezvous was for seven o'clock at a house outside the
Inner Zone.

It was then a little after four. They had had no lunch. They
bathed awkwardly and, when they had changed, walked over
to the hotel restaurant. There was a noisy group of Dutchmen
drinking in the veranda bar, and they did not stay there long.
With some difficulty they found a waiter and persuaded him
to produce some food. It was a warmed-over rice dish and not
very appetizing, but they were hungry enough to persevere
with it. While they were eating, darkness fell, and the square
on the far side of the gardens, which had been deserted before,
suddenly came to life. Market stalls were set up among the
trees, people congregated, and food sellers appeared. A boy,
squatting on his haunches by the roadside, began to play a
bamboo xylophone.

It was a gentle, plaintive sound and curiously moving. Dorothy looked at Greg and he smiled at her understandingly. They
were in a strange, far-off land, with no tourists within hun-
dreds of miles of them. For a moment the discomforts of the
day were forgotten. It was a brief moment.

Mrs. Lukey had said that it would take half an hour to
walk to the rendezvous, and that they would probably be back
at the hotel by eight o'clock. When they had had their coffee,
they returned to the bungalow.

As soon as they switched the lights on, a large insect flew
in and blundered about the sitting room, hitting the walls and
light fittings with the force of a ricocheting pebble. Greg

killed it eventually by knocking it down with a towel and treading on it. It was like a huge grasshopper made of brown plastic. Its hard shell crunched sickeningly beneath his foot. Two more came in immediately after.

Mrs. Lukey said that they were harmless and that it was best to ignore them; but Dorothy had seen the one Greg had killed and was afraid of the things getting into her hair. The prospect of remaining there by herself while Greg and Mrs. Lukey went off to their business appointment was becoming more unattractive every minute. She announced her intention of shutting herself inside one of the screened bed cubicles while they were gone.

Greg looked at Mrs. Lukey. "Is there any reason why all of us can't go? If we took a cab, Dorothy could sit and wait outside while we did our business."

"Of course, if she will not be bored."

"I'd sooner be bored than fighting these things," Dorothy said.

They had some difficulty in getting a taxi, but the reception clerk sent boys out and eventually one was captured. Shortly after seven they set off.

The taxi was a diminutive Fiat, and Greg and Dorothy, crouching in the back, found it difficult to see where they were going. After they left the Inner Zone there were fewer lights in the streets, and soon they lost all sense of direction. They had glimpses of the port, of the flashing beacon at the end of a mole mirrored in the water, and of a cluster of oil-storage tanks. Then they turned onto a road with a bad surface and broken fences on either side, bumped along it for two or three hundred yards, and stopped.

The house was about twenty yards from the road, and surrounded by an untidy litter of banana trees. It was built on teak piles and there were steps leading up to the veranda. Light showed through the plaited window blinds.

Greg pressed Dorothy's hand. "You'll be all right here?"

"Of course."

As Greg clambered out to join Mrs. Lukey, she said something to the taxi driver. He switched off his lights. As they walked toward the house, Greg asked her if she had used this rendezvous before.

"Once," she said.

The car's arrival had been heard, and, as they approached, a door opened and a man came out on the veranda. He had a flashlight in his hand. He shone it in their faces for a moment before motioning them up the steps.

He was very small and thin, with slightly bowed shoulders. He wore a black *petji*, a sarong, and bifocal glasses. He inclined his head courteously to Mrs. Lukey, and then looked at Greg.

"Mr. Nilsen?"

"Yes."

He held out his hand and said in good English: "I am Mr. Hamid. That is not my real name and this is not my house, of course, but you will understand that I have to be careful."

"Sure."

"Please come in."

The walls were of corrugated iron. Nightfall had not brought any noticeable drop in temperature, and the single room interior was like an oven. In one corner there was a bed with a mosquito net looped back over it, but most of the space appeared to be used as an office. There was a desk, a steel filing cabinet, and a table piled high with small cartons apparently in the process of being labeled. Against one wall were stacked some larger cartons with the words FRAGILE— MADE IN JAPAN stenciled on their sides.

There were two men in the room: one Indonesian, one European. The Indonesian was a slender, graceful man and tall for his race. The skin of his face was stretched tightly over a prominent bone structure, and the veins on his forehead stood out too plainly. There was a look of hunger and tension about his face that seemed to contradict the ease and grace of his body. His hair was long and unkempt. The European was thick-set and muscular, with cropped gray hair, lined gray cheeks, and a thin half-smile which exposed a set of stainless-steel false teeth. Both men were dressed in sweat-stained khaki shirts and slacks, and wore pistol belts. The Indonesian was sitting by the desk. The European lounged on the bed.

As Greg and Mrs. Lukey came in, the Indonesian got to his feet.

"This is Major Sutan," said Hamid.

The Major did not offer to shake hands. "The woman can wait outside," he said.

Mrs. Lukey looked at Hamid, who nodded and ushered her out again. The Major moved across and shut the door after them before turning to face Greg again.

"Your passport, please," he said.

Greg took the passport from his hip pocket and handed it over.

The Major examined the photograph in it and handed it back. "This is Captain Voychinski," he said.

Greg nodded. "How do you do, Captain?"

The man on the bed stared at him without speaking.

"Captain Voychinski is Polish," said the Major. "He is one of our technical staff advisers. Sit down, please, Mr. Nilsen."

He himself sat down behind the desk. Greg got the Singapore check out and laid it on the desk. Major Sutan glanced at it.

"We have not done business together before," he said. "You will not object if I ask you some questions?"

Greg smiled amiably. "As long as you don't object if I ask you a few, no."

Major Sutan considered him for a moment before he said: "Perhaps you had better ask your questions first."

"All right. To begin with, why do I have to come all this way to get a check signed? Captain Lukey says you like to know whom you're dealing with. I don't get it. Don't you trust him?"

Major Sutan shrugged. "We trust ourselves."

Captain Voychinski got up off the bed and came over. "That's right, mister," he said. His English was only just intelligible. "That fool in Singapore know nothing."

"He knows how to drive a bargain."

"Does he know agent provocateur when he see?" Captain Voychinski demanded. He spat the French words out as if they were fish bones.

"Are you suggesting that's what I am?"

"How we know? You sell arms. How do we know you not take our money and tell the Central Government?"

"I went through all this with Captain Lukey," Greg said patiently. "It's not my business to deliver the arms here. I sell them in Singapore. When and how they reach you is your business."

Major Sutan leaned forward. "We have lost too many shipments lately, Mr. Nilsen."

"Sorry about that, but I don't know what it's got to do with me."

"I am explaining our caution, Mr. Nilsen."

"Well, I'm not proposing to tell the Indonesian Government about the deal, and I don't know anyone who is. That's if there is to be any deal to tell about."

"If, Mr. Nilsen?"

"That's right—if. You like to know whom you're dealing with. So do I."

Captain Voychinski laughed unpleasantly.

Greg turned and stared at him. "You're a long way from home, Captain," he said.

"Home?"

"Isn't Poland your home?"

"What is meant by that?" Captain Voychinski's hand had gone to his pistol.

Major Sutan intervened. "Captain Voychinski is an ardent fighter against Communism," he said. "He fought in Russia and Italy and Vietnam."

"Italy?" Greg raised his eyebrows.

"Captain Voychinski was an officer in a Polish division of the Wehrmacht."

"I see."

"Any more questions, Mr. Nilsen?"

Greg shook his head. Captain Voychinski smiled grimly and took his hand from his pistol.

"Very well." Major Sutan picked up the check and looked down at it. "Where did these arms come from, please?"

"Manila. Why?"

"You are not a regular dealer, Mr. Nilsen, and the composition of the shipment is unusual. Naturally, we are curious."

"I got the stuff from a man who'd taken it as collateral for a loan. He was left with it on his hands and wanted to get rid of it. I understand that it came originally from Red China."

"How?"

"I was told that it was intercepted at sea on its way to Malaya."

"At sea?"

"That's right. Does it matter? Captain Lukey has inspected the stuff."

"Arms from China to Malaya do not go by sea."

"Well, these did."

"What is the name of the person who told you?"

"Tan Tack Chee."

Major Sutan looked down at the check again and then took a pen from his shirt pocket. "I do not know this Tan, Mr. Nilsen, but I would suggest you do not deal with him again."

"Why not?"

"If you are not lying to me, then he lied to you. I do not think you can be lying."

"Thanks."

"On that point you would have no reason to lie." He signed the check and pushed it across the desk. "That is all, Mr. Nilsen. Will you be returning to Singapore tomorrow?"

"Yes." Greg picked up the check and slipped it inside his passport.

"Then the transaction could be completed the following day?"

"It could."

Major Sutan got to his feet and held out his hand. "Next time," he said, "I think that our dealings will be more friendly. It will not be necessary for you to come here again, I think."

"Thanks." Greg shook hands with Major Sutan, nodded to Captain Voychinski, and went to the door.

Mrs. Lukey and Hamid were waiting on the veranda.

"Is everything in order?" Hamid asked.

"Yes, the check's signed." Greg glanced at Mrs. Lukey. "Shall we go? Good night, Mr. Hamid."

They had reached the bottom of the veranda steps when he heard Dorothy cry out.

He started to run toward the road.

There were lights there now, and he saw the soldiers almost immediately. Two of them were dragging the driver out of the taxi. Three more were coming toward him across the clearing. From behind, near the house, there was a sudden confused shouting and then the ear-shattering din of a submachine-gun burst.

At that moment one of the soldiers saw him, yelled to the others, and started to bring his carbine up to his shoulder.

Mrs. Lukey was screaming at him to stop.

Greg stopped; and then, as the other two soldiers ran toward him, he took a step backward and put up his hands.

CHAPTER VII

GENERAL ISKAQ ate a second honey cake and poured himself a third cup of coffee. It was cool enough to drink, but he left it to get still cooler. He was in no hurry. He knew that he was going to enjoy the day which lay before him. A little delay in approaching it could only serve to increase the ultimate satisfaction. Meanwhile, there were more modest pleasures at hand. He picked up his binoculars.

From the window of his apartment on the top floor of the Stadhuis he could see the port, the river delta, and the sea beyond. The sky was cloudless, and at that early hour there was little heat haze. The previous day's rains were pouring down from the hills, and the silt-laden water was swirling out in fantastic patterns across the choppy waters of the bay. When the river was in flood like that, the currents interacted with the tides to produce a mill-race effect at the harbor mouth. Plans had been made to eliminate this navigational hazard by extending the mole; but the Government had refused to pay for the work. Now a tanker in ballast, trying to get alongside the oil company's wharf, was having to be warped in cautiously a foot at a time. The morning sun was glittering on her wheelhouse windows, and the General could see the white-topped caps of her European officers out on the wings of the bridge. Other white blobs on the wharf marked the presence of the oil company's Dutch undermanager and the English representative of the tanker's owners. They, too, would be impatient at the delay.

147

The General watched through his binoculars and was content. Admittedly, the situation had richer possibilities. For some minutes he had toyed with the vision of one or, better still, both of the warps parting under the strain, and of the tanker drifting helplessly across the basin to crunch into the side of a dredger moored there; but that, he knew, had been idle daydreaming. One should not expect too much of life. It was enough that the Europeans were inconvenienced and irritated. Enough for the present, anyway. One of them, the Englishman, was British vice-consul in Labuanga, and there were further tribulations in store for him.

The tanker was nearing the wharf now, and the brown water eddying around her sides was losing its power over her. The General continued to watch, but his thoughts began to stray. There was an important question to be decided. Whom should he tell first—the American vice-consul or his British colleague?

It was not easy. The Englishman, Mr. Wilson, was the local agent of the North Borneo and Federation Shipping Company, and his post as British vice-consul was merely honorary. In fact, it was said that the only reason for appointing a British vice-consul in Labuanga had been to enable Mr. Wilson to import his supplies of whisky and tobacco duty free. When told that a female British citizen had been arrested the night before and was in jail on charges of conspiracy against the Government, illegal trading in arms, illegal entry, consorting with criminals, and espionage, the inexperienced Mr. Wilson might well become confused and behave incorrectly. That would be most enjoyable. On the other hand, he might consult with the British consul in Medan or, worse, ask Mr. Hallett, the American vice-consul, for advice. They were very friendly. In that case, Mr. Hallett would have less of a shock when he discovered that there were two American citizens also in jail on similar charges.

The General wanted Mr. Hallett to have a big shock. Mr. Hallett's post was not honorary. He was a career member of the Foreign Service of the United States, and acted not only as his country's vice-consul, but as a local information officer as well, organizing subversive things like American book centers and documentary film shows, and corrupting prom-

ising young Indonesians by arranging for them to take
courses in American technical institutions. He was also closely associated with the World Health Organization office in
Labuanga, and had been known to accompany malaria-con-
trol and B.C.G. field units into the interior. On several occasions he had even penetrated into insurgent-held areas with
such units, returning not only unscathed but impertinently
unwilling to talk about what he had seen. There were a number of American technicians working in the oil fields; and
when they came into Labuanga, they could be as riotous as
Dutchmen. Mr. Hallett had a disagreeable way of making
the arrest of one of these drunken gangsters appear as either
a calculated affront to the President of the United States or
the result of some ridiculous mistake on the part of the security forces under the General's command. The prospect of
confronting Mr. Hallett with two American arms smugglers,
disguised as tourists and caught redhanded in the company
of notorious traitors, was infinitely alluring.

From the other end of the apartment he could hear his
wife upbraiding one of the servants for not answering the
doorbell promptly. A moment or two later he heard the
voice of Major Gani. He decided to hear his aide's report
before making up his mind how he would handle the situation.

The General did not really like Major Gani, who had
spent a year as a student at a Japanese university and did
not always trouble to conceal his belief that he was cleverer
and more cultivated than his commanding officer. He had,
too, an annoying habit of quietly snapping his fingers while
the General was speaking. The General, a religious man
himself, had also realized by now that Gani was a Communist. However, it was impossible to get rid of him at this
juncture. The man had made himself indispensable; and so
had the Communist Party.

The idea of seizing the insurgent arms shipments in the
Labuanga area had been a good one; he was at once arming
his secret militia and denying arms to the enemy; but without the Communist intelligence network to discover the
times and places of the shipments it would have been impossible. The insurgents had lost four substantial shipments be-

fore they had changed their delivery arrangements; and now, thanks to Gani and the Party, the new arrangements would soon be as unprofitable to the Committee as the old.

It had been Gani, who had noted, in the immigration service's reports, the frequency and brevity of the visits to Labuanga of the British woman Elizabeth O'Toole. A more detailed study had then shown that O'Toole had always arrived from Singapore, and in the company of a male European of one sort or another. She had always left with him the following day. Out of five visits, one had been made with a Belgian, one with an Italian, one with a German, and one each with two different Australians. Since nobody in his senses, Asian or European, would regularly choose Labuanga as a place of assignation for any amorous purpose, Gani had made a further investigation and noted a relationship between the dates of three of O'Toole's visits and the dates of three interceptions of arms shipments. The Party had alerted the comrades in Singapore and inquiries had been made about her there. Two days ago a report of her true identity had been received, together with the information that she was about to make another visit to Labuanga. Arrangements had been made with the immigration service to delay the woman and her companion at the airport when they arrived, so that the necessary steps could be taken to place them under surveillance.

Major Gani came in briskly. As usual, his salute was more like an acknowledgment of applause than a mark of respect; but the General did not care today. He was hungry for information.

"Well, Major?"

Major Gani took off his cap and sat down before he answered. "The traitor Hamid Osman," he said, "died of his wounds an hour ago, sir. It is a pity because I had hoped for much information from the man. The house they were meeting in belongs to a small importer. He is believed to be in Medan at the moment. We shall find out. Hamid Osman's house was most interesting."

"Ah."

"He is unmarried and lived with his brother, who is a radio technician. We found a radio transmitter there. It was still warm from use."

"You arrested the brother?"

"He had escaped. The two houses are only three hundred yards apart. He must have heard the firing."

The General frowned. "The radio was still warm, you say. Would he have had time to report to the traitors in the hills?"

"Perhaps."

"It would have been better if we could have had complete secrecy."

Major Gani shrugged. "There cannot be complete secrecy, sir. The American and British consuls here will have to be informed. And I believe there is a Polish consul in Medan." There was a hint of malice in the way he said the last sentence. The General would have to be careful. If it became generally known that there were four non-Dutch whites under lock and key in Labuanga jail on charges other than disorderly conduct, the area commander in Medan would remove them from the General's jurisdiction within hours. The area commander had a weakness for personal publicity and would certainly not permit a subordinate to take charge of a situation of such lively interest to the press.

"I will deal with the American and British consuls myself," the General replied casually. "They will want to be discreet. The Polish consul does not matter." He brushed the subject aside with a wave of his coffee spoon. "Now, about the prisoners. What information do we have from them?"

"It is a little soon, sir, to expect real information. I interrogated the taxi driver who took them from the hotel. He heard only that the house had been used as a meeting place once before. Nothing of value. I released him." He saw the General stiffen and added curtly: "He is a good Party member."

"But the O'Toole woman—what does she say?"

"Nothing, sir." Major Gani began snapping his fingers.

"And the Americans?"

"Also nothing. The man Voychinski advised them to say nothing until instructed by their consuls. It is not important. They are not important."

The General threw his coffee spoon down with a clatter. "Not important?" he demanded. "Four European gangsters engaged in smuggling arms to the traitors, not important?"

Major Gani sighed patiently. "Very important, sir, for propaganda purposes. But for our purposes we have someone much more useful—Major Sutan."

The General controlled himself. In his daydreaming about the white prisoners he had almost forgotten that a member of the insurgent Committee had been taken, too.

"What does Sutan say?" he asked.

"He refuses to speak."

"Where are the prisoners?"

"In the police jail, sir."

"Sutan as well?"

"Yes, sir." And then Major Gani made a mistake. "He is a strong man," he went on blandly, "and will not talk easily. I have put two good men onto the preliminary interrogating work, but we do not want to injure him too much, in view of the public court-martial that must follow, and it may be twenty-four hours or more before he can be persuaded. I thought it safer not to interrogate him at your own headquarters. He has many friends in the army."

"Yes." The General pushed his cold coffee away and got to his feet. "I was one of them."

"Ah, then you understand, sir."

Major Gani was an able and astute officer with a glib command of the Marxist dialectic and a keen eye for the weaknesses of other men; but he was also a deeply conceited man and in some respects grossly insensitive. To him, General Iskaq was merely a brutish and reactionary strong-arm guerrilla leader whom circumstances had thrust into a temporary position of authority—a thick-skulled clod to be deferred to and pandered to now so that he could be exploited later. The possibility of the General's disliking the idea of torturing a former comrade had not occurred to him.

The General looked him in the eyes. "Yes, I do understand. I shall take charge of these interrogations personally."

"In the case of the foreigners, sir?"

"In the cases of all these prisoners. Then we will see who will talk, and who will not."

ii

At the time of the arrest Greg had been too bewildered to be really frightened; it had been as if they were in some nightmare traffic accident involving a truckload of uniformed maniacs instead of another car. Later, when Dorothy and Mrs. Lukey were being yelled at, prodded with guns, and searched in front of a roomful of policemen, he had been too angry. The butt of a carbine slammed into the pit of his stomach had ended that phase. Out of the consequent pain and nausea had come at last a cold realization of their predicament—and, with it, fear. On the way to the jail Mrs. Lukey had wept hysterically. It had been Dorothy, calm and collected, who had found the words of reassurance. Handcuffed to Voychinski and Major Sutan, he had sat there in numbed silence.

At the jail, a single-story brick building in a walled compound on the outskirts of the town, Dorothy and Mrs. Lukey had been hustled off to the women's quarters. Major Sutan had been held in the control section. Greg and Captain Voychinski had been put into a cell containing one iron-framed bed, an urn of water, and a bucket. The whole place had a strong ammoniac smell thinly mingled with that of disinfectant.

Voychinski had taken their arrest philosophically, and, now that Greg's good faith had been so strikingly proved, his attitude became almost friendly. Unfortunately, he was one of those men who, in the face of danger, affect a sardonic facetiousness as nerve-racking after a while as any display of fear.

"How did they get onto us?" Greg asked him as soon as they were alone.

"When I know, I send you letter."

"What do you think they'll do?"

"To me? Pop-pop-pop." He grinned, showing his steel teeth. "Or perhaps . . ." He made the motion of castrating himself. "With you? Big trial after six months. After two years, perhaps, they let you go. With the women? If they let you go, they keep the women. If they let the women go, they keep you. Don't worry."

"Well, they'll have to inform our consuls, anyway."

"Oh, yes. Next week, perhaps."

"What about Major Sutan?"

"He no have consul here. Like me."

As there was nothing to sit on except the bed, neither of them had any sleep. Voychinski seemed unconcerned. He began to talk about his experiences with the German army in Russia and Italy. His facetiousness never flagged, but there was an unpleasant undercurrent of reality to all he said. Greg, who had served with the Fifth Army in Italy and understood what he was hearing about, listened with a mounting disgust that he found difficult to conceal. He had seen an Italian village after a unit of the sort Voychinski seemed to have enjoyed serving with had left it. He tried not to listen, and to pin his thoughts onto the moment when Dorothy and he would be regaling their friends with the hilarious account of how they were arrested in Labuanga and had to spend a night in the local hoosegow; but it was not a very convincing fantasy and was too easily overlaid by another in which Dorothy and he did not figure personally. In this, their friends were discussing with gloomy perplexity what the newspapers were referring to as "the Nilsen arms-racket inquiry" and wondering how come Greg Nilsen had made such a horse's ass of himself.

Soon after dawn a guard brought them a pot of rice and fish, which they had to eat with their fingers. Greg ate very little. His bowels were beginning to cause him uneasiness and he had been obliged more than once to make use of the bucket. Voychinski had some jokes to make about that, too. Greg's dislike of him was now complete.

The barred window of the cell gave onto an inner court, and as the sun rose, they were able to see through the zinc mosquito screen that it was an exercise yard. About twenty male prisoners, barefooted and wearing sarongs tucked between their legs like loincloths, wandered about aimlessly or squatted in groups under the supervision of guards with carbines. Inside the cell, the heat and smell were becoming unbearable. When, shortly before noon, a guard unlocked the door and beckoned to him, Greg's fondest hope was that he was to be allowed out into the yard with the other prisoners. Instead, he was taken by two guards to a room off a corridor leading to the main entrance. Except for a long table and six chairs, it was bare. The windows were barred. One guard entered with him, motioned him to a chair, and stood by the door with his carbine at the ready. After a brief interval the door opened and an army officer entered. Greg recognized him as the officer who had attempted to interrogate him the previous night, a handsome man with angry eyes and an air of carefully controlled impatience. Behind him was a man of Greg's own race, in a very clean white shirt and gabardine slacks. He was about thirty-five, stocky, and balding, with a round, chubby face and square shoulders. He stood in the doorway with a lopsided smile on his face and looked curiously at the guard.

As Greg got to his feet, the officer inclined his head. "I am Major Gani," he said.

Greg nodded. "Major."

"And this, as you requested, is the American vice-consul in Labuanga."

Greg gave an audible sigh of relief and smiled. "Am I glad to see you, Consul!"

The man in the doorway nodded, but without looking at him. "I wish I could say the same, Mr. Nilsen. My name's Ross Hallett."

Greg started to move toward him, but the guard raised his carbine threateningly. Hallett took no notice. He looked from the guard to Major Gani.

"Good-by, Major," he said.

Major Gani's lips tightened and he began to snap his fingers. "The formalities have now been complied with," he said. "You have seen the prisoner. He is unharmed. It is now your duty to inform him that it is in order for him to be interrogated and to answer all questions."

Hallett shook his head. "Oh, no, Major. That isn't my duty."

"This is Labuanga, not Washington, Mr. Hallett. The prisoner is under our law, and so are you."

"Sure we are," Hallett replied easily, "and you have every right to ask Mr. Nilsen any questions you like. But that doesn't mean he has to answer them. You see, I've had no opportunity yet of talking privately to him. I don't think that I can advise him to co-operate with you at this stage."

He turned away as if to go, then paused as the Major said something sharply in his own language. Hallett answered him in the same language.

"What did he say?" Greg asked.

Hallett ignored him. Greg stood there, uncomprehending and irritated, while they argued. Finally the Major gave a reluctant nod and motioned the guard out of the room.

"You may have ten minutes," he said in English. "There will be a guard on the door."

He followed the guard outside.

Hallett's smile faded as the door closed.

"Sit down, please," he said.

"Now look, Mr. Hallett," Greg began, "all I'm worried about at the moment is my wife. You see . . ."

"I know, Mr. Nilsen. But we don't have that much time, so supposing you let me run things. I've seen your wife, and she seems to be okay. The British vice-consul is seeing Mrs. Lukey, and she's okay, too."

"You mean Miss O'Toole, don't you?"

Hallett sighed. "Mr. Nilsen, I don't have time for games. Whatever her passport says, these people know she's Mrs. Lukey."

"How did they find out?"

"I don't know. Anyway, that's unimportant. If you'll just answer my questions, we may get somewhere." He took a notebook from his pocket. "Now, then. Mrs. Nilsen gave me some basic facts, and, according to her, you have a joint American passport. Where is it now?"

"They took it away."

"The police or the military?"

"That officer who was just in here was in charge."

"What else did they take from you?"

"Everything—money, wallet, watch, the lot."

"They claim they have documentary evidence linking you with Major Sutan. What would that be?"

"I had a check for sixty-two thousand five hundred Malay dollars in my passport. It was drawn on the Hong Kong and Shanghai Bank and signed by Sutan."

Hallett's lopsided smile returned for a moment, but it was anything but friendly. "Do you know what sort of a spot you're in, Mr. Nilsen?"

"I have a pretty good idea."

"I wonder if you have. All right, give me the background. I want the whole history of this transaction."

Greg gave it to him.

When he had finished, Hallett was staring at him in sour wonderment.

Greg shrugged.

Hallett drew a deep breath. "Mr. Nilsen," he said, "I wish you could tell me something. Why is it that when an apparently normal, intelligent, law-abiding citizen like you gets hold of a passport and a steamship ticket, he suddenly turns into a juvenile—"

"Okay, Mr. Hallett," Greg broke in irritably. "You can't say anything I haven't already said myself."

"I wouldn't be too sure of that. Our country spends millions of dollars trying to help these people become a nation of free men, trying to give them confidence in democratic processes, trying to persuade them that some version of our way of doing things offers them a better chance of happiness than the Communist Party, and then people like you . . ." He broke off. "I'll give you the rest of the lecture another time. Right now we've got to try to get you and Mrs. Nilsen out of this mess."

"Well, Mrs. Nilsen, anyway."

"As they see it, she's guilty by association." Hallett leaned forward. "Now, tell me again. Your arrangement with Lukey was just as you've stated it? You had nothing to do with the delivery of this war material and know nothing about the arrangements that were to be made for that delivery? Is that right? Don't fool with me, Mr. Nilsen. I have to know. Is that the true picture?"

"It is."

Hallett sighed. "That's too bad."

"What do you mean?"

"The military governor's terms for your release are that you inform them when and how the stuff is being delivered, so that they can intercept and confiscate it."

"But that's crazy. How can I tell them? Lukey doesn't even own the stuff until that check is cashed in Singapore."

"They won't believe that."

"But they'll have to."

"There's no 'have to' about it."

"Major Sutan'll tell them I don't know anything. Voychinski, too."

"A traitor and a hoodlum? Why should they believe what they say?"

Greg was silent for a moment. Then he nodded. "I see. It looks as if my wife and I are going to be here quite a while."

Hallett made no comment. "How much money did you have with you?" he asked.

Greg told him.

"All right, I'll try to get that released. While you're held without trial you can pay for a more comfortable cell and have food sent in from outside, if you want."

"Will I be able to see my wife?"

"I'll ask, but I doubt it."

"I don't know how Mrs. Lukey's fixed for money. If we can get these privileges for her, too, I'd be glad to pay."

"I'll speak to the British consul about that. Now, then. You're going to be interrogated by the governor personally. His name is General Iskaq, and what he'd really like to do is beat the daylights out of you. He won't, because he knows I'd raise hell in Medan and Djakarta if he did, but bear it in mind and don't push him. Do you know what xenophobia is?"

"Yes."

"Well, the General has it badly. So watch yourself. Tell him the truth. He won't believe you, but go on telling it anyway. That check is your best talking point."

"How do you mean?"

"It substantiates your story that the transaction was incomplete, and that there were, therefore, no delivery arrangements. Tell him about the second signature needed. Say that, if he doesn't believe you, he should send the check to the Indonesian consulate in Singapore and ask them to try and cash it as it is. Ask him if he thinks you fool enough to trust Lukey with the goods before you had been paid."

"He knows Lukey?"

"Of course. Lukey's a crook. The oil company filed embezzlement charges against him two years ago, but couldn't make them stick. The Government deported him."

"I see."

"Another thing: don't get into any sort of political discussion. You had the stuff to sell. You were approached in Singapore. You thought you were dealing with an agent of the Central Government."

"You said I was to tell the truth."

"The Communist Party here will make all the propaganda use they can out of this. They'll try to say you're an American agent and that we're secretly backing the insurgents while pretending friendship with the Central Government. The less help they have from you, the better."

"How do I account for the meeting with Major Sutan?"

They could hear footsteps approaching along the corridor outside. Hallett began to speak quickly.

"You thought he was a Government official trying to get a secret commission on the deal. Play the innocent. You shouldn't find that too difficult." He waved Greg into silence with a gesture. "Do you smoke, Mr. Nilsen?" he went on loudly.

"A cigar occasionally. Why?"

"I'll send you in some cigarettes anyway. They are currency here. There's a pack to go on with. Liquor is not allowed, I'm afraid."

"Do you have something for an upset stomach?"

"I'll get you some pills from my doctor."

The door opened as he was speaking and Hallett got to his feet. Greg rose with him.

The man who came into the room had a stunted, barrel-chested body the ugliness of which was only partially concealed by an immaculately laundered uniform. He had a heavy, pock-marked face with thick, rubbery lips and ears. His eyes were watchful and his movements deliberate, like those of some powerful yet cumbersome animal. He wore a scrubbed webbing pistol belt, and carried a short leather-covered cane of the type Greg had seen carried by British officers during the war.

Just inside the door he stopped and looked distastefully from Hallett to Greg.

"This is Mr. Nilsen," Hallett said, and added to Greg: "The military governor of Labuanga, General Iskaq."

The General went over to the table and sat at the head of

it. He was followed by Major Gani, who motioned to Greg to stand facing the General.

Hallett said: "General, I have advised Mr. Nilsen to make a frank and full statement."

The General seemed to take no notice.

"You will find that he acted in good faith and that no possible charge against him can be substantiated," Hallett continued.

Major Gani smiled ironically and began to translate what had been said into Malay. Only then did Greg realize that the General could not understand English.

When the translation was finished, the General looked at Hallett and said something in a harsh, guttural voice.

Hallett inclined his head politely and turned to Greg. "I am requested to leave now, Mr. Nilsen," he said. "You will, of course, answer the General's questions as best you can. I have no doubt that you and Mrs. Nilsen will be released very soon. In any case, I shall be watching your interests and will see you as often as I can. If it becomes necessary, I will get counsel for you."

"Thanks."

With a slight bow to the General, Hallett went. As the guard shut the door behind him, Major Gani sat down by the General.

Greg turned to face him.

Major Gani nodded. "We will begin," he said briskly. "First, let us hear what you and Mr. Hallett have arranged that you shall say. After that we will hear the truth."

iii

The General listened absently to the white man's voice speaking the language that always sounded to him like the chattering of apes, and watched the sweat pouring off him as he talked. In his mind's eye, however, all he could see was the room he had left ten minutes earlier, and his old friend Mohamad Sutan lying on the stone floor in a pool of bloody water, moaning and choking, with blood running from his mouth and nostrils and his stomach heaving. He had told the proudly smiling men who had done it to stop for the present and let the prisoner rest; but he could not leave matters there. Soon he would have to tell them to go on again. Unless, of course, one of the whites should talk first.

As Major Gani started to tell him what the white man was saying, the General picked up the cane he had placed beside him on the table and began to tap the palm of his other hand.

iv

"It's really my fault," Dorothy was telling Mrs. Lukey. "We'd been planning this trip and looking forward to it for so long that the reality was bound to be an anticlimax. I was prepared for that, but Greg wasn't, and I let him get angry and bored. I should have had more sense. When a man's worked so hard and successfully for so many years, and been such a wonderful husband and father, you tend to forget some things about him. Or maybe tell yourself that they're no longer there."

"What sort of things?"

Dorothy sighed inwardly with relief. After the American and British consuls had been there, Mrs. Lukey had been calmer for a while; but gradually the effect of their visits had worn off and she had begun to weep again. She was going to be tortured, she was going to be raped, she was going to be shot. She had done nothing. She did not want to die.

As almost everything she had said expressed Dorothy's own presentiments and fears, it had not been easy to re-assure her with any sort of conviction. Despair can be infectious, and Dorothy had begun to cast about feverishly for some means of diverting her companion's thoughts from their immediate situation. She had found it, unexpectedly, in the subject of her relationship with Greg. Mrs. Lukey was almost avidly curious about it. Dorothy guessed that she was trying indirectly to find the key to a more secure relationship with her own husband. It was the difficulties of marriage that interested her most. Her eyes were dry now, and, although she still held the damp white ball which had been Dorothy's last piece of Kleenex, her nose had at last stopped running.

"What sort of things?" she repeated.

"Oh, I don't know," Dorothy said. "Nothing very bad, really. You know those dolls with round weights at their feet? The ones that always stand up straight again, however much you push them over? As long as he has work that's important to him, a man like Greg hardly ever does anything really silly. It's only when the weight is suddenly taken away that things go wrong. It was like that when he came home from the army. He'd been away four years working with mine-detection equipment and explosives. It was dangerous work, but it had fascinated him. All that time he'd hardly thought of anything else. When he came home safely to me and the boys, I was so happy. I thought that all our troubles were over." She paused. "The first thing that happened was that he fell in love with another woman—or, rather, a nineteen-year-old girl."

Mrs. Lukey looked at her quickly; but Dorothy's expression remained placid.

"I suppose that if it hadn't been for the children," she said, "we'd have broken up. But we didn't. Greg got his business going, and gradually everything was all right again."

"What about the other woman?"

Dorothy shrugged. "The last time we talked about it was five years ago. Greg became very upset."

"Because he was still in love with her?"

"No. Because he couldn't remember her second name."

Mrs. Lukey stared at her uncertainly for a moment. Dorothy was looking preternaturally solemn. Then Mrs. Lukey began to laugh. After a moment Dorothy began to laugh with her. They did not hear the footsteps of the guard approaching, and were still laughing when the cell door opened. Mrs. Lukey's laughter became a strangled cry as they turned.

Standing in the doorway were the old woman who acted as wardress and one of the armed guards from the control section.

The wardress said something in Malay, and Mrs. Lukey began to back away.

As Dorothy started to go to her, the guard came into the cell and, reaching out, grabbed Mrs. Lukey by the arm. She screamed and tried to pull away. With a shout he flung her across the cell to the wardress and then, using his carbine with both hands, thrust them out into the corridor. The cell door slammed behind him.

As the sound of Mrs. Lukey's screams receded, Dorothy sat down on the bed and searched her bag frantically to see if by any chance there was one more piece of Kleenex that she had overlooked. There was none. She sobbed once and tried holding her breath. Then she ceased trying. Kleenex or no Kleenex, it was better perhaps to cry.

v

When Greg was taken back to his cell, Voychinski was stretched out asleep on the bed.

He awoke at the sound of the cell door closing, but made no attempt to move. Greg took no notice of him. Heat, lack of sleep, stomach cramps, and the insistent questioning had exhausted him to the point of indifference to discomfort. When he had used the bucket, he sat down on the floor and rested his back against the wall.

Voychinski sat up lazily and yawned. Greg took Hallett's cigarettes and matches from his shirt pocket and tossed them onto the bed.

"Compliments of the American consul," he said.

Voychinski picked up the cigarettes and smirked. "You leave soon, hah?"

"Just as soon as I tell them when and how that stuff you were going to buy is being delivered."

"They think you know?"

"That's right. They think I know."

Voychinski swung his feet off the bed and looked down at him. "Who question you?"

"General Iskaq and that major."

"So!" The pale eyes searched for hidden clues. "What you say?"

"What could I say? I told them all I know. I told them fifty times."

"About the delivery?"

"I don't know anything about the delivery. You know that as well as I do."

"But you tell them something, a good story perhaps?"

"I told them what I know and that's all."

"Nothing about delivery?"

"That's right."

"You lie."

Greg shut his eyes wearily. "Anything you say."

Voychinski got up off the bed and stared down belligerently. "Gani would not permit you to say nothing."

"Gani wasn't conducting the interrogation."

"You are lucky."

"It's not Gani I'm worried about."

"That peasant Iskaq?" Voychinski spat derisively. "Listen, my friend. Iskaq is a soldier, a good soldier, but stupid politically. Oh, yes, he would wish to break your face, but he is not serious. Gani is the dangerous one. He want those guns to arm more of his Party men."

"What party men?"

"You do not know he is a Red?"

"How would I?"

"Mrs. Lukey know it."

"What difference does it make?"

"My friend, if Iskaq had political sense, he would have come over to the Committee. Now he secretly help to arm the Reds and think he is fighting us when he only make firing squad for himself. It is stupid." He sat down again and stared at Greg suspiciously. "You did not tell Gani anything?"

"About the delivery? Don't be silly. I don't know anything. Is there anyone who does? Does Major Sutan? Do you?"

Voychinski's eyes narrowed unpleasantly. "Did Gani tell you to ask that?"

"Oh, for God's sake!"

Voychinski shrugged. "When a man is afraid and has nothing to lose, he will do many things. And Gani mean to find out from one of us."

Greg glowered at him. "What do you mean, 'nothing to lose'?"

"Your arms are still in Singapore."

"Exactly! So there's nothing for Major Gani to find out. That's what I keep trying to tell you."

Voychinski sighed impatiently. "My friend, do you think that you are the only man in the world who sell us arms?"

It took Greg several seconds to get the point. Then he remembered something Captain Lukey had said. "You only
have to go the first time. After that it's plain sailing." With
only one deal to consummate himself, he had not taken
much notice of it then. He looked up at Voychinski.

"You mean there's another shipment from someone else
already on the way?"

Voychinski showed his teeth, but did not reply. From along
the corridor there was the sound of a door opening and a
rattle of keys. A moment later the cell door was opened and
a guard outside motioned to Voychinski.

He got up slowly, stretched himself, and walked out. He
did not even glance at Greg. The door shut behind him.

vi

Ross and Fran Hallett were playing bridge with Dr. Subramaniam, the Indian director of the tuberculosis clinic, and
his wife that evening when the lights went out. It was a little
before eight o'clock.

They were not unduly concerned. Power failures were
common enough. Dr. Subramaniam lit some oil lamps, and
they went on with the rubber. Twenty minutes later the
lights were still out, and Dr. Subramaniam, wondering if the
failure could after all be due to a fuse in his own house,
went out to the road to see if there were lights elsewhere.
He saw immediately that the failure was general; but as he
walked back he heard the sound of distant machine-gun
fire. It seemed to come from the other side of the town, by
the port.

He called Ross Hallett. The sounds of firing were becoming more insistent, and intermingled with them now there
were faint thudding noises.

"What is it, do you think?" asked the doctor. "Another
raid on the storage tanks?"

"Possibly. Difficult to tell from here."

"What else could it be?"

"I wouldn't like to say. Anyway, I think I have to get
back."

"Why? There's nothing you can do. We've got a spare bed
you and Fran can have for the night."

Hallett shook his head. "I'll be grateful if you'd let Fran stay, but I have to get back."

"They'll have shut the Inner Zone."

"I'll get through on my pass."

Fran Hallett recognized what she called the "State Department" look on her husband's face when he returned to the house, and made no attempt either to dissuade him from going or to insist on going along herself. She did not even tell him to take care. She merely reminded him that there were fresh eggs in the water cooler and kissed him good night.

He drove very slowly. Once, when a column of army troop carriers began to pass him, he pulled off the road and stopped. During these emergencies the Labuanga garrison became trigger-happy, and moving vehicles, including their own, were frequently shot at. As he approached the Inner Zone check point, he became even more cautious. A hundred yards short of it, he stopped the car and, leaving the headlights on, got out and walked toward the guardhouse. With the lights behind him, the sentries could see clearly that he was unarmed and alone.

The N.C.O. in charge of the check point had never seen a diplomatic pass before, and could not read. An officer had to be summoned to approve the pass before Hallett was allowed through. The sounds of firing were louder there, and it was possible to determine the direction from which they were coming. The officer was excited and on edge, but Hallett decided to take a small risk.

"What do they want?" he asked. "To burn one more oil tank?"

There was a local joke implicit in the form of the question. From time to time Government spokesmen had accused the oil company of secretly subsidizing the Party of the Faithful. Insurgent propaganda leaflets had indignantly denied the charge and listed the attacks made on oil-company property. The list had been unconvincing, and a Government newspaper had run a sarcastic article about it. Why was it, the writer had asked, that the insurgents were never able to blow up more than one oil-storage tank at a time? Why didn't they use a little more explosive while they they were about it and blow up two or three? And why did they bother with oil-storage tanks at all when they could, at much less risk to themselves, cut the pipelines? The writer had gone on to offer helpful suggestions of how this might be done, and to suggest that the insurgents apply to America for technical assistance. Even the strongly pro-Faithful had smiled a little at this.

The officer looked at Hallett uncertainly.

Hallett said: "Maybe they brought two sticks of dynamite this time.

The officer grinned. "Tuan, it will take more than two sticks to blow up the power station."

Hallett chuckled, but said nothing more. He had confirmed an earlier suspicion.

He went back to his car and drove through into the Inner Zone.

CHAPTER VIII

KEITH WILSON, Her Britannic Majesty's honorary vice-consul in Labuanga, had been born in Shanghai. When he was eight, his parents had sent him "home" to school in England. When he was eighteen, he had returned to the Far East. Most of his working life had been spent in Borneo and Malaya. He looked and, in a sense, was a typical middle-class, pipe-smoking Englishman. His wife had died in a Singapore internment camp during the war, and he had never remarried. The ruling passion of his life was cricket, and his only complaint against Labuanga was that there were not enough cricketers there to form two teams. He had a powerful radio receiver and spent much of his spare time listening to broadcast cricket commentaries on the Australian and B.B.C. short-wave services. He held that the political stability of India and Pakistan owed as much to the legacy of cricket as to the existence of the British-trained Indian Civil Service. When not on the subject of cricket, he had an agreeable sense of humor. He also had the insight necessary to translate obscure Malay and Chinese jokes into meaningful English. The Halletts, who had read their Somerset Maugham, referred to him, not unaffectionately, as "The Taipan."

He answered Hallett's telephone call promptly. "I tried to get you at the Subramaniams," he said. "They told me you were on your way back. Are you at home now?"

"Yes." Hallett could hear the breathing of the switchboard operator listening to their conversation, and knew that

Wilson could hear it, too. "What about a drink?" he asked.

"Fine. Why don't you come over here and enjoy the view?"

"Be with you in a couple of minutes."

Wilson's apartment was on the top floor of the oil company's building and overlooked the western half of the city. That was the area in which the power station was situated. Earlier, when the firing had started, he had been able to see through his binoculars a sparkle of tracer bullets in that direction. By the time Hallett telephoned, however, the firing had almost ceased. He had switched the radio over to battery operation, and was listening to the voices on the garrison communication frequency when Hallett arrived.

"What do you make of it, Keith?" Hallett asked.

"As far as I can gather, the Faithful sent a strong force in to take over the power station, and the army got in first. The Faithful took up encircling positions. Now they're all just sitting there. I don't understand it. If they wanted to dynamite the place, why didn't they use a small party and their usual hit-and-run tactics?"

"Why indeed?"

Wilson was lighting another candle. Something in Hallett's voice made him look up. "Any ideas?"

"A hunch. You know the night defense plan. The moment there's an attack alarm, the main body concentrates in the Inner Zone. No dispersal of forces. All that's left outside is the mobile column. Where's that now?"

"Holding the power station."

"Which is on the opposite side of town from the jail."

"What about it?"

"That power-station attack could be a diversion. The Faithful could be going for the jail to spring Major Sutan."

Wilson thought for a moment. "It's a possibility," he said finally. "Do you think Sutan's worth it to them?"

"He's an important member of the Committee. Besides, if they do nothing, don't they lose face?"

Wilson thought again. "If they did get inside that jail," he said, "what they'd do there wouldn't be very nice."

"That's what I was thinking. Once they started killing . . ."

"Yes. You know, I tried to call our consul in Medan earlier. I wanted him to go to the area commander and get Mrs.

Lukey moved out of here. They wouldn't put me through. Said the line was down."

"I know. They gave me the same treatment. I'd made up my mind to fly over there in the morning if necessary. As it is . . ."

"What do we do? Call General Iskaq and request him to move troops out to the jail just in case?"

Hallett frowned. "I don't know. Let's think. Supposing he did take the idea seriously enough to send part of the garrison out there. Is that necessarily better for our people? Supposing the troops were given orders to shoot all prisoners in the case of an attack. It's happened before. Supposing someone like Major Gani decided to use them as hostages. Look at it another way. The more fighting there was, the more killing there would be after the fighting was over. After all, the jail doesn't matter to us, only those three persons inside it."

"I gather you're against requesting reinforcements," said Wilson dryly.

"I'm against hypothetical reinforcements in that hypothetical situation."

Wilson switched the radio off. "Well, it may be hypothetical, but I must confess you have me worried. Mrs. Lukey's a highly strung woman. Anglo-Indian, you know. Even with your Mrs. Nilsen to help, she's in a pretty bad state. I didn't like leaving her there today."

"Do you think she knows anything they want to know?"

Wilson hesitated before he said: "I'm afraid she might."

Ross Hallett nodded. Mrs. Lukey was a British subject and, common humanity aside, no concern of his. He thought about the Nilsens, who *were* his concern. To Fran he had referred to them as "rogue tourists." They had been irresponsible and stupid—more irresponsible and more stupid than the booziest oil driller spoiling for a fight. So far, he had been able to view their predicament with a certain amount of detachment. Now it was beginning to frighten him. Men like General Iskaq and Major Gani were not easily deterred from violence by the fear of diplomatic consequences. The Nilsens could be murdered that very night, and he would be powerless except to protest and listen to polite expressions of regret.

"I'm going out to the jail," he said. "Do you want to come with me?"

"What are we going to do?"

"Ask to see the prisoners."

"At this time of night? They won't let us."

"No, but we'll be there. It can't do any harm, and if there is going to be trouble, it just might do some good."

"Then we ought to put on a show. Flags on our cars, neckties, lots of protocol."

"Whatever you say, Sir Anthony."

They had to make a wide detour to avoid going through the Inner Zone, and approached the section in which the jail was situated from the Chinese quarter to the south of it. It was probably that which saved them. If they had been coming from the Inner Zone, they would almost certainly have been fired upon before they had had time to identify themselves.

As Hallett's car was the more imposing, it had been agreed that he should lead the way. Skirting the Chinese quarter there was a deep drainage canal that was bridged in only two places. He was driving very slowly over the ruts and potholes of the approach road to one of the bridges when something he saw in the headlights made him pull up quickly. He heard Wilson stopping behind him.

They were about fifty yards from the narrow earth ramp which led up to the bridge. At the foot of the ramp was an overturned cart completely blocking the way. Hallett got out of his car. Wilson joined him.

"What do you think, Keith?"

"We could probably move it out of the way between us."

"Think we ought to try?"

"I don't know. Does it look like an accident to you?"

"Pretty funny sort of accident."

On one side of the road there were a few small houses, but they were in complete darkness. The only sounds were those of crickets and of the car engines idling.

"What about leaving the cars here with the lights on and going a bit closer to have a look?"

"Okay."

They walked forward into the beam of the headlights, heard the quick rustle of sandaled feet, and saw the long shadows of the men behind them flickering across the road ahead. As they swung around and stopped with their hands in the air, the men closed in.

iii

It had been mid-afternoon when Voychinski had been taken away, and Greg had immediately used the opportunity to get some sleep.

It had been dark when he had wakened. Voychinski had not returned. After a while, a guard had come in with food and water. With it had been a package from Hallett containing a carton of cigarettes, two paper-backed novels, a tube of Entero-Vioforme, and a note saying that he hoped to secure further amenities the following day. The package had been opened and most of the cigarettes stolen. Greg had given one of the remaining packs to the guard and received in return a cup of weak tea. His watch had been taken from him with the rest of his personal belongings, and he had had no means of telling the time. It had been about two hours later, it seemed, when the lights had gone out. He had thought that this must be part of the jail routine. Then, through the grille in the cell door, he had seen oil lamps being brought to light the corridor.

The cells had been left in darkness. As he could no longer read, he had gone to sleep again.

To Dorothy the power failure had brought a curious kind of relief.

Some time after nightfall Mrs. Lukey had been brought back to the cell sobbing incoherently. It appeared that after being questioned for over two hours by Major Gani she had been taken to another room and confronted by Captain Voychinski. Already he had been so badly beaten by his guards that he was scarcely able to stand; then, in front of her, they had knocked him down and kicked him until he became unconscious. After that, she had been taken out and warned, meaningly, that her own interrogation would shortly be resumed. Meanwhile, she should try to remember useful facts.

Dorothy had done her best to calm her, but without success. It had been all she could do to remain calm herself. If they could beat Captain Voychinski, they could beat Greg. The American consul had said that Greg would not be physically harmed; but how could he be sure? These horrible little madmen might do anything.

"But what do they want to know?" she had asked. "Mr. Hallett said he was going to tell Greg to make a full statement."

"There is another shipment already on the way." Mrs. Lukey had hesitated. "They want to know about that."

"Did you know about it?"

"Yes, I knew."

"Did you tell them what they wanted?"

"I told them what was in the shipment. That is all I know. But they want the route so that they can intercept it. They said that if I did not know the route myself, I must tell them who did know."

"What did you say?"

Mrs. Lukey raised her panic-stricken eyes to Dorothy's. "I told them Captain Voychinski knew."

"And *does* he?" Dorothy was beginning to feel sick.

"He might." The eyes pleaded for understanding and forgiveness. "I could not help it. I had to say something or they would have beaten me."

And then the lights had gone out, and Dorothy had no longer had to watch Mrs. Lukey's eyes and wonder if, the next time she were questioned, she would become desperate enough to implicate Greg as well as Captain Voychinski.

There were two beds in that cell. After a while Dorothy said: "It looks as if we're not going to have any more light. I think we ought to try to get some sleep."

"They will be coming for me again."

"If you don't listen for them, maybe they won't."

"I could not sleep."

"Try."

A few minutes later Mrs. Lukey began, in a quiet, ladylike way, to snore.

Dorothy dozed fitfully. Hours seemed to go by. She was half awake, half asleep, when she heard a sound like a huge air-filled paper bag bursting somewhere near at hand. A moment later the sound came again. This time the bed shook a little. Mrs. Lukey woke up and started to whimper.

iii

Only convicted prisoners serving sentences of less than
ninety days, and suspects on remand or awaiting trial,
were held in Labuanga jail. It was built around two small
quadrangles which were used as exercise yards—one for the
male prisoners, one for the female. Separating the two quadrangles was the so-called "control section." This contained
the guards' quarters, some interrogation rooms, a kitchen,
and the head jailer's office. A high outer wall enclosed the
whole compound. The main gates, two imposing slabs of
iron-braced teak, were opposite the control-section entrance.

What Dorothy had heard were the explosions of two
P.I.A.T. mortar bombs, stolen some months earlier from a
British army ordnance depot in Kuala Lumpur and purchased from the thieves by Captain Lukey. They were fired,
with some accuracy, from a projector which looked like a
truncated Lewis gun, and the first one hit the junction of the
gates just by the drop bar. Two of the brackets which supported it snapped, and a piece of the flying metal wounded
one of the duty guards. The second bomb completed the
work. The drop bar fell to the ground, and one of the gates
swung open. The unwounded guard was too dazed by the
blast of the explosions to do more than stare as the attackers
poured in. Then, as he turned and started to run, he tripped
and fell to his knees. An instant later a parang sliced
down into the muscles of his neck, and he slid forward to
die.

The grilles at the entrance to the control section were less
imposing than the outer gates, but more efficient. A Very
pistol was fired to give the P.I.A.T. crew light to aim by, but
the bomb only bent and jammed the long sliding bolts. A
second bomb aimed at the hinges was equally unsuccessful.
By this time, too, the defenders had come to their senses. A
flare was lobbed from the roof of the building onto the road,
and a burst of rifle fire from behind the grille forced the
P.I.A.T. crew to take cover behind the outer wall, where
they could do no more damage. The flare from the roof was
now followed by grenades. Caught in the narrow space be-

tween the outer wall and the jail itself, the assault party began to suffer casualties.

However, they were well trained and ably led. The surprise attack having failed, they set about blasting their way in. With the aid of smoke grenades and covering fire from across the road outside, more men were rushed through the broken outer gates. They had orders to work around the sides of the building, deal with the defenders on the roof, and then dynamite their way through from the rear.

Inside the control section, Major Gani, whose interrogation of Voychinski had been interrupted at an interesting point, was on the telephone to General Iskaq at his headquarters in the Inner Zone.

"No, sir," he was saying, "I cannot tell you how strong the attacking force is. It is impossible to estimate. But they are well armed, with machine guns and an anti-tank weapon of some kind. Our guards are armed with only rifles and grenades. It is imperative that you send armored cars and troops."

"Anti-tank weapons?"

"They burst open the main gate with two shots."

The General hesitated. Only four of his ten obsolete armored cars were at that moment capable of taking the road. The rest had mechanical trouble of one sort or another. Three, which were awaiting spare parts from Italy, had been out of commission for months. The thought of exposing even one of the effective cars to the fire of anti-tank weapons made his heart sink.

He put a touch of impatience into his voice. "Unless they destroy the outer wall first, they cannot use such long-range weapons against the building. The jail is of brick. Every window is barred. You have the main gate covered. Why do you need more troops?"

"These guards are not troops," Major Gani replied. He knew that he had made a mistake in mentioning the anti-tank weapons, and tried to regain the initiative. "I must remind you, sir," he went on quickly, "that we are holding important prisoners here. This is an attempt to free them."

"Of course. But they will not be freed."

"Then send troops, sir."

"They will not be freed," the General repeated sharply.
"Better if they should all be killed."

"You authorize me to kill those five prisoners, sir, including the American and British subjects?"

"It would be the insurgents who would be held responsible.
But that will not be necessary. We will keep them. Has the
white man talked yet?"

"No, sir. He . . ."

Somewhere overhead a grenade burst, and slabs of plaster
fell down from the ceiling of the head jailer's office from
which Major Gani was speaking. As the plaster dust billowed
up, he heard the General asking if they had been cut off.

He managed to croak into the mouthpiece: "Send troops,"
before the dust forced him to start coughing; then he hung
up. If the General were left wondering what had happened, so
much the better. The troops would be dispatched with more
urgency.

He had misread the General's thought processes. The General was a hard man to stampede. So far, only half of the
available Party men had been armed with weapons from the
intercepted shipments, and they had very little ammunition.
Subsequent interceptions would no doubt improve that position, but, until they did, the "militia" was not effective. As
far as the General was concerned, the Inner Zone plan was
still in force. That meant that the garrison did not dissipate its
small strength by chasing off in all directions to fight wherever the rebels chose to attack. The thrust at the power station was obviously a diversion for the attempt on the jail;
but that knowledge changed nothing. The power sation was
difficult to defend. The jail was virtually a stronghold. Gani
was an Intelligence officer, unused to battle and therefore
overanxious. His reckless demand for armored cars showed
that. He must learn that there was more to soldiering than he
had realized. The experience might make him more respectful.

The General's only misgiving at that moment concerned his
authorization to kill the white prisoners. It would be annoying
if Gani lost his head and killed them prematurely. For a moment or two he considered telephoning the jail and countermanding the authorization; but he concluded finally that any
hint of indecision on his part could be misinterpreted just then.

If there were a serious change in the situation at the jail, Gani would obviously report it. Meanwhile, it was best to leave things as they were.

At that moment, in fact, the situation at the jail was changing more rapidly than even Major Gani knew. There had been fighting on the roof, and the jail guards up there had been cornered by the water tank. It was only a matter of time before the enemy winkled them out and gained access to the stairs leading below. With a steadiness and decision which would have surprised the General, Major Gani prepared to evacuate the control section and fall back behind the grilles and steel doors of the men's cell block. What he did not know was that, under cover of the roof fighting, a party had made its way to the rear of the building and was at that moment setting demolition charges in one of the drains.

Orders had been given to remove Sutan and Voychinski from the interrogation rooms and transfer them immediately to cells in the men's block, when the man who had tapped the charges lighted the fuse.

iv

Greg's cell was less than a hundred feet from the explosion. The blast wave slammed him against the wall, smashed the light fitting, and snatched the zinc screen out of the window embrasure as if it had been paper.

Since the attack had begun, he had been sitting there as wretched and perplexed as a child listening to a quarrel between adults. Outside in the corridor, there had been some confused shouting at first, and then the guards, apparently in response to an order, had all left. The other prisoners in that section had begun to carry on excited conversations in Malay through the door grilles. The exercise yard had been quiet. The sounds had been coming from the other side of the jail. He had started then to worry about Dorothy. If, as it seemed, there were some sort of jail riot going on, she could be in danger.

Now, as he got to his feet and went to the unscreened window, he could see a cloud of dust and smoke drifting across the moonlit yard. At the same moment there was the crash of a grille opening along the corridor behind him and the sound of running, struggling, shouting men. Then the air was shattered by a long burst of submachine-gun fire and the shouts changed to screams.

v

The Committee member in charge of the raiding force was a former army officer, Colonel Oda, whom Hallett had met on one of his trips into insurgent territory.

The Colonel had a protruding lower lip which curled inauspiciously at the smallest hint of opposition to his wishes; but he was not wholly unreasonable, and had been persuaded in the end that the proposal of his second-in-command to kill the American and British vice-consuls and commandeer their cars was both politically unsound and tactically unnecessary. On the subject of those in the jail, however, he had been adamant. He and he alone would decide what was to be done with them, prisoners and guards, white or brown. After further discussion he had agreed, reluctantly, to allow the foreign diplomatic representatives to accompany the attacking force. They would go as neutral observers of the justice meted out by the Committee of the Faithful.

The reason for even that concession had soon become apparent. Neutral or no, the observers had been ordered, before the assault began, to park their beflagged cars bumper to bumper fifty yards from the jail entrance, in order to provide cover for the Colonel's battle headquarters among the trees beside the road. During the early stages of the fighting, Hallett and Wilson had been obliged to crouch behind the cars while carbine bullets from the roof of the jail had ripped through the door panels into the upholstery.

Half an hour after the first P.I.A.T. mortar bomb had been fired, the demolition charge blew out the rear wall of the control section. Two minutes after that, the sound of firing ceased. There was some shouting. Then the second-in-command appeared at the main gate and called out that the place was taken. The Colonel walked across the road. He took no notice of Hallett and Wilson. They exchanged questioning glances, then left the cars and followed him.

As they went through the main gate, the damaged grilles

beyond were being levered open by the men inside. Lanterns had been brought. By their yellow light it was possible to see a group of guards huddled by an office door with their hands clasped behind their heads. The bodies of the guards who had been killed in the forecourt were lying face downward at the foot of the steps. Their blood had drained into a broad puddle. The Colonel did not trouble to walk around it.

The blast of the demolition charge had brought down a great deal of plaster. The dust of it hanging in the air made Hallett and Wilson cough. It did not seem to affect the Colonel. He was talking to his second-in-command. When he saw the captured guards, however, he stopped and glanced over his shoulder at Hallett.

"Do you know where your American and British prisoners are in this place?" he asked.

"I know where they were, Colonel." Hallett began coughing again.

The Colonel looked at one of the soldiers covering the guards. "Keys," he said.

The soldier looked at the six terrified guards. Three of them had long key chains at their belts. The soldier grinned and took out a knife. Then he stepped forward and swung the knife upward. The guard screamed as the double blade of the knife slashed through the belt and across his stomach simultaneously. As he doubled up in agony, the soldier snatched the belt away and handed the keys to the Colonel. The other two guards with keys hastily unfastened their belts and let them drop to the floor. The soldier with the knife laughed.

The Colonel pulled his lip in and nodded to Hallett. "You may release your prisoners," he said, "but do not try to take them away from here."

"Very well, Colonel."

But the Colonel was already walking on. "Voychinski can wait," he was saying to the second-in-command. "The one who matters is our Sutan."

The guard with the stomach wound had sunk to the floor and was looking down stupidly at the blood pouring over his hands. Wilson picked up one of the belts and took the key chain off it. His face was white as he looked at Hallett.

"If you want to see that Nilsen's all right," he said quietly, "I'll look after the two women."

Hallett nodded. "Okay."

He took the remaining set of keys and went on down the corridor. The demolition charge had wrecked the building here, and he had to pick his way over piles of rubble to get to the passage leading to the men's cell block. The soldiers there had seen him with their officers and made no move to stop him. In any case, they were too busy stripping the bodies of the dead guards to care much about a white man. He stumbled on, using the flashlight from his car to light the way and shutting his ears to the cries of two men who were not yet dead. From beyond the open grille ahead of him came the sound of prisoners calling to one another and pounding on the doors of their cells. One man was screaming hysterically that the place was on fire and that they would all be burned alive. As Hallett went along, trying to make out the cell numbers, he shouted in Malay that everything was all right and that all prisoners would soon be released. Under cover of the excited cries that followed this announcement he called out quietly: "Mr. Nilsen."

"Here."

He had already passed the cell. He went back, fumbling with the flashlight and keys, and called again. "Where are you? Keep talking."

"Right here. Is that Hallett? What's going on? Is my wife all right? What's happened?" He was trying, not quite successfully, to keep a tremor out of his voice.

Hallett began trying the keys. "Take it easy, Mr. Nilsen. I've got to find the right key. The jail's been taken over temporarily by the insurgents. The British consul's gone along to get your wife and Mrs. Lukey."

"Is she all right?"

"There was no fighting on that side. They may be scared, but I'm pretty sure they're not hurt. Wait a minute. This looks as if it might be the right one."

A moment later he had the cell door open and saw the prisoner's face livid and desperate in the beam of the flashlight.

Hallett made himself smile. "Dr. Livingstone, I presume," he said and then: "Steady, Mr. Nilsen. Sit down a moment."

"I just want to get out of here." But he did as he was told.

"It sounded as if they'd blown the whole place up," he added weakly.

"Only a bit of it. Now, listen. We're in a curious sort of spot. Sutan's friends came to get him. Okay, they've got him. They won't hold this place for long, though. As soon as it starts to get light, they'll be high-tailing it back to the hills. Where that leaves you and Mrs. Nilsen, I don't know, unless you ask them to take you along. Even if they'd agree, I wouldn't advise that."

"You mean we've got to stay here in jail?"

"I hope not. I don't know. I'm just warning you. At the moment it's all up to the commander of the raiding party, and he's a tough proposition. I'm taking you to him now. He doesn't speak much English, so he won't question you direct, but don't say anything unless I tell you to. Above all, don't get mad or try to protest. Just keep quiet. Is that clear?"

"I don't have a protest left in me."

"Good. How's your stomach?"

"Queasy."

"Well, keep close to me and don't look around too much, or it may give you trouble."

He led the way out of the cell and back toward the control section. He went quickly, holding the flashlight ahead of him and ignoring the prisoner's complaints that he could not see where he was going. Hallett judged that the man had reached a point of mental exhaustion at which he could very easily become unnerved. Anger was sometimes a useful restorative.

"Come on," he said impatiently, "we don't have much time."

"Time for what?"

Hallett did not have to reply. They had reached the main corridor of the control section and Colonel Oda's second-in-command was approaching. He was a square, muscular man with a wispy mustache and bright, stupid eyes. He had not forgotten that the Colonel had earlier accepted Hallett's arguments in preference to his own. He looked at the prisoner contemptuously.

"Is this your American?"

"This is Mr. Nilsen, yes."

"You will both come to see the Colonel immediately."

"Very well."

The second-in-command turned on his heel, and they followed him along the corridor. Hallett felt the prisoner's hand on his arm.

"What did he say?"

Hallett frowned warningly and told him loudly in Malay to hold his tongue. The second-in-command spoke no English and Hallett did not want to irritate him unnecessarily.

The room into which they were taken was the one in which Hallett had last seen Major Gani; and Major Gani was the first person he saw there now. He was standing against one of the barred windows, with a soldier on either side of him and blood running from his head and left shoulder. Sitting at the table beside Colonel Oda was a man whom Hallett guessed to be Major Sutan. His head was drooping and his face a deathly yellow in the lamplight. It was obviously all he could do to remain upright. The Colonel was talking to him quietly.

Across the table from them was Wilson with the two women. Mrs. Lukey was crying. As soon as he saw his wife, Nilsen went over and put his arms around her. She began to cry, too. The Colonel looked up in exasperation.

"Ah!" He rapped on the table as if for silence. "I have told Mr. Wilson. Now I tell you, Mr. Hallett. Major Sutan has confirmed the friendly status of these European prisoners. You may take them with you and go. That is all."

Hallett's eyes met Wilson's. The latter shrugged resignedly. The Colonel frowned. "That is all," he repeated sharply.

"Thank you." Hallett bowed slightly. "May I ask where you suggest they should go to?"

"That is their affair. They are free to go."

"Just a moment, Colonel." Hallett went forward to the table. "You asked Mr. Wilson and me to come here as neutral observers to witness the administration of justice by the Committee of the Faithful. You say now that Major Sutan has confirmed the friendly status of these persons. Yet you are prepared to send them away from here, without protection, to be rearrested by the Central Government, put back into prison like common criminals, perhaps shot as your collaborators. Is that the justice of the Committee of the Faithful?"

"They are free to go. I do not understand what you want."

"He understands, all right," Wilson said in English. "I've just finished explaining it to him."

Hallett kept his eyes on the Colonel. "It has been instructive to see how the Committee of the Faithful keeps faith with its friends," he said. He put a sarcastic inflection on the word "Faithful."

The second-in-command stepped forward. "You do not have to hear these insults, Colonel. Give the order and I will see that they cause no further trouble."

The Colonel ignored him. "What can we do?" he demanded angrily. "What do you expect?"

"A safe-conduct for these perons to the airport, and permission to embark on the first Malayan Airways plane to Penang or Singapore."

"You are a fool or mad."

"I don't believe so."

"This is a raiding force, not an army of occupation. Only General Iskaq could give such a safe-conduct."

"I know that."

The Colonel laughed shortly. "Then you must know also that you are wasting my time. We have released these persons. They are in your care. We can do no more."

"You can obtain a safe-conduct for them from General Iskaq."

"Impossible."

"Is it? Why not ask Major Gani?" Without waiting for a reply, Hallett looked across the room at the man by the window. "Major, do you think that General Iskaq values your services highly enough to grant a safe-conduct for Mr. and Mrs. Nilsen and Mrs. Lukey in exchange for your release unharmed?"

He saw Gani's eyes flicker. Then there was a crash as Colonel Oda stood up quickly and his chair shot back against the wall.

Wilson started to move toward Hallett. The second-in-command snapped back the cocking handle of his machine pistol.

Hallett looked from the machine pistol to the Colonel's lower lip and shrugged. "Violence is the fool's answer for every difficulty," he remarked. "I did not think it was yours, Colonel."

"Get out, before we think too much."

Hallett inclined his head. "Very well. It is a pity. I had

hoped that Mr. Wilson and I could have been of help to you."

The Colonel's lip curled proudly. "We did not need your help to take this prison. We will not need your help to take all Labuanga when we wish."

"Maybe not. But you will find that taking Labuanga is easier than keeping it. One day—soon, perhaps—you will proclaim an autonomous government here and declare your independence of Djakarta and Medan. It is then you will need the help of friends."

"These are our friends." The Colonel tapped his pistol holster.

"They will not win your government recognition. Think, Colonel. The Central Government will denounce you as brigands and bandits and destroy you as they destroyed your comrades in Celebes. To whom will you appeal for justice? To the United Nations? The Central Government is there before you. To the Soviet Union? You are anti-Communist. The only ears that will hear you are in the United States and Britain. Our countries, Mr. Wilson's and mine, admire good fighting men, but they also value moderation. No doubt Major Sutan has been viley ill-treated by this man Gani. But how will you explain that, merely in order to have your revenge by torturing and killing Gani, you endangered the lives of two Americans and a British subject? Supposing General Iskaq puts them back here tomorrow, has them killed, and then tells the world that they were savagely murdered by you when the jail was attacked. How could you deny it?"

"You would know that was not true," the Colonel said indignantly.

"Would I? It seems to me that there is a very small difference between that and what you are planning. And how foolish that plan is. Simply by using Gani as a hostage, you could not only cause General Iskaq to lose face, but also show yourselves as humane and honorable men, infinitely more worthy of governing Labuanga than these lackeys from Djakarta. These things are not forgotten. When the day comes on which you need the friendship of the United States and the nations of the British Commonwealth, which memory will you prefer—that of killing Major Gani or that of having saved American and British lives?"

The Colonel stared at him for a moment and then sat down again. He looked at Sutan inquiringly.

Sutan's haggard eyes looked up at Hallett. "Captain Voychinski has died from the beatings this man gave him," he said slowly in English. "Perhaps the gentleman does not know that. Voychinski was a white man. Perhaps if the gentleman saw Voychinski's body, he would not feel so merciful."

"It's not mercy he's asking for," Wilson put in, "but some protection for these people who came here to do business with you."

"They came at their own risk."

"Oh, no. They came because you wanted them to. They were told there was no risk. Personally, I feel they were unwise, but I also feel that you people have a responsibility. Besides, have you thought about what would happen to your future arms deliveries if you turn these three persons over to the authorities? You wouldn't be able to buy a bow and arrow after that."

The Colonel hammered on the table with his fist. "We are *not* turning them over to the authorities," he shouted.

"In effect you are." Hallett had taken over again. "That is, unless they have a safe-conduct out of the country."

The Colonel turned to Sutan again.

Sutan shrugged wearily. "Gani learned nothing that matters. Do what is best."

The Colonel looked with disgust from the white men to Major Gani. His eyes hardened.

"We had good plans for you, Gani," he said. "Perhaps, if your General does not love you enough, we shall still carry them out. Or perhaps, if you stay in Labuanga, there will be another day."

"Perhaps," said Major Gani.

The Colonel motioned to the telephone. "Then, see if your fine General will speak to you."

vi

General Iskaq had not been unduly worried by the absence of news from the jail. An explosion had been heard in that direction; but the sounds of firing had later ceased. He had assumed that the situation at the jail was now similar to that at the power station. When he heard Gani's voice on the telephone, he was prepared to be calm and matter-of-fact. By making no reference at all to Gani's hysterical behavior earlier, he would emphasize its absurdity far more effectively than by drawing attention to it.

When he heard what Gani had to say, a spasm like an electric shock seemed to jolt him from his heels to the top of his head. His ears began to sing.

Through the singing he became aware of Gani's repeating urgently: "General! General! Can you hear me?"

He controlled himself carefully before he answered: "You say you are a hostage?"

"Yes, General. You see, sir, the position is this. . . ."

"Answer my questions!" He had heard the brisk self-assurance flowing back into Major Gani's voice, and, in a sudden rage, shouted the order.

"Certainly, General. But you see . . ."

"What steps were taken about the white prisoners?"

"Unfortunately, Captain Voychinski died. The others are alive. It is about those persons . . ."

"And Sutan?"

"Major Sutan is beside me, sir, and Colonel Oda."

"Why have they not killed you?"

"If you will permit me to explain, sir."

He explained.

The General listened with mounting bitterness. Fantasies began to crowd into his mind. He would countermand his standing orders about night operations and the Inner Zone, take his armored cars and field guns out, and blast the jail into a heap of rubble. He would kill everyone in it, including Major Gani. The anti-tank weapons of the raiding force would be crushed beneath the wheels of the armored cars. There would be a holocaust. Or, simpler, he would refuse the safe-conduct, tell them to kill Gani, and then hang the three whites publicly in front of the Stadhuis. Or, wiser, more cunning, he would put a cordon around the jail area, cover it with the field guns, and starve them all into submission. He knew that none of those things was really going to happen, that he could never be sure that the power station and jail attacks were not tricks to lure him out of the Inner Zone so that the garrison could be chopped to pieces by the main body of the insurgents. He also knew that, however much he might want to discard Major Gani, the time had not yet come when he could safely do so. Without Gani, the arming of the militia could not be completed, and he, the military governor, would be left again to plead impotently for reinforcements which would never arrive. He knew, too, that he could never justify, even to himself, the proposition that the life of one Indonesian officer was worth sacrificing for the pleasure of punishing three whites.

He heard himself saying: "Very well. I understand. But what guarantees do we have that they will keep the agreement?"

"One moment, sir."

"I had better speak to Oda myself."

"One moment, please, sir."

There was a pause and silence. Gani had had the impertinence to put his hand over the mouthpiece. Then another detested voice addressed him.

"General, this is Ross Hallett. I am at the jail in order to protect the lives of two American citizens. Colonel Oda, who commands the troops now in control of the jail compound, has requested my assistance and that of the British vice-consul in the matter of this proposed exchange of prisoners."

"What kind of assistance?"

"As referees, General. It will be five hours before a Malayan Airways freight plane leaves that could take Mr. and Mrs. Nilsen and Mrs. Lukey out of Indonesian territory. During that period Colonel Oda's troops will leave the jail compound. They will take Major Gani with them. So that there will be no misunderstandings or unfortunate incidents, Mr. Wilson will accompany Major Gani and remain with him. I shall remain at the airport with Mr. and Mrs. Nilsen, Mrs. Lukey, and three of Colonel Oda's officers until the plane leaves. I shall then telephone Mr. Wilson, and the exchange will be completed. Major Gani will report to you. Colonel Oda's officers will report back to him."

"You expect me to trust you?"

"Colonel Oda is prepared to trust us, General. However, should either side attempt to take advantage of the situation, Mr. Wilson and I will personally offer ourselves as hostages until the agreement is carried out."

The General thought for a moment. The possibilities of trickery inherent in such a situation were many. Mr. Hallett had obviously envisaged some of them. For instance, he had stipulated a Malayan Airways plane. That precluded the use of an Indonesian plane to take the prisoners into the air and set them down at Labuanga again after Gani's release. But, what was to prevent Oda, on learning that his white accomplices were free, from killing Gani and laughing at Mr. Wilson's protests? The lives of three expendable junior officers? The General sighed. He knew the answer to that. No insurgent leader who hoped to survive would dare to abandon so treacherously even the most useless of his men.

"How can I believe that you will not favor the traitors in arranging this exchange?" he said at last.

"Do you really believe, General, that Mr. Wilson and I are dishonest?"

The General examined his inner thoughts and found, somewhat to his surprise, that his truthful answer to that question would be "no." He decided to ignore it.

"Very well," he said coldly.

"Then perhaps I may discuss the detailed arrangements for the exchange with a member of your staff?"

"I will discuss the arrangements personally."

When the conversation was finished, the General made a few notes and sent for his senior colonel.

Only one thing puzzled him. Gani had tortured Sutan. Sutan and Oda were friends. How was it that such men, whom he himself knew and had once respected, could forgo the satisfaction of tearing Gani to pieces with their own hands in order to permit three whites to escape without a scratch on their ugly skins? It seemed incredible. And yet, from another point of view, it showed how easily Asians became weak and corrupt through association with white men. It showed how right he had been himself to resist the temptation to come to terms with the Party of the Faithful. The thought was comforting.

vii

It was four o'clock in the morning when Hallett set out in his bullet-scarred car to drive Greg, Dorothy, and Mrs. Lukey from the jail to the airport. Following him, in Major Gani's personal jeep, were the three insurgent officers who would replace them as hostages when the plane took off three and a half hours later.

Hallett had managed to retrieve the two passports and an envelope with the prisoners' valuables in it from the wreckage of the head jailer's office; but, at his lukewarm suggestion that some way might later be found of picking up their other belongings from the Harmonie Hotel, Greg had shaken his head.

"We've caused enough trouble," he had said. "As far as Dorothy and I are concerned, they can keep everything, camera included. We just want out."

Mrs. Lukey had not been so accommodating. Hallett had explained briefly to Greg and Dorothy the substance of the negotiations for their release; but Mrs. Lukey had understood them at the time and, as a result, had acquired an exaggerated idea of the strength of their position.

"I do not see why someone should not be sent from the hotel to the airport," she had said. "I have a very nice overnight case. It was very expensive. I do not want to lose it. These people are all thieves."

Hallett had started to remind her that the Inner Zone was still closed, when Dorothy had firmly taken Mrs. Lukey aside. Neither man had heard what she had said, but thereafter Mrs. Lukey had been subdued, and there had been no more talk of her overnight case.

The General had evidently decided that the opportunity of impressing three insurgent officers with the strength of the Labuanga garrison had been too good to miss, and the airport building was bristling with troops when they arrived. As Hallett presented himself to the officer in charge, an armored car moved in menacingly, if pointlessly, to cover the approaches to the bus yard.

They were taken to a large storeroom in the customs section to await the arrival of the plane. Hallett asked for food and tea, and, rather to his surprise, some was presently brought. Access, under escort, to a nearby washroom was also granted, providing that not more than two persons went at a time. Dorothy and Mrs. Lukey were away taking advantage of this concession when Greg raised a question that was beginning to trouble him.

"Does everybody know about all this?" he asked. "I mean, will it get in the newspapers back home?"

Hallett's smile was not entirely free from malice. "If it gets in the newspapers here," he said, "you can bet your life it'll be picked up back home. So far, it's all been kept secret. I don't imagine the General'll want to give it any publicity now. The press do what they're told here, anyway. Where you'll have to be careful is in Singapore."

"How do you mean?"

"Well, you'll be put on this plane under armed guard. You can't stop the crew talking when they get back. You might be questioned when you arrive. If I were you, I'd have a nice dull story ready in advance for the pilot."

"Like what?"

"Technically, your visa's not in order. You were only cleared for Bali. You've been held here under guard. You could be pretty mad about it. Why didn't Garuda Indonesian Airlines check your visa carefully before flying you out from Singapore? Goddam Asian inefficiency. That sort of stuff. I'm not telling you to say that, mind. That's just advice."

"Thanks. I wish there were something I could do for you."

"Don't worry about that, Mr. Nilsen. There's no real harm been done."

"Major Gani's going back to work, isn't he? That's harm. You can't have enjoyed making that deal."

"No?" Hallett laughed. "I was never so relieved in my life. When the General agreed to swap you three for that sadistic bastard, I thought he must be kidding."

Greg stared. "Why?"

"You don't know General Iskaq. I'd have said he'd have ditched his own wife for the chance of keeping his hands on you three. He hates the whites. Always has."

"So you said. But you knew he couldn't ditch Gani."

"Couldn't? I was almost sure he would. You don't know how lucky you are."

"But in view of what he and Gani are doing, surely he *had* to have him back."

Hallett frowned. "What are you talking about?"

"Well, aren't they hijacking all these insurgent arms shipments to arm the Communists? Isn't Gani the Party go-between?"

Hallett said nothing for a moment, then looked across at the three officers. They were curled up on top of some packing cases, asleep. He looked again at Greg.

"Who told you that?"

"Voychinski. Didn't you know? He spoke as if it were common knowledge."

"Well, it isn't. Can you remember exactly what he said?"

Greg could. He would remember every moment he had spent in that jail for the rest of his life.

"Is it important?" he ended.

"If it's true—and that could easily be checked—it's important enough to relieve Iskaq of his job and start a clean-up. Assuming the area commander in Medan were to find out, of course."

"Will he?"

"That's not for me to say. All I'll have to do is send an information report through. You'll be quoted as the source, naturally."

"Do I have to be?"

"I'll have to send through a report about your arrest and the reasons for it." His smile was no longer unfriendly. "This could just about square the account," he added.

"That's something, I suppose."

"It is. By the way, was that check of Sutan's with your other things? I didn't look to see."

"I don't know." Greg got his passport out and opened it. The check was still there. He looked up at Hallett. "Did Major Sutan mention it to you at all?"

"No."

"That's funny. He must have known they'd found it, but he said nothing to me before we left. I know he was in pretty bad shape, but you'd think he'd have been anxious about that."

"Perhaps he took it for granted that an experienced arms peddler like you would have asked for another check if he needed it." There was a gleam of amusement in his eyes.

Greg was silent for a moment; then he folded the check carefully and put it in another pocket. "Did you see Voychinski's body?" he asked.

Hallett seemed to find nothing inconsequential in the question. He nodded. "Major Sutan evidently felt that a mutilated corpse ought to prove something about the Central Government. All it proves really, of course, is that in civil wars there are always men around like Major Gani."

"I think that Voychinski was that kind of man himself." Greg remembered something. "By the way, did you or Wilson tell Dorothy *how* he died?"

"I didn't, and I don't imagine Wilson would. Maybe Mrs. Lukey told her. Why?"

"Well, she didn't appear to worry too much about those guards who were killed. But Voychinski dying—that really seemed to upset her."

viii

The freight plane from Koetaradja and Medan landed at seven-thirty and took off again for Singapore at eight. The captain was a New Zealander. Greg had no difficulty in boring him with complaints about Indonesian red tape and a garbled tale of mislaid overnight bags. He listened absently, lent Greg an electric shaver, and returned to his seat in the nose. They did not see him again.

Most of the interior space was taken up by pieces of machinery going to Singapore and beyond for repair, and mail bags. The plane was unpressurized, cold, and noisy. They sat on the mail bags, dozing fitfully, until the Malay radio operator came aft to warn them that in five minutes they would be landing in Singapore. The plane taxied in to the freight sheds and the operator led them across to the passenger arrival section so that they could go through immigration and customs. He left them there, politely declining the tip Greg offered him.

It was the first time the three of them had been alone together and able to talk freely since the evening of their arrest. Mrs. Lukey, hollow-eyed and plaintive when she had been awakened on the plane, now became flustered and embarrassed. As soon as they were through the customs, she hurried off to telephone her husband.

Greg sighed. "Oh, my God! Do we have to wait for her?

All I want in the world at the moment is the Raffles Hotel, a bath, and a drink."

"Me, too, darling," said Dorothy, "but I think we have to wait a moment."

"I suppose so. Don't you think one of us ought to tell her that we're not holding her responsible for anything?"

"I don't think so." Dorothy's tone was surprisingly firm.

"Just as you say. Only she looked perfectly miserable to me."

"I don't think we're feeling exactly gay, are we, darling?" He kissed her, but she drew away.

"Don't. We both smell of that place still."

"I know."

They stood there unhappily until Mrs. Lukey returned.

"I had to telephone," she explained breathlessly. "I knew he would be terribly worried when we did not get back yesterday. He sent a cable off, but there was no reply. He is coming over immediately with the car."

Dorothy nodded. "That's good, but I don't think we'll wait, Betty."

"Oh, but you must."

"No. We'll get a cab to the Raffles."

"That's right," said Greg. "Maybe we'll talk later, or tomorrow morning when we're rested up a bit."

"But he said he wanted to see you."

"Sure, but not right now, eh? We'll be in touch."

She seemed both relieved and distressed to see them go.

In the taxi they were silent until, as they were nearing the hotel, Dorothy said: "Did you get that check back?"

"Yes, it was still in the passport." He paused. "We don't even have a toothbrush," he went on. "I suppose we'd better stop at a drugstore and buy a few things."

By the time they had bathed, it was twelve-thirty. Greg rang down to the bar for double dry Martinis, but neither he nor Dorothy wanted any lunch. While they were drinking the Martinis, he telephoned Cook's.

"This is Mr. Nilsen. . . . Yes, we're back from Indonesia. . . . Yes . . . Well, we decided to cut it short. Now, look. I'd like you to check up for me on boats sailing during the next couple of days for Calcutta. . . . No, that doesn't matter. British, Norwegian, German, anything you like, as long as it's comfortable. We'd want a large stateroom with bath, air-conditioned if possible. . . . I see. Okay, but not too slow, and it's got to be comfortable, with good food. At the same time, I'd like to know about flights to Calcutta. . . . Via Bangkok. We might want to stop over there for a couple of days. . . . Yes, that's right. . . . No, not today. We'll come around and see you in the morning. . . . Thanks."

He hung up and his eyes met Dorothy's.

"Could we afford the Bangkok trip?" she asked.

"I don't know. Let's see what it would cost, anyway."

He smiled at her, but she was looking down at her drink now.

"Greg, what are you going to do about Captain Lukey?"

He got up with a sigh. "I don't know. While we were in the plane I tried to think about it. We went to get a check signed and—" he hesitated—"get off the beaten track. Well, we did both. Logically, all I have to do now is go to the customs office with Tan and Lukey, sign some papers, and collect sixty-two thousand five hundred dollars. But . . ." He broke off.

"But you don't know if you want to be logical."

"That's right. What do you think?"

She went over and kissed his cheek. "Maybe we should get some sleep," she said.

CHAPTER IX

GREG WOKE at six-thirty in the evening. His body ached all over and he had a metallic taste in his mouth. Dorothy was still asleep. He went into the sitting room, shut the bedroom door softly behind him, and rang for some ice. When it came, he got out the remains of the bottle of whisky purchased for his first meeting with Captain Lukey, and made himself a drink. As he drank it, he realized that he would be feeling very hungry, but for one thing: he could still smell the jail.

He thought carefully about that. Before they had gone to bed, both he and Dorothy had thoroughly washed every inch of themselves, their hair included; and they had given every stitch of clothing they had been wearing to the room boy with orders to burn or otherwise dispose of it. There could be only one reason for the phenomenon. "Thank *you*, Dr. Freud," he muttered sourly.

He reached for the telephone and asked the operator to see if Mr. Lane Harvey of the American Syndicated Wire Service could be found at his office or at the American Club.

Harvey was at the club, and sounded as if he had been there for some time.

"And how was fabulous Bali?" he asked.

"Great."

"And those nubile young ladies with the fecund breasts and the sidelong looks? How were they? Or maybe I'd better ask Mrs. N. about them."

"Maybe you had. Look, I want to have a word with Colonel Soames. Do you mind telling me how I can get in touch with him?"

There was a momentary pause before Harvey answered. "The Policeman? Sure. Just call up police admin. They'll put you through to his office."

"I meant this evening."

"Oh. Well, I don't have my book with me right now, but I'll be going back to my office sometime. Supposing I call you later."

"Thanks. I'm at the Raffles."

"I'll call you."

His tone was careless and he hung up almost before the last word was out. Greg suspected that the promise had already been forgotten. He put some more ice in his drink and then looked up the word "Police" in the telephone directory. There was a long list of entries, none of which was "Police admin." He was edging his way through the listings under "Government" when the telephone rang.

"This is Soames," said a well-remembered voice.

"Colonel Soames, I was just trying to contact you."

"So I gathered. That's why I'm phoning. What can I do for you?"

"I need advice. I'd like to see you as soon as I can."

"Won't the morning do?"

"I was hoping . . ." Greg broke off. "Look, I've been in Labuanga. I got back today. It's sort of urgent."

There was a pause. "Very well, Mr. Nilsen. I'll meet you in the Raffles lounge in fifteen minutes. Will that be all right?"

"Fine. Thanks."

He went back into the bedroom. Dorothy was fast asleep. Very quietly he collected the clothes he needed and returned to the sitting room. When he was dressed, he left a note for Dorothy telling her where he was, and went down to the lounge.

ii

Colonel Soames arrived with the sandwiches Greg had ordered. He was wearing a white dinner jacket.

"Hope this won't take long," he said briskly. "I'm due at a dinner party at eight-thirty."

"It's a longish story," said Greg, "but I'll cut it as short as I can. What are you drinking?"

"Is that coffee you've got there?"

"Yes."

"I'll have some of that. Now, what's the trouble?"

The Colonel was a good listener. He did not stir as Greg told him the story of his dealings with the Tan brothers, Captain Lukey, and the Party of the Faithful. Twice only, he interjected brief questions to obtain a clarification of detail. Once he signaled to the waiter to bring some more coffee. When Greg had finished, he sat back.

"That all?"

"Yes."

"What did you say that fellow's name was? Gani?"

"Yes, Major Gani."

"Very interesting. Might come in handy to our people sometime. Much obliged to you." He paused. "You said you wanted advice, though."

"Help would be a better word."

"For a rank amateur, you don't seem to have done so badly without help. You've been lucky, of course, but didn't someone say luck was a form of genius?"

Greg leaned forward. "Colonel, you said at lunch the other day that you'd considered having me deported."

The Colonel chuckled amiably. "If I'd known what I know now, I probably would have. Can't have amateurs fooling about in the arms racket. Disgraceful state of affairs!"

"Supposing you had deported me," Greg went on, "and supposing I'd just been on the point of concluding a piece of business that netted me sixty-two thousand five hundred Straits dollars. Would I have been allowed to complete it?"

The Colonel's smile faded and he eyed Greg curiously. "That would have depended. I was only gingering you up a bit. You wouldn't have been deported unless the Indonesians had made a formal and specific complaint against you. In that case, naturally, we'd have tried to stop you completing."

"Once I was out, could I have come back?"

"Of course not."

Greg nodded. "That's what I wanted to know. Right, Colonel. As a favor to me, I'd like you to have a deportation order made out against me."

"I beg your pardon."

"Naturally, I'd like it done without any fuss or publicity. I figure there wouldn't be any, unless I tried to contest the order, and, obviously, I wouldn't do that. I'm sure that if I were to have a word with the American consul first there'd be no trouble there."

The Colonel was staring at him angrily. "If this is your idea of humor, Nilsen, I think it's in very poor taste."

"I'm quite serious."

"Then you must be up to some game I don't know about. I think you'd better tell me what that is."

"Certainly. I want to call this whole deal off."

The Colonel scowled. "I see. Had a better offer for the stuff. My dear chap, if you think you're going to use me to get you off the hook, you're very much mistaken."

"I haven't another offer. I don't want another offer. I just want out from the whole filthy business."

"But not neglecting to take your commission, I imagine."

"No deal, no commission, nothing."

The Colonel shook his head wearily. "All right, what are you up to? Come on, let's hear it."

"I've told you. I want out." Greg paused, then shrugged. "You may as well know the whole idiotic truth. When I went into this thing, it was a sort of a joke. I was told those arms had been hijacked from the Communists. I thought it would be highly amusing to help put them into the hands of anti-Communists. Don't ask me how I managed to sucker myself into thinking that I was doing something pretty smart. That's another cute little story. The thing is, I fell for all that double talk of Tan's in Manila like a kid. No, that's unfair. My own sons would have had more sense." He paused again. "Well, then I got what I deserved. I had a chance of seeing a bit of both sides of this fascinating little war. Oh, yes, I found a Communist bastard, all right, and he was right where you might have expected him to be. But I found a Fascist bastard there as well."

The Colonel laughed shortly. "And wasn't *he* where you might have expected *him* to be?"

"I guess he was." Greg's lips thinned. "But you have to remember this, Colonel. I'd been dealing in make-believe. Now, for a real hundred-per-cent Rover Boy like me, just a lick of reality can be terribly uncomfortable and disturbing. To say nothing of the fact that Rover Boy managed to put his wife as well as himself into a very dangerous situation, where they not only became a source of acute embarrassment to their country's representative, but had to be rescued by him as well. So you see, Colonel, the joke's now over. My wife's a very tolerant woman. She hasn't said 'I told you so,' and she won't. But I have a bad conscience, and she knows it. I think she'd like me to do something about that. So, that's what I'm trying to do."

The Colonel sneered. "I see. You'd like to wash your hands of the whole thing and make believe none of it ever happened."

"Yes, that's about the size of it, I guess. More make-believe, as you say. Well, maybe that won't work, but there are some things I can do."

"Like having yourself deported? What would that accomplish?"

"One thing. It would put Tan back right where he started. Originally, he couldn't move those arms from Manila because of some legal snag, or so he said. I'm his sole authorized agent. If I'm expelled from here, I can't sign them out of bond or transfer ownership. That means he can't move the arms from Singapore because of a legal snag. So he's back where he was before I came along, and those arms are back behind the eight ball. He can't take legal action against me because the circumstances are beyond my control. He can have his check for a thousand dollars back. Finish."

The Colonel looked perplexed. "I see your point, but, my dear fellow, you're not seriously asking me to have you deported, are you?"

"I am."

"I'm not Himmler, you know. I'd have to justify such a request, and I don't see how I could."

"Why not? You said yourself that a complaint from the Indonesian Government could do the trick. I bet there's one on the way right now."

"If what you say about General Iskaq is true, I should think that extremely unlikely. He'd have to send his com-

plaint through Medan, and that'd mean he'd have to answer
a lot of awkward questions first." He shook his head. "No,
I'm afraid it won't do. If that's your idea of washing your
hands, you can forget about it."

"Well, thanks for listening, anyway."

The Colonel glanced at his watch. "I'll have to be off." He
hesitated. "Of course, it's none of my business really, but I
can't help thinking that you're being a bit hard on yourself,
Nilsen."

"Yes?"

"And on one or two other people as well."

"Including Tan?" Greg asked sarcastically.

"I wasn't thinking of him. You see," the Colonel went on
thoughtfully, "I'm something of a prig myself, too,
on occasions, so I can understand how you feel. But one
thing I have noticed. When all the hand-washing, clean-slate
stuff begins, it usually has the effect of landing someone
else in the soup. Funny thing, moral indignation."

Greg said nothing.

"This idea of yours, for instance." The Colonel broke off
to murmur something in Malay to a passing waiter. "It wasn't
such a bad idea really, selling Communist supplies to anti-
Communist forces, hoisting them with their own petards or
whatever the phrase is. Not bad at all."

"Maybe. If they really had been Communist supplies."

"They were that, all right."

"You don't mean to say you believe that story of Tan's
about collateral for a debt?"

"No, but I had one of my chaps take a closer look at the
stuff. The types of weapons, the manufacturers, the ammunition batch numbers, the quantities—it all corresponds
to a very familiar pattern."

"What pattern?"

"Terrorist arms cache. That's exactly the kind of parcel
the Chinese were shoving across the Thai border into Malaya
four or five years ago. Couldn't mistake it."

"Where did Tan get it, then?"

"How should I know? Probably stole it. Does it matter?"

"No, except that, if he did, that makes me a receiver of
stolen goods as well."

The Colonel sighed. "As well as what, my dear fellow? Of

what other crimes against God or man are you accusing yourself?"

"Arrogance, ignorance, stupidity, and trying to make a fast buck out of men trying to kill one another. Will that do for the moment?"

The waiter put down two stengahs in front of them.

"As I doubt if I shall reach my hostess in time to be offered a drink before dinner, this is just a precaution," the Colonel explained. "After all the breast-beating you've been doing, you could probably use one, too."

Greg was silent.

The Colonel drank half the contents of his glass, and then dabbed his lips with a black silk handkerchief. "Nowadays," he said, "we don't hear the phrase 'merchants of death' very much. It's all very sad. The idea that the act of selling arms somehow tricked people into making wars they didn't want never really stood up to very close inspection, did it? But it was good to have a fine, top-hatted bogeyman to put all the blame on. The trouble is we've learned a thing or two since nineteen thirty-nine. Now we can't even blame the politicians—not with much conviction, anyway. The real bogeyman crawled out of the mud with our ancestors millions of years ago. Well, we all have a piece of him, and when we start to put the pieces together, it's like one of those nuclear-fission things—when the mass reaches a critical point, a chain reaction starts, and poof!"

Greg raised his eyebrows. "I always thought there was a standard justification of any sort of illicit peddling, whether it was in drugs, smut, or arms. 'If I don't, somebody else will.' Isn't yours a bit new?"

"I wasn't talking about illicit peddling," the Colonel replied huffily, "and I wasn't attempting to justify anything. I was merely trying to correct your rather muddled view of your obligations at this moment. Selling arms or selling the wherewithal to make them—what's the difference? What does your government do with the die-castings you make for them—feed the hungry or put them into ballistic missiles?"

"The United States Government isn't selling arms for profit."

"I must remember that when the nuclear war starts. It'll be a great comfort."

Greg's temper was beginning to fray at the edges. "As I said before, Colonel, you change hats rather easily. Which one are you wearing at the moment?"

"Major Sutan's, probably."

Greg looked at him, startled.

The Colonel picked up his drink and examined it dubiously. "Of course," he said slowly, "you've had a trying time, a surprise or two, and not very much sleep. Apt to warp a man's judgment, those things. Same as a hangover. Alcoholic remorse and all that." He looked up with a small smile.

"What are you getting at, Colonel?"

"Well, now. Let's suppose I'm Sutan. Rightly or wrongly, I'm buying arms with which to fight for something—freedom, power, social justice, or one of the other delusions. You offer to sell me arms and I accept your offer. We're both men of good faith, eh? I give you a check. Then something unforeseen happens. As a result, I and my friends have a choice. We can wash our hands of you and your wife and leave you both to rot, or we can, at some cost to ourselves, see that you go free. It's not an easy choice, but we decide in your favor and you go free. To show your appreciation, you promptly call off the deal we've made, and try and arrange things so that nobody else can call it on again. How does that sound to you?"

Greg sighed. "As it was intended to sound, of course. However, the facts are a bit different."

"I'm sure they are. But you began by asking for advice. Then you asked me to help you. I couldn't do that, so perhaps you'll accept some advice after all. It's not your conscience that's troubling you, Mr. Nilsen, but a slight injury to your self-esteem. Officially, I'm not particularly interested now either in you or in what happens to those arms. Unofficially, though, I would suggest that you do something about recovering your sense of humor."

"So that I can laughingly go ahead with the deal as planned?"

"Oh, I've no doubt you'll find a way of penalizing yourself in the process, like sending that thousand-dollar check back to Tan." He got to his feet. "I really must be going now. I think I'll let you pay for my drink."

"Good-by, Colonel."

The Colonel hesitated, then sat down again. "I don't like to leave you in this despondent mood," he said. "If it's laughter you need, it's just possible that I may be able to help you."

"I'll stop you if I've heard it."

The Colonel ignored the remark. "What was your arrangement with Tan in Manila about payment?" he asked. "What were you to do with the money from Lukey?"

"Pay it into the Merchants' Security Bank here for the credit of his account."

"Was anything particular said about what you were to do if you received the money in cash?"

"No. Why? I seem to be missing the point of this story, Colonel. You know, I doubt very much if we laugh at the same things."

"How about poetic justice? That can sometimes be quite entertaining, can't it?"

"Oh, sure."

"Well, your Mr. Tan in Manila wasn't what you might call frank with you, was he? Don't you think you're entitled to a little joke at his expense?"

"What sort of joke?"

"You could give Tan Yam Heng here the money to bank for his brother."

"And give him a chance to take his double commission after all? Is that the idea?"

The Colonel pursed his lips. "Something like that. Of course, you'd make the fellow give you a receipt in duplicate for the full amount. Keep one copy for yourself, send the other to Manila."

Greg smiled doubtfully. "Well, it's not exactly the biggest belly laugh of the year." He shrugged. "In fact, it's sort of petty, isn't it?"

"I can assure you that Mr. Tan won't think so."

"You mean he'll lose face, or whatever they call it?"

"Undoubtedly."

"Well, I'll think about it. There's no chance of Tan Yam Heng being restrained by any feelings of family loyalty, I suppose?"

The Colonel grinned. "Don't worry. I know a little about that chap. No chance at all."

When he had gone, Greg remained there for a few minutes, finishing his drink and thinking about what the Colonel had said.

He had, he reflected, been called, directly on by implication, a prig, a simpleton, a hypocrite, a pompous ass, a self-satisfied ingrate, and a man who could mistake his self-esteem for his conscience. Together with the adjectives he himself had applied, it all made quite a picture. Dorothy would have been highly indignant. The odd thing was that he did not feel at all indignant himself. For the first time in several days, in fact, he felt like laughing—not at anything in particular, certainly not at the Colonel's feeble vision of poetic justice, but because he had suddenly seen his own face.

He signed a chit for the sandwiches and drinks, and went back up to the suite. Dorothy had not stirred. He undressed, brushed his teeth, and got back into bed beside her.

iii

The following morning he met Captain Lukey and Tan Yam Heng at the Orchard Road branch of the Hong Kong and Shanghai Bank.

The Captain was boisterously cheerful, and countersigned the check with a flourish. The "spot of bother in Labuanga," as he had called it over the telephone, had now, it seemed, been forgotten.

Greg watched Tan as the money was being paid out. His face did not move, but his eyes followed every bundle of notes as it was pushed across the counter, and the fingers of his right hand twitched in sympathy with the Captain's as he checked the bundles. It was more than likely, Greg decided, that the Colonel had been right. Once Tan Yam Heng had his hands on the money, brotherly love would not deter him from taking a triple or even quadruple commission if he had a mind to.

From the bank they went to the Customs House. There Greg signed the necessary papers transferring the ownership of the arms and ammunition to Captain Lukey, and received the bulky canvas bag containing the money.

Captain Lukey beamed. "Signed, sealed, and delivered," he said fatuously. "What about a drink to celebrate?"

They went to the lounge bar of a nearby hotel. When the drinks had been ordered, Captain Lukey left them to go to the toilet. Greg looked at Tan.

"I think this is where you give me another check for a thousand and fifty dollars," he said.

"Ah, no." Tan pointed to the bag on the table in front of Greg. "That must be paid into the Merchants' Security Bank first."

"Where is the bank?"

"In Coleman Road. We will take a taxi there."

Greg frowned. "I've got a lot to do today. Look, you're acting for your brother. Why don't I give you the money, and you pay it in? Then we can square everything away right now."

He had been prepared for some visible indication that the suggestion met with Tan's approval, but had not expected the reaction to be so manifest. It was remarkable. Not a muscle of the man's face moved; but suddenly it was glistening with sweat.

His lips moved slowly. "If that is what you wish, Mr. Nilsen, yes, I will go to the bank."

"Fine. Just a moment." Greg got up and, going over to one of the writing tables, wrote out on hotel stationery two copies of a receipt for sixty-two thousand five hundred Straits dollars cash received from Gregory H. Nilsen as payment in full for the goods listed on bill of lading number so-and-so, and the date. Then he addressed an envelope to Tan Tack Chee in Manila, marked it "airmail," and went back to the table.

Captain Lukey had stopped to talk to someone on his way back from the toilet, and they were able to complete the transaction before he returned. Tan filled in the bill-of-lading number on the receipts, signed both copies, and handed Greg a check for a thousand and fifty dollars. Greg put the check and one copy of the receipt into his pocket. Across the other copy he wrote "Compliments of Gregory H. Nilsen," then put it in the envelope and sealed it.

Tan was sitting tensely, watching. Greg pushed the canvas bag over to him and smiled. "I guess you don't want to count that again."

"No." Tan took the bag and rested it on his knees.

Greg held up the envelope. "You don't happen to have an airmail stamp for Manila, do you?"

"I will get one from the barman."

"Don't trouble. I'll get one later."

"No trouble, Mr. Nilsen."

Tan put the bag under his arm and went to the bar. Captain Lukey came back to the table and began talking about the "dear old chum" he had just run into. "White man through and through, which is more than you can say for some of the murky types who work for Afro-Asian nowadays."

Tan came back with a stamp and put it on the table at Greg's elbow. He did not sit down.

"If you will be good enough to excuse me now," he said with strained civility, "I think I will go to the bank."

"Won't you have a drink first?"

"No, I will go to the bank." He was still sweating, and obviously yearning to be gone.

"Okay. I'll be seeing you."

"Good-by, Mr. Nilsen, Captain."

He hurried away.

Captain Lukey chuckled. "You must have a trusting nature, old boy. If it was mine, I wouldn't let him hold that money even while I tied a shoelace."

Greg smiled. He was putting the stamp on the envelope. "I don't think I need worry," he said.

As they were leaving, Greg went over to the hotel mailbox. He was about to drop the envelope in it when Captain Lukey stopped him.

"By the way, old boy. Couldn't help noticing, but if you want that to go airmail to Manila you'll have to put some more stamps on. That's the surface rate. It may take a week or more to get there."

Greg shrugged and put the envelope into the box. "It's not particularly urgent," he said.

iv

On his way back to the hotel, Greg called in at the Chase National, who were his own bankers' agents, paid in Mr. Tan's two American-dollar checks, and asked for special clearance on them.

At the hotel he wrote out a check for two thousand one hundred dollars payable to the Wilmington Chapter of the American Red Cross. Dorothy, who knew a woman on the Volunteer Service Co-ordination Committee, wrote a covering letter. They mailed it on their way to see the man at Thomas Cook's.

CHAPTER X

TAN TACK CHEE and Tan Siow Mong were bland men with level heads and strong nerves; but the arrival of Yam Heng's receipt in Manila threw them into a state of flustered consternation that Greg would have found gratifying, if puzzling.

Tack Chee took one long, appalled look at the receipt and then put through an overseas call to the Raffles Hotel in Singapore. He was told that Mr. and Mrs. Nilsen had sailed two days previously on the S.S. *Camboge* for Colombo and Bombay. Next he tried to call Yam Heng at the union office where he worked. A clerk there told him that Yam Heng had not been to his office for several days. He was presumed to be indisposed. Yam Heng had no telephone at his home, and Tack Chee knew that it would be useless to cable. Despairingly, he put through a call to the Merchants' Security Bank. The manager was helpful and efficient. No payment of any kind had been made into his account for the past month. Tack Chee hung up, turned his air-conditioner on FULL, and told his secretary to place a person-to-person call to his brother in Kuala Pangkalan.

Siow Mong had not been unduly concerned at the delay in collecting the twenty-five thousand dollars due to him in respect of Girija's check. He had received a satisfactory progress report from Singapore, saying that the sale was about to be completed. As there was still a clear week to go before the Indian could present the check for payment, he did not expect to have to draw upon his own resources in order to honor it. Only one thing was troubling him a little. So far, the clerk had shown himself to be shrewd, careful, and discreet. But would he go on being shrewd, careful, and discreet with twenty-five thousand dollars in the bank? Money could affect people strangely, and for a young man in his position this would be a fortune. What did he propose to do with it? Something foolish, like buying an expensive sports car and driving about ostentatiously advertising his sudden wealth? And, if so, how was he proposing to explain where he had got it? Tan Siow Mong had decided to have a talk with him before the thirty days were up, to caution him if that seemed necessary, and to make sure that any explanations the young man contemplated using did not compromise either the Anglo-Malay Transport Company or its proprietor.

The telephone call from Manila came through late on Thursday afternoon.

As soon as he heard his brother's voice, Siow Mong knew that something was wrong; but Tack Chee was an ingenious breaker of bad news, and it was two minutes before Siow Mong fully realized what had happened. Then he lost his temper, and for a further minute there was a loud and demeaning exchange of generalities in which words relating to the excretory organs and functions of the body were freely used. Finally, however, Siow Mong began to recover his self-possession and to think again.

"It is the American who is responsible," he declared. "If the money is gone, he must pay."

"Impossible," Tack Chee replied. "Yam Heng signed the receipt as my authorized agent. We can only hope that he has not yet lost it all. You must go to Singapore immediately."

"Both of us must go."

"My expenses in this business have already been heavy enough. Twenty-one hundred dollars American plus entertainment, and now overseas telephone calls."

"Those are trifles, brother." Siow Mong was becoming angry again. "When I stand to lose twenty-five thousand dollars Malay, plus five hundred dollars Hong Kong, plus shipping and other handling charges, I am surprised that you commit the indelicacy of speaking about them."

"There is nothing indelicate about two thousand dollars American. The whole transaction was your idea."

"You had no criticisms of it. If you had properly instructed this Nilsen . . ." He broke off. "There is no sense in our bickering. It is a waste of time. Obviously, we shall get nothing unless Yam Heng can be persuaded to co-operate. You know what that means. This time it may be necessary to bring in the police and threaten charges of embezzlement. You are the legal principal in this, and the receipt will be required as evidence. You must be there."

"The police? He would know we were bluffing."

"I am not bluffing," Siow Mong said. "This time he has gone too far. Charges of misappropriation of funds brought against him by that union would have been damaging to our names. We should have lost face. Charges brought against him by us would give rise to no such indignity, except for Yam Heng."

"They might cause pain to our mother."

"She has endured worse," Siow Mong said unfeelingly. "If I leave immediately for Kota Bharu, I can get a plane to Singapore tonight. I will meet you at the Cathay Hotel tomorrow morning."

Yam Heng had had a bitterly frustrating week on the pickle market, and was querulous when the brothers eventually confronted him. He had, he explained indignantly, merely borrowed the money for a few days. Was not part of it due to him anyway, for all his work on their behalf? Why was he hounded in this way? Yes, he had incurred certain losses; but these would at any moment be more than offset by substantial gains. In three days' time he would be able to give them a hundred thousand dollars if they needed money so badly.

Mention of the police, however, changed the character of the debate. There was abuse, and much harsh, contemptuous laughter and snapping of fingers. It was only when he realized that his brothers were not simply ready to press charges against him, but beginning to feel vindictive enough to relish the prospect of doing so, that Yam Heng agreed sulkily to an accounting.

Of the sixty-two thousand five hundred dollars there remained seventeen thousand, three hundred; and threats of violence as well as police prosecution were necessary to persuade Yam Heng to part with that. His brothers left him, glutinous with self-pity, and returned to the Cathay Hotel.

Minor expenses disregarded, they were fourteen thousand dollars (Straits) out of pocket on the deal. They were also tired. They had little difficulty in agreeing how they should divide the salvaged remains. Tack Chee took the equivalent of eight hundred American dollars to set off against his outlay of twenty-one hundred. Siow Mong, as the heavier loser, took the balance of fifteen thousand dollars (Straits).

He arrived back in Kuala Pangkalan late on Friday night. When he went to his office the following morning, he found a message. Mr. Krishnan had telephoned and would like to see Mr. Tan. In the hope that Mr. Tan would find it convenient, he would call in on Saturday afternoon at four p.m.

ii

Mr. Tan, sitting gloomily at his desk, watched the Indian cross the yard from number-one godown and thought that he detected a certain impudent jauntiness in the fellow's walk.

In spite of its obvious absurdity, he could not quite rid himself of the fear that the Indian had somehow learned of the Singapore disaster and had come there merely to gloat over and humiliate him. If that should indeed be the case, he told himself darkly, the fellow would regret his temerity.

As matters now stood, he, Siow Mong, was prepared to be generous. The Indian would be solemnly warned of the dangers of so much sudden wealth, and of the impossibility of his being able to account satisfactorily to the police for its acquisition. It would then be relatively simple to persuade him to return the check. In exchange, he would be given a deed of annuity guaranteeing him a yearly income of two thousand five hundred dollars for ten years. Mr. Tan was reasonably sure that he could buy such an annuity for around fifteen thousand dollars.

Should the fellow be in any way disagreeable, however, Mr. Tan had an alternative scheme ready. He would stop payment of the check and invite the young blackguard to sue him in open court. There, if his challenge were accepted, he would tell the judge that the Indian had undertaken to buy for him, through a relative, a certain valuable tract of tin-bearing land, and that the postdated check had been written, at the Indian's request, to impress the relative and to use as a deposit if the purchase went through. When he had discovered that the Indian's land-owning relative was nonexistent, he had stopped the check. Perfectly simple. If the Indian chose to tell the truth, he would either be disbelieved and lose his case, or believed and prosecuted for selling arms. Mr. Tan did not think that he would be fool enough to risk either of those alternatives.

When he was announced, Mr. Tan assumed the mask of courtesy and ordered tea.

Girija flashed a smile as they shook hands. "I am sure that if Mr. Wright had been aware that I was to have the pleasure of seeing you, Mr. Tan, he would have wished me to convey his personal regards." He had a box file under his arm. He placed it on the floor beside him as he sat down.

"Mr. and Mrs. Wright are well and happy, I hope."

"Oh, yes, thank you. I trust that your own fine family are equally blessed."

The tea came and was consumed to further light conversation. Then Girija picked up the box file and rested it on his knees. Mr. Tan accepted this as an intimation that business might begin.

"I was hoping to have the pleasure of seeing you again in the near future, Mr. Krishnan," he said. "In fact, when I returned from Singapore yesterday, it was already in my mind to telephone you."

"Perhaps there was the same thought in both our minds, Mr. Tan."

Mr. Tan stiffened involuntarily.

"I refer," Girija continued, "to the thought, sad for me, that, under present arrangements, our very satisfactory association will shortly end."

Mr. Tan relaxed. He had noted the words "under present arrangements" and decided to wait for the Indian to explain them.

"I am assuming," Girija added politely, "that the association also proved satisfactory from your point of view."

"Oh, yes. Very satisfactory," Mr. Tan replied manfully.

"And Mr. Lee's?"

"Sufficiently so, I believe."

"I am glad of that," said Girija, "because it gives me the courage to submit a further problem to you, in the hope of receiving further good advice."

Mr. Tan was silent.

Girija flashed another smile. "I am so sorry to have to tell you that the friend I spoke of to you before has since died."

Mr. Tan permitted himself a faint twitch of the lips. "You have my sympathy."

"Thank you. However, as you know, my friend had money. That now passes to me. Unfortunately, he left no will. My difficulty at the moment is to find a substitute for that will."

Mr. Tan hid his satisfaction perfectly. "I can appreciate the difficulty," he said. "In fact, if you will allow me to say so, I had anticipated it. I even had a possible solution to suggest to you if you were interested."

"I am indeed most interested."

Mr. Tan proceeded, somewhat elliptically, to explain his annuity proposal. As he began to enlarge upon its virtues, however, he was disconcerted to see, for the first time, a smile of pure amusement spread over the Indian's face. He felt himself getting angry, and stopped in the middle of a sentence.

The smile vanished instantly and Girija leaned forward. "Mr. Tan, I beg your pardon. Perhaps I should have explained first. For the project that I have in mind, twenty-five thousand dollars will be the minimum capital required if we are to operate at a profit."

Mr. Tan never discovered whether the Indian had used the words "we" and "profit" at that moment intentionally; just as he was never quite clear how it had come about that, twenty minutes later, the contents of the box file had been scattered over his desk and he had been listening bemused to a dissertation on the economics of public transport operation in rural areas. It had been quite difficult to break in and regain the initiative; and even then he did not keep it long.

"Why don't you begin with one bus? Why must you have two?"

"People must learn quickly that the buses are reliable or

they will keep to their bicycles. The service must become indispensable, Mr. Tan. With only one bus it cannot be guaranteed."

"But if you were to buy one new one, you would have the reliability you want."

"We cannot afford an experienced mechanic full time, to begin with. Therefore we cannot carry out maintenance at night, as the big operators do. What I propose is that we buy two of these reconditioned buses. I know this firm at Acton in London. They have long experience of the work. The chassis are old, but very good. The engines are new. The bodies have been adapted for Far East work. Look, here is a picture."

Mr. Tan waved the picture aside. "Yes, yes. It is all very interesting. But why have you brought this project to me?"

Girija returned to his seat on the other side of the desk before he replied, slowly and methodically: "Firstly, Mr. Tan, because a bus service such as I have described would be a logical extension of the Anglo-Malay Transport Company's business. Secondly, because of the trade journals I subscribe to, Mr. Wright knows of my interest in such matters. He knows of my respect for you. He would not think it too strange that a new bus company which you owned should employ me as manager. Thirdly, because if a new company called Kuala Pangkalan Transport Limited were formed, with a nominal capital of fifty thousand dollars, and if, in consideration of my signing a service agreement as managing director of that company, I were allotted fifty per cent of the ordinary shares free, I could return your check to you without presenting it for payment. Fourthly, because a company with your reputation behind it would have no difficulty in securing a franchise to operate the service. Fifthly, because I think you know that I can be trusted and would serve our interests well."

Mr. Tan thought carefully. What the Indian had said about the need for a bus service was undoubtedly true. As a business venture, it was probably sound. The capital of a new company would not have to be fully paid up. Fifteen thousand would buy the two reconditioned buses. On the other hand, if the project were a success, a fifty-per-cent interest in it was eventually going to be worth a lot more than twenty-five thousand dollars. He would certainly be wise to keep the ordinary shares in his own hands. A counter-offer of non-voting preference shares might be the answer. Ingeniously worked out, it could, he was sure, be made to seem advantageous. Meanwhile, he would employ delaying tactics, wear the Indian down by keeping him waiting, and then, if necessary, dictate the terms. He fingered the papers from the box file as if they were of small importance, and then pushed them aside.

"Very well," he said. "I will look through these estimates and proposals, and perhaps make some other inquiries. Later, possibly, we could meet again and continue the discussion."

Girija nodded. "Of course, Mr. Tan. On the terms I have mentioned, the whole matter can be very easily settled—" he paused and flashed his most annoying smile—"any day before your check falls due for payment next week."

iii

The day after Greg and Dorothy arrived back in Wilmington, Kuala Pangkalan Transport Limited took delivery of its first vehicle at Singapore.

W. W. Belden, the maker's Far Eastern representative, was on hand to promote an atmosphere of goodwill. The new owners' managing director, G. Krishnan, was there to sign the necessary documents on behalf of his company.

A ten-ton crane picked the bus off the deck of the ship and placed it on the dockside.

Privately, Mr. Belden thought that the thing looked like a cattle truck; but, as most of its passengers would presumably be coolies, that probably did not matter. The important thing was that the Indian seemed to be pleased. With all this German competition in the low-price field, you had to be on your toes. When the second reconditioned unit had been delivered, he would start plugging their own new economy job. Meanwhile, he had a luncheon date at the Yacht Club. As soon as he could gracefully do so, he left.

The two drivers Girija had brought with him had both spent some years on army vehicles, and knew the type of chassis well. When everything had been checked, the new battery installed, the temporary registration plates fitted, and the tank filled, the engine was started. It had a leisurely, powerful sound that was very satisfying.

One driver got up into the cab, the other sat behind him on one of the passenger benches.

The driver at the wheel grinned down at Girija. "Can we drive the tuan to his hotel?"

Girija smiled and shook his head. "I'll be waiting for you in Kuala Pangkalan," he said.

He did not ride in buses; he operated them.

But he stood there, listening and watching, as the big gears grated, the big tires began to turn, and the bus rumbled away toward the dock gates and the journey north. He wished that his father, the subahdar, could have been there.

ERIC AMBLER

"THE GREATEST SPY NOVELIST OF ALL TIME!"
—SAN FRANCISCO CHRONICLE

RAYMOND CHANDLER
Dean of the
Modern Crime Story!